FIXX

TERENCE BLACKER

BLOOMSBURY

First published 1989

Bloomsbury Publishing Ltd, 2 Soho Square, London W1V 5DE

British Library Cataloguing in Publishing Data

Blacker, Terence
Fixx.
I. Title
823'.914[F]

ISBN 0-7475-0270-6

Typeset by Hewer Text Composition Services, Edinburgh
Printed in Great Britain by Butler and Tanner Ltd, Frome and London

FOR CAROLINE

If you could see me now, you'd probably wonder what all the fuss was about. Is this not a man in control, at peace with himself, a man who has it all?

Take this chair. Mahogany. Eighteenth century, Chippendale. For generations, it belonged to a family firm of tea importers, until the last incumbent – a charming, slack-jawed aristo whose name I forget – found himself in a spot of bother with a Third World supplier and came to yours truly for help. The old firm's gone now, slimmed down, goosed up, sold off, but the desk has remained to become the scene of many a victory both entrepreneurial and (after all, it has the size if not the comfort of a double bed) personal. The thought of the chairman's Chippendale being put to such contemporary use has always amused me.

Then there's this loft. You won't find many like it in London. Spacious – only slightly smaller than a fair-sized football pitch, I'm told – yet with a certain stylish austerity to it. My designer Tony Snowdon, an old family friend, has done a wonderful job here, emphasising its remarkable view over the River Thames and the City, that great stamping ground of Jonathan Peter Fixx.

The name may or may not be familiar to you. Frankly it makes not the slightest difference to me either way, the need for recognition by the common herd never having been one of my weaknesses.

If you do know of me, one word of advice. Ignore what you have read in the papers. Their various caricature versions – J. P. Fixx, maverick tycoon; Jonty Fixx, bold-eyed Lothario and despoiler of virgins; 'F', mysterious intelligence operative; the Honourable Jonathan Fixx, new aristocrat; even FIXX THE FUGITIVE FINANCIER of the headlines – bear little resemblance to the man of simple desires and ambitions who stands before you.

Not that it was all lies. Promoter, playboy, philosopher of the market-place, risk-taker, Romeo, role model to a generation – you name it, I've done it, I've had it, I've been there. But there's more, much more, and this modest account of my life thus far is an attempt to set the record straight simply, honestly and directly.

I shall, of course, be dealing with my enemies. No man who has broken the mould of contemporary life on his way up fails to attract the odious attentions of the loser, the underachiever, the naysayer, and I am no exception. For years, I have tolerated allegations against my good name, suggestions that I have strayed on to the wrong side of the law, obscene innuendi concerning my personal life, whining, more-in-sorrow-than-in-anger editorials, private lies and public libels.

A lesser man might have been tempted to scatter his foes with the help of a battery of well-briefed lawyers. Such is not the way of Jonathan Peter Fixx. Like the famous Frenchman, I shall reply to my critics with a dignified, written response, a *J'accuse* for our times. *La littérature* will be my *mot juste*.

There's a murmur from the sleeping quarters, not far from where I am sitting. The love of my life, Katrina, is lost in dreams, the hint of a wanton smile upon her lips. Who knows, is she dreaming of our past adventures, the many exquisite pleasures of the flesh to which I have introduced her? A shaft of sunlight catches the golden tresses that spill over the dark satin sheets and, for a moment, I am distracted. In the House of Fixx, Signor Libido rarely slumbers. Shortly she will stir, stretch and wander over to where I am working. She may massage my shoulders, her every touch a sleepy request.

'Not now,' I'll say tenderly. 'I'm busy.'

Maybe later I'll let her help me with this manuscript, typing it out, phoning contacts, researching minor points of detail. It's good to make people feel involved.

If you could see me now, you might even be a touch jealous of all that's me and mine. An achiever at work, a man in his prime, an agreeable bachelor penthouse overlooking the Thames, Katrina. What could be more pleasant?

As I embark upon this memoir, the sun is rising over the Bank of England. It is my favourite time of day. Normally, while the world slumbers, I would be planning, making overseas calls, orchestrating dawn raids, stealing a march on my dozier rivals. Today I am the writer, surrounded by the basic tools of my trade: a dictating machine, a working library (dictionary, book of quotations, *The Faber Book of Literary Anecdotes*), and a jotting pad.

It was Count Leo Tolstoy, was it not, who used to insist on writing in top hat and tails as a sign of respect to his readers? Likewise, I sit at my desk in my smartest City suit, ready to address you, the common reader, to inspire you with my story, to convince you of my innocence.

Soon the lie-a-beds will be awakening. I shall look down from my office at the thousands of ordinary people going about their business. Among them, who knows, there may be a young wealth-creator with a dream, with that sense of destiny which I know so well, a young eaglet poised to take wing into the bright blue sky of free enterprise.

It is to this young achiever of the future, his eyes bright with hope, his mind aswarm with schemes, deals and sudden money projects, that I dedicate this book.

One

'He was fiercely vital from the cradle, with
a life-thrust that gave neither himself nor those
around him much peace. His greed for life
approached gluttony.'
Hugh Martin, *Winston S. Churchill*

I
Humble stock

Although, looking back, I can see that my parents let me down badly in almost every department throughout my young life, I bear no grudge. Raising a gifted child is never easy, even for a normal couple. For Mother and Father, it turned out to be impossible.

Not that my father had much to do with my early years, since I was fully seven years old before I was granted the dubious pleasure of an introduction. The shock of that first meeting with Major Colin Fixx VC, MC, war hero and only begetter of yours truly, remains with me to this day.

I had just returned from school, entering our modest abode at 32 Elm Tree Drive, Biggleswade with my normal boisterous good humour. It had been a good day; a virus was going around the school, to which all but the most robust had succumbed. The survivors had been rewarded with extra games and art with old Miss Wortham, whose increasingly hysterical attempts to keep us in order were always amusing.

On a normal day, Mother would have greeted me at the door, perhaps making, as I brushed past her to comb the kitchen for biscuits, a half-hearted attempt at conversation. But now she stood palely in the hall, her finger to her lips. I remember noticing that she looked different, almost smart. She had done something striking and unusual to her hair – combed it perhaps.

Without a word, she led me to the room we called the Snug. It must have been winter because I remember that the room was quite dark. Even on this special occasion, Mother, ever the worrier, had rationed our electrical output to one lamp with a weak bulb. A figure sat slumped in a chair by the fire. It was an old man in a dressing-gown and he was staring rather oddly into the flames. He looked up slowly as we entered the room, like someone waking from a deep trance.

'This is your father, Jonathan,' said my mother in a silly, wobbly voice.

Manfully, I stuck out my little hand, as I had been taught to. I said, 'How do you do, sir.'

As my father rose slowly from his chair, I was alarmed to see that his face was wet with tears. He made as if to shake my hand but then, with a sort of muffled groan, he grabbed me and, falling to his knees, embraced me in a suffocating bear hug. Mother looked on, a dotty half-smile on her face as, for what seemed an age, the old man held me, weeping uncontrollably on my shoulder, drenching my school blazer.

Standing there in the Snug, with both parents blubbing openly, I began to feel a growing sense of disappointment, annoyance even. So this was my father, the hero, the man who had killed all those Germans, who had defeated Hitler, who had risked his life for his country! This old codger, boohooing away on my shoulder, was the almost mythical figure of whom I had heard so much. 'His father's a VC, you know,' I would hear my friends' parents say as I walked home from school. 'Got shot up in Normandy.' And I'd stick out my little chest and pretend I hadn't heard.

But this was not at all what I had been expecting.

Eventually Father extricated himself and, after a certain amount of snuffling and nose-blowing, smiled goofily.

'How are you, my boy?' he croaked.

I held out my little hand again, as if to show that at least one member of the family was able to keep his dignity.

'How do you do, sir,' I repeated, more firmly this time.

Father looked at me with surprise, even alarm. He shook my hand nervously.

'How do you do, Jonathan,' he said. 'I'm very pleased to meet you.'

Let's get one thing straight. I do not for one moment hold against my father the fact that I was obliged to spend the first seven years of my life without the all-important paternal influence. He had a job to do, a career that involved a certain amount of travel in Northern Europe, and naturally his family had to take second place. It's true that, throughout my formative years, I was deprived of the rough good humour of masculine company but I could hardly blame Father for that. Indeed, to put a positive gloss on what others might regard as an entirely negative situation, it's quite possible that my later understanding of, and sympathy for, the fair sex has much to do with those years spent in the exclusive company of Mother, not to mention various twittering female relatives who have no place in this narrative.

If I were not bound by a strong sense of family loyalty, I'd be obliged to describe Father as something of a loser. Even before he got caught in the crossfire during the Rhine offensive, he was one of life's walking wounded. Of course, he had what they call a 'good war', earning himself something of a reputation for courage and leadership. In 1940, he won a medal of some sort – an MC, I believe – and was generally thought to be sound at doing the sort of thing soldiers are meant to do in wars.

The circumstances of his early retirement as a regular soldier have never been made entirely clear to me, but apparently there was this hill on which there were some Germans who had to be removed. Father volunteered to take a few men and do the necessary. The glory was great, the cost in human life was high, the hill was taken. One of the few survivors, Father was brought home, riddled with bullets, and something of a basket case. They awarded him the VC while he was still in the hospital where he spent two years after the war. Naturally, his military career was over.

'Your father's a very sick man,' my mother used to whisper to me, when I expressed childish impatience with the gloomy regime which had been imposed on the family since his return from hospital.

It was an impossible situation for a boy as curious and high-spirited as I was. Raised on stories of derring-do, I now had access to a real war hero, yet whenever I pestered him for stories from the front, he became tetchy and evasive.

Paradoxically, he was haunted by the war. A cowboy film on the television would have him leaping about like a loony. He was unable to sleep for nightmares. He became morbidly afraid of insects. Even an aircraft flying low over the house would send him diving under the nearest table screaming 'Cover!' Mother would eventually manage to coax him out and we would all behave as if nothing had happened. No wonder I avoided bringing my young friends home.

So were the early years of Jonathan Peter Fixx entirely a catalogue of deprivation? Regrettably the answer must be 'yes', although I would be the last person to blame my parents for failing to provide me with a good start in life. They were humble folk, ill-equipped for the onerous task of bringing up an exceptional child in the dark, austere days of post-war Britain.

To make matters worse, we came from a part of Biggleswade where, sociologists today would agree, underprivilege was rife. Not poor, not rich, we were nonetheless more disadvantaged than all of those around us.

From the end of Elm Tree Drive, you could hear the clamour of children on the nearby council estate, kicking tin cans, abusing one another, chasing cats, or whatever children on council estates do. Even then I was deeply jealous of them. For although most of them were destined to be no more than spear-carriers in the great drama of the late twentieth century, they were, in their insignificant way, enormously privileged. They had something to overcome, to fight against, to aspire to. The very fact that they were born in squalor, raised in a sleazy one-bedroom flat by oafish, chain-smoking parents on a diet of TV, child abuse and baked beans on toast could, in a world that adores the self-made bootstrap-puller, be turned to advantage. Men of the people, touting their accents like passports to credibility – they had it easy.

Then there were our other distant neighbours, the rich folks on the outskirts of town. Biggleswade was already something of a commuter dormitory. Within a couple of miles of Elm Tree Drive, behind stone walls and privet hedges, surrounded by rose gardens, tennis courts, croquet lawns and kidney-shaped garden ponds, in Jacobean farmhouses, Georgian residences, Victorian rectories and mock-Tudor mansions, lived the *haute bourgeoisie* of Biggleswade.

I saw little of the boys and girls from these families – they were usually away from home, being groomed for a life of privilege, responsibility and easy living – but, even at the age of seven, I knew that I wanted what they had. Of course, most of them would grow up to accept the easy living, squander the privilege and buckle under the weight of the responsibility. Like the council children, they would be ciphers in the grand plan, achieving no more in their pointless existence than a comfortable income, an occasional stamp-sized photograph in the *Tatler* (drunk at a charity ball), an acceptable marriage. Only rarely would one of them find it in himself to rise above the whinnying, braying clamour of the inbred jackasses that surrounded him, to exploit his position and step easily, confidently into the spotlight.

The suburban toff riding his luck. The yob on the make. How ridiculously straightforward it was for them.

Elm Tree Drive (and environs) was not at all like that. The houses there had neither the sturdy Victorian utilitarianism of the council blocks nor the spacious elegance of the country residences. Typically, in imitating both the style of the mock-Tudor mansions and the manageable size of a working-class hovel, they ended up merely pretentious and poky.

On our street, the children were never heard to scream and shout and rarely, if ever, amused themselves with cats or tin cans (although I confess I instigated an amusing pet kidnapping service – Moggy disappears, reward offered, Moggy found by plucky local children – which kept me in pocket money for a while). Nor, of course, did we spend months away from home at exclusive boarding-schools. If we were quiet, it was because we were uneasy as to our position in the world. In the class war, we were stranded in No Man's Land. We talked in unconvincing accents, neither toff nor yob. We had no team to support, no school worth mentioning in polite society. We faced a future with neither a niche in society nor an escape route from mediocrity, having been born, to all intents and purposes, *sans* background.

No wonder I was the only achiever to have been raised on Elm Tree Drive. My contemporaries have all, so far as I know, settled for the dull anonymity of life as teachers, accountants and book publishers.

'The child is father to the man,' they say. How very true that is. In the months that followed Father's return home, I played a significant part in putting his poor, shattered life back together again.

It was not an easy process, and his malaise – persistent feeble-mindedness, interrupted by bouts of spectacular hysteria – tested Mother and me to the limit.

Doctors came, doctors went. They interviewed him in low, sympathetic voices. They shone little torches in his watery blue eyes. They prescribed pink pills to pick him up, blue pills to bring him down. Over countless cups of tea in the kitchen, they talked to Mother of War Trauma, Trench Fever, Delusional Alienism, Psycho-this, that and the other. Patience, they said, Time the Great Healer. In the meantime, keep your voices down and dose him up with these nice brightly coloured bombers.

With the sort of instinct for the right course of action which was to serve me in such good stead later in life, I ignored the doctors' advice in a game attempt to bring him out of himself. I collected war comics and acted out bloody skirmishes in the sitting-room. Using a toy rifle, painstakingly modelled during woodwork lessons at school, I would hide around corners and in cupboards, acting out an elaborate fantasy involving a deadly sniper behind enemy lines. I took up butterfly collecting, experimenting with different types of stunning gas in the kitchen.

A healthy enough approach towards a bad case of the middle-aged collywobbles, you might think, but the medical opinion of the time decided otherwise. I was a disturbing influence, if you please; I was 'holding Father back' in his rehabilitation into the world of everyday life.

'No more Tommy guns, Jonathan,' the medical booby of the moment told me, peering over his half-moon specs. 'No more bang-bang games through the banisters. And why don't you collect stamps instead of butterflies, eh?'

Tears may have welled up in my innocent, young eyes.

'Tell you what,' said the doctor. 'I'll give you my old albums to start you off. I think I've even got a Penny Black. Eh? There's a good boy.'

He patted me on the knee and ambled off, under the mistaken impression that he had convinced me to mend my ways. He was one of the first, but certainly not the last, to underestimate the inner resources of Jonathan Peter Fixx.

The doctor's stamp album, it was true, would have provided a fine start for the young collector. In fact, the antique dealer who bought it from me for £14.10.0 will have had no difficulty in selling it, while the money was useful for bribing my schoolmates to bring me as many butterflies and moths as they could catch. A couple of bob for a dozen live specimens was the price I hit on, so far as I remember.

After a week, I had hundreds of butterflies in the garden shed. My master plan, possibly the first example of the impish sense of humour for which I've since become well known, was about to unfold.

Every day after lunch, Father would retire to the Snug to recover from his morning's exertions (weeping, wringing his hands, diving under tables). There he had what he insisted on calling 'a zizz' in his favourite armchair.

If there was a touch of childish resentment, if I could be said to have gone too far that Sunday afternoon when I released several hundred sleepy, fluttering insects in the room as he slept, it could hardly be held against me. I was, after all, a solitary child with only my games and my butterfly collection to keep boredom at bay. And now, thanks to my inadequate and thoroughly unsatisfactory father, I was to be deprived of even those.

Mother was out for the afternoon and as I waited outside the Snug, reading a copy of the *Eagle*, the minutes dragged by interminably. But it was worth it.

Suddenly there was a strangled cry. Father was awake. There was the sound of thuds and gasps from the room as he fought his way through the winged invaders to the door. Feverishly he pulled at the doorhandle, which came away in his hand. I had been meaning to mention that loose screw to Mother, but somehow had never got round to it.

'Help!' my father cried. 'Jonathan, help! Get them off me! Quick!'

How odd it was, I remember contemplating as the sounds of Father's increasingly hysterical tussle with the butterflies echoed throughout the house, how *very* odd it was that a man who could lead others to their death, who could stand up to the might of Hitler's stormtroopers, who had actually won medals for bravery, could have so much difficulty with a few insects.

'Please, Jonathan, where are you?'

It was the same with our holidays, I recalled. Once I had dreamt of a tour of Northern France, with Father showing us over some of the sites of his much-vaunted heroism, perhaps even tottering up the famous hill, but all my pleas had been ignored. Despite being decorated by his country for facing up to the enemy, Major Fixx no longer had the nerve to face anything, not even his own past.

'JONATHAN!'

Sighing, I got to my feet and opened the door. My father was lying on the floor in a mess of pollen and broken wings.

'What happened, Father?'

There was a sob from the floor.

'Get them out. Quick.'

'I certainly will,' I said, grabbing a cushion.

My father looked up. 'Don't harm them,' he whispered. 'Get me out – but don't kill them.'

'Don't worry, Father,' I shouted, flailing left and right at the butterflies. 'You'll soon be safe.'

There followed a spectacular scene of confusion: the child of the family beating back the invaders, inflicting massive losses on them; the father, now covered in butterfly wings, clawing at his son's legs, imploring him to stop.

'There,' I said, surveying the devastated room with some satisfaction. 'It's all right, Father. You're safe now.'

It was not long after the Battle of the Butterflies that my eventful, difficult childhood took another unexpected turn. By selling a few items of family jewellery, Mother had laid her hands on enough money to enable her to hire a home help which, with typical adult selfishness, she thought would bring peace to our little ménage.

It was a woefully misconceived notion.

The arrival at 32 Elm Tree Drive of Miss Whiting, also known as Aunty Bar-Bar, the Iron Powder Puff, the Coventry Climax and Bar-Bar Black Sheets, affected me in a way from which, in a very real sense, I have never fully recovered. Harsh yet fragile, a leader yet easily led, a disciplinarian yet almost wholly lacking in self-discipline, as appealing one moment as she was utterly repellent the next, Aunty Bar-Bar has, over these past thirty or so years, endured as a fragrant, fearful symbol of all things feminine.

In a feeble attempt to spare my feelings, Mother would refer to this creature as 'the housekeeper', but I was never fooled. Her area of responsibility was not the house, but the child. Aunty Bar-Bar – the name she insisted I called her by – was to be my nanny.

I was almost eleven years old now, a late age, as most child psychologists will agree, to come to terms with a new adult presence in the house, and, while I went along with the new arrangement, I experienced a certain resentment, an anger even, that the perfumed bulk of Aunty Bar-Bar stood between my parents and me.

At first, these quite understandable feelings were expressed in small but significant accidents of rebellion – a toad down her bed, a broken glass under the front wheel of her Morris Minor, the contents of a stink bomb emptied into a bottle of her precious scent.

To my intense disappointment, the Iron Powder Puff failed to respond to these provocations with the tears, hysteria and flailing right hand that I expected.

'Tumtee,' she would say, surveying my latest effort quite calmly. 'Who to bless and who to blame?' And, with a grim little smile, she would take me to my room and lock me in, sometimes for hours.

My parents, too self-absorbed to notice the casual sadism being inflicted on their only son, would occasionally congratulate Aunty Bar-Bar on her work.

'What's your secret, Bar-Bar?' Mother asked once, smiling at me with idiot affection as we ate our modest high tea.

'No secret, Mrs Fixx,' said the nanny. 'It's just that Jonathan and me, we understand one another. Don't we, Jonathan?'

'Yes, Aunty Bar-Bar,' I said, miserably.

– And Mother?

– Who? What are you talking about?

– Your mother. Isn't she important? You've hardly mentioned her. You're not going to move straight on to Aunty Bar-Bar without mentioning her, I hope.

– Good God, do we have to? She's told it enough times herself.

– That's her version.

– I suppose so. And Mother has never enjoyed more than an arm's-length relationship with the truth. Perhaps I ought to set the record straight.

How far do we go back to trace the influences that shape a person's life? Parents? Grandparents? Were the ingredients of the cocktail of chromosomes that is you, the common reader, being mixed in some small way as your ancestors trod their undistinguished path through life centuries ago? I know not. I leave such questions to the experts. Yet, leaning on old Ma Experience, I would venture to say that it varies. We are all different, in our own way.

There's little doubt, for example, that I owe virtually nothing to my forebears, having acquired what qualities I possess through my own efforts and experience. Father, on the other hand, probably drew heavily from the Fixx heritage. Generation after generation, they served their country in the armed forces with dog-like loyalty, before dying – often prematurely, always in obscurity – with no more to show for their lives than the occasional mention in despatches. Patriotic, reliable, stupid – that was the way of his family. The mental instability was, as far as I can tell, all his own work.

Mother's family, who went by the name of Williams, also stamped its stock with a grim predictability. From the time of the Restoration, there has always been at least one Williams mooching self-righteously about this sceptr'd isle, making trouble on behalf of his or her (and how) fellow man. No research needed here; Mother would warble on about her hatchet-faced forebears at the slightest excuse. Quakers, levellers, chartists; the family's stock in trade was a grey, joyless radicalism, a rock-hard belief that There Must Be a Better Way. Good-hearted but fundamentally pointless, they spent half their lives preaching, the other writing pamphlets for people who, more often than not, had yet to master reading. Moaning was in the blood; no wonder Mother turned out as she did.

She was one of two daughters born to Henry Williams, a teacher who, true to the family tradition, spent his life rocking the boat and generally making a nuisance of himself. Despite being a free-thinker and a liberal, Williams was not a bad old stick in his own eccentric way. He used to bring me 2/6d every time he visited us, stipulating that it should be spent on improving my education with books, an instruction that I interpreted with a precocious sense of enterprise by spending the money on encouraging a local swot to help me with my homework.

I learned at an early age that the best way to keep the half-crowns coming was to feed him the occasional wide-eyed question that would prompt a wise, deeply dull homily. 'Why do the people who live on the Peabody Estate dress so badly, Grandpa?' 'Why are boys doctors and girls nurses, Grandpa?' 'What's a bread-line, Grandpa?'

'Ah, my boy,' my grandfather would smile, shake his head sorrowfully and, nodding stupidly, he would try to brainwash me with some dangerous item of soppy, love-thy-neighbour claptrap. It is a considerable tribute to my sturdy youthful independence that I remained uninfected, despite these tiresome little sermons. 'So, my boy, you try to remember that when you get older.'

'You mean that . . . ' I screwed my face up, as if to master the point that he had just made. 'I think I see. Perhaps I can read about it, when I've saved up enough pocket money.'

'Perhaps,' said the old duffer, reaching into his trouser pocket, 'you can.'

For most of the sixty-five years he spent on this earth, before keeling over stone dead from a heart attack during the closing stages of an Aldermaston march, my grandfather had apparently espoused a succession of hopeless left-wing causes. At one point, during the thirties, he had actually gone so far as to stand as an Independent Peace Army candidate for parliament in some obscure constituency. According to Mother, he would have made a fair showing at the polls, had the Conservative candidate not made much of his brief, unwise flirtation with the free love movement in the twenties. Apparently, Grandfather and free love never advanced much further than a spot of light foreplay but he had written a couple of pamphlets advocating the wider availability of sex for everyone, including the working classes, and that was more than enough for the folk of Leicestershire.

As Grandpa grew older, his political views became more extreme, frequently teetering on the brink of out-and-out communism. Today I can look back on his intellectual excesses with a certain degree of leniency. Even in those days, there was something about a life given over to drumming the rudiments of education into the thick skulls of grimy-faced children that turned many a teacher's mind towards pseudo-bolshevism, and anyway those Williams chromosomes gave the old boy no chance. To understand all, as they say, is to forgive all, and I'm a big enough man not to blame my grandfather for the woefully misguided direction his life took.

Yet, for his daughters Phyllis and Mary, the effect of all this milk of human kindness slopping about the Williams family home was nothing short of disastrous. From the earliest age, their susceptible female minds were filled with dangerous, revolutionary tosh, so that by the time most respectable girls were preparing themselves for a life of service to the home, attending finishing school, learning how to dance and knit, reading *Little Women* and *The Green Hat*, they were immersed in the works of Wells, Shaw and Vera Brittain. While their saner contemporaries were getting engaged to nice young men with prospects, a decent accent and at least one suit, Phyllis and Mary were mixing with labourers, serving at soup kitchens, handing out leaflets to striking miners and generally behaving in an irresponsible way. As to whether their father's ill-fated enthusiasm for free love influenced the later behaviour of the two girls, it is not for me to say. There's no reason to doubt that old man Williams expounded his views to the family over dinner on this as any other topic – if 'War We Say No' was an acceptable topic for young girls, why not 'Sex We Say Yes'? – and my suspicion has always been that the seeds of Mother's late-blooming interest in matters physical were sown by her father. Certainly my Aunt Phyllis was an ardent campaigner on behalf of free love both before and after her marriage although in her case – and this is unusual for a Williams – actions have spoken louder than words.

How Mary Williams became, and remained, Mary Fixx is one of my family's more enduring mysteries. They met in 1938 on a train – he, the straight-backed junior officer, a man ill at ease with anything you couldn't shoot, ride to hounds or boss about; she, the young teacher, with more brains than sense, on her way to change the world – and, quite extraordinarily, they established some sort of relationship.

Later, at the slightest excuse, they would engage in sickening banter about the exact circumstances of the meeting.

'He just offered me his *Daily Express*, you know. As if we'd known each other for years.'

'You mean, you asked for it. I was quite taken aback.'

'Nonsense. I was keeping myself to myself. A respectable young girl. The last thing I expected was to be accosted by a serving officer of the crown.'

'Saucy minx, even then.'

'The other passengers were *very* suspicious. Started giving us disapproving, jealous looks. They could see what was going on.'

'Damn lucky I didn't miss the train.'

'Heaven knows who you would have picked up on the next one.'

'Mary!'

And so on.

At a normal time, the mutual attraction of strangers on a train would have quickly cooled off as his stupidity and her bolshiness bubbled to the surface, but these were not normal times. The gathering storm made strange bedfellows, and none stranger than Mother and Father. To say that Adolf Hitler was responsible for their marriage, and therefore my birth, may appear harsh, but it is not far from the truth.

In January 1939, Lieutenant Colin Fixx and Mary Williams were married. By May he was away from home on active service.

– Of course, you might have been born anyway.

– Without Hitler?

– Maybe you were why they married.

– It's true that I was born in August. Mother always said I was premature. It somehow seemed in keeping with my character.

– Overpunctuality?

– Young man in a hurry. Ready to jump the gun if necessary, to steal a march on the opposition. I was competitive, even before I breathed air.

– But you could be, technically anyway, a –

– A bastard, yes. Or a semi-bastard. I would only have been conceived out of wedlock. But personally I find the idea of Father and Mother locked in a premarital embrace somewhat ludicrous.

– The sex lives of our parents always are.

– Quite.

If the Führer was not the prime mover behind my parents' engagement and marriage, he certainly had a posthumous hand in keeping it intact during those troubled post-war years. For, apart from a couple of months in 1939 before he marched off to war (Mother claims these days that on several occasions he returned home on leave, but I'm damned if I can remember it), husband and wife were never to know one another as they really were. With parts of his already limited cerebrum scattered over a Normandy hillside, Father frankly lacked the wherewithal to be the blinkered authoritarian old bigot he would otherwise have become and Mother, required by any standard of decency to be a nurse rather than a wife, had no alternative but to rein in her wayward and bloody-minded intellect (although it found an underhand, clandestine outlet, as I was later to discover). From 1947 until my father's spectacular last offensive, they lived in a fantasy world, in which the normal hostilities of the average marriage were suspended indefinitely. In fact, it was not so much a marriage as a hospital soap opera, a protracted game of doctors and nurses.

No wonder I took to playing truant from school, to wandering the streets of Biggleswade looking for adventure, to passing the time by imitating a machine-gun behind Father's chair. I was a determined child, I admit, not above expressing myself by going on hunger strike for more pocket money, or refusing to sleep anywhere but between my parents in their large bed, where my bed-wetting caused many a memorable early morning scene. Maybe such behaviour was nothing less than a cry for help, possibly the last cry for help in Jonathan Peter Fixx's life. At any rate, it's the sort of thing mothers are meant to be able to handle.

But Mother couldn't. Or, as I now believe, wouldn't.

Rather than face up to her parental responsibilities, she enlisted the help of Nanny Whiting, the most enthusiastic and expert wet-nurse any eleven year old could wish for.

2
Youth's heavy burden

Aunty Bar-Bar lasted at 32 Elm Tree Drive for almost two years, and I confess that, all things considered, my life improved somewhat during her final six months with us.

In a vain attempt to encourage Father to rejoin the human race, Mother had begun to take him out to the local cinema on Friday nights. These weekly excursions into the realms of Hollywood, Disneyland and Ealing had no noticeable effect on Father, who continued to live in his own private fantasia, but it did allow my nanny one evening's solo babysitting, which she put to good use.

'Bathtime,' she'd announce gleefully, within moments of my parents leaving the house.

'Going, Aunty Bar-Bar,' I would say quickly, perhaps aware that this new interest in my cleanliness was somewhat unhealthy, considering that I was already a mature lad for my age.

'I'll be up soon.'

'But Aunty – '

'I know you boys. Splish-splash and out you get. You probably don't even clean behind your ears.'

So it was that – reluctantly, bashfully – one Friday, I allowed Aunty Bar-Bar to help me in my ablutions.

It had to happen, I suppose. Me, innocently lying back in the warm water as she, eyes sparkling with pleasure, a thin film of sweat on her upper lip, busied herself with her soapy ministrations on my lean young body.

'Goodness me,' she said coarsely as, to my inexpressible embarrassment, something proud and surprising appeared through the bubbles like a small but lethal inter-continental missile. 'It's Mr Doodah come up for a look around.'

With the natural shyness of a boy my age, I attempted to disguise my state with a little cloud of bubbles, but Aunty Bar-Bar would have none of it. 'No,' she said, with a softness in her voice that was quite new to me. 'He doesn't want to hide.' She leant down and softly blew the bubbles away from me. I closed my eyes in shame and fear. 'I think,' said Aunty Bar-Bar, soaping her hands purposefully, 'Mr Doodah's come out to play.'

These are painful details to relate. Indeed I only relive the strange events of those Friday nights in order to cast light on my later life. Child abuse scars for ever. Sometimes, I find myself wondering by what miracle it was that I have grown up to be so normal.

Not that I was an entirely unwilling victim. In fact, it was I who suggested the following week, as Aunty Bar-Bar bobbed about the bathroom, her sleeves rolled up like a peasant washer-woman, soaking herself as she attended to Mr Doodah, that we might be comfier in her bedroom.

She looked up, rather sharply. 'Quite the little man of the world, eh?' she said, not entirely pleased that I had regained the initiative. Reaching for the towel, she dried her face. 'Chop chop then. Up sticks.'

And so we took what Aunty Bar-Bar still referred to as the High Road to Bedfordshire, where my education in the ways of the flesh took new and ever-surprising turns. In the brief moments of repose during those evenings as we lay uncomfortably in her single bed, Aunty Bar-Bar would conduct a monologue around the theme of her deprived past and her rosy future.

It was rather interesting, to tell the truth. The back streets of Coventry, the large Bar-Bar family, the drunken father, the brutish elder brother whose concern for her was more than fraternal, the local cinema where, as far as I could see, she had spent most of her teenage years on a crash course in the care and maintenance of most of Coventry's Mr Doodahs, her escape south to become a nanny (without, I discovered, the slightest qualification for the job), how she was going to settle down one day and have lots of kiddies ('and no bloody nanny, that's for sure'), in a nice house with a garden . . .

At this stage, as the reminiscences began to pall, my precociously virile young body would frequently come to my rescue.

'Ooh,' she'd say, with mock coyness. 'Naughty. *Very* naughty. Now what does he want?'

My eyes averted her hungry look. I may have blushed. After all, I was still a child. 'Kissy-kissy?' I'd mutter shyly, having discovered that there's nothing quite like kissy-kissy for Mr Doodah when it comes to putting a stop to tedious bedtime conversation (a lesson, incidentally, that has stood me in good stead throughout my adult life).

'Chop chop, Aunty Bar-Bar,' I said, enjoying my new-found power. 'Down the little red lane.'

–It's a bit implausible, this.

–Take it or leave it. That's what happened.

–A superstud before you reached puberty?

–It's not that unusual, in fact. The young Byron was seduced by his nurse when he was nine. Aristotle Onassis tried it on with the family laundress when he was eleven. Something happened to Baudelaire, I believe. A lot of us start early.

–You seem to have made quite a study of it.

–One picks up these things, if one happens to have a photographic memory. Personally, I wish it hadn't happened. I'd like to skip the whole thing.

–But you owe it to history to provide the seamy details.

–No. A sketchy broadbrush account should do the trick.

How did you lose yours? On some star-spangled night in the arms of a teenage sweetheart? Amidst a happy confusion of tangled limbs and underwear in the back seat of Daddy's car? Maybe a romp in the hay with an older cousin and, whoops, it was gone. Or did you drink too much at a party and give yourself to a stranger on top of a pile of overcoats? Where was it, the setting for that momentous never-to-be-repeated event? Your parents' bedroom while they were out enjoying an agreeable Tracy and Hepburn double feature at the Gaumont? Or perhaps it was you at the Gaumont, finishing round the back what you started in the cheap one and nines. And your precious gift, your flower not exactly untouched by human hand but still more or less intact, was it given freely, or was it snatched from you, pilfered while your thoughts were elsewhere, or simply nagged out of you? And how was the great moment? Nasty, brutish and short, or did it seem to go on for ever, like a long and bumpy journey? And when it was over, did you cry, or did you dust yourself down briskly and assume things could only improve? I bet you remember it, even if you're old and past it now.

How I envy you your sweet, normal memories.

It was my twelfth birthday and, in spite of my parents' cackhanded attempts at jollity, the day had passed more or less like any other. I had always been a solitary lad and, ever since I had first taken control of my mother at the age of four, I had steadfastly refused the annual humiliation of a birthday party. This was not shyness and, to tell the truth, I could have used a few extra birthday presents, but my contemporaries bored me and, beyond using them for homework, I was determined to have as little to do with them as possible. This precocious sense of my apartness from the common herd is, I believe, not unusual in the young achiever. Einstein's first words ('The soup's cold') were spoken at the age of sixteen. When asked by his parents the reason for his long silence, the young genius replied, 'Because up to now everything was in order.' Thus it was with me, although everything was far from in order. Aloof, contemplative, my own man.

So, there had been a cake, a few presents (mostly money, I was glad to find), and that was just about it. With a hint of desperation, Mother suggested that we go out to the cinema as a birthday treat but, by the end of the day, I was bored with the false *bonhomie* and politely declined, preferring to retire early to bed, feigning a headache.

'Going to Bedfordshire at this hour? On his own birthday?' Aunty Bar-Bar hovered threateningly over my bed, as she wished me goodnight. 'No treats for the birthday boy?' I shrank down under the covers, somewhat relieved that Mother and Father were downstairs and that my nanny was therefore unable to slake her unnatural lusts on my poor, abused young body. Truth to tell, the novelty of bathnights was beginning to wear off.

'I've had a lovely day, thank you, Aunty Bar-Bar.'

'Bye-byes time, Jon-Jon. Maybe – ' as she tucked me in, she casually pressed her right breast into my face, 'maybe treats will come later.'

She winked at me vulgarly from the door, and turned out the light. Oh no, I thought, lying there in the dark, she can't, she wouldn't – not with my parents there. Could she?

How young I was. How innocent. Today I know that sex, for the average woman, is like a drug. Most men they can take occasionally and lightheartedly – a puff here, a snort there, nothing serious. Others (and, luckily for them, we are few and far between) they take once and are hooked. The more they have, the more they want. Of course, it can be a mixed blessing, having a body that for the fair sex is totally addictive, the hardest of drugs. Mine really should carry a government health warning. The first of many, Aunty Bar-Bar was in need of her private little Fixx.

I remember it all with the vividness of a dream. It must have been two or three in the morning when I was awoken by the unmistakable aroma of the cosmetics counter at Woolworth's. There, beside my bed, like a vast, white ghost in her billowing nightgown, stood Aunty Bar-Bar. She smiled and put a finger to her lips and I noticed, by the light of the moon shining through my window, that, although it was the middle of the night, she had what she called 'put on her face'.

'Birthday treats for Jon-Jon,' she said, looking down at me hungrily.

'It's not my birthday any more,' I said weakly.

'*Little* one.' To my horror, Aunty Bar-Bar pulled her nightdress over her head. Huge and naked (this was the first time I had been confronted by her awe-inspiring bulk in its totality), she pulled back my bedclothes and slowly began to unbutton my pyjamas.

It's a funny thing, the human body, isn't it? These days Signor Libido knows who's boss. He obeys orders. Need to slow things down? Drop a little hint maybe by a show of passive non-cooperation downstairs? Easy. I shift my mind away from the action to contemplate a suitably neutralising topic. My share portfolio. Who to sack next. The first ten lines of 'The Charge of the Light Brigade'. Semolina at Melton Hall. The death of Father. My ex-wife. Exit Signor Libido, tail between his legs.

But then my young body was an impulsive thing. It lived a life of its own. There was no telling it. As Aunty Bar-Bar addressed herself huskily to my pyjama cord ('And *down* with the pywags'), it was giving her all the wrong messages.

'Now,' she said, with a little satisfied smile, 'are you ready to give it all to Bar-Bar?'

Mouth dry, eyes squeezed shut in shame, I nodded dumbly.

'Lie still then,' she said more briskly as, swinging her leg over me, she placed a plump knee on each side of my body. Through half-closed eyes, I saw her lowering herself carefully on to me. As, with a surprising lightness, she made contact, momentary confusion ensued – there was, after all, a lot of her and not that much (we're talking early days here) of me. Vaguely aware that I was meant to make some sort of contribution, I rummaged around the folds of flesh that were attempting to envelop me, as if I were searching for the best present in the bran tub at Christmas. Somewhat roughly, Aunty Bar-Bar pushed my hand aside and, with a girlish intake of breath, she had me just where she wanted me.

'Up and down, up and down,' she crooned softly.

It can't have lasted long – five minutes, maybe less – and, once the terror had subsided, it was not entirely unpleasurable.

'This is the way the ladies ride.' There was now a daffy cradle-rocking expression on Aunty Bar-Bar's face. 'Trit-trot . . . trit-trot . . . trit-trot.'

Then, quite suddenly, she winced as if in pain and, placing a chubby hand firmly on each of my shoulders, gasped through gritted teeth, 'Keep still, Jon-Jon, don't move.' ('What *was* that?' I asked her during a quiet moment the following week. 'That was Aunty Bar-Bar having her climax,' she said primly. I was none the wiser.) Seconds later, she sighed gigantically, like a great overblown tyre being let down, and shuddered to a halt. Such was my surprise, that, at the same moment, I found my own release. It was a poor, low-key affair compared to hers but not at all bad under the circumstances.

For a minute or so, Aunty Bar-Bar lay draped over me, crooning softly, running a clammy hand through my hair. She was not so light now, and it was some relief when she clambered off and, with brisk professionalism, slipped on her nightdress, put me back in my pyjamas, straightened my bedclothes and tucked me in.

'Better now?' she said, as if the whole thing had been my idea. She kissed me on the nose, whispered, 'You're a man now, Jon-Jon,' and tiptoed out of the door.

So, in my little wooden bed, on my gaily coloured Dan Dare bedspread, I bade farewell to the flower of my innocence, my remarkably short-lived virginity.

And that was how I lost it.

My nanny sat on me.

It is not my intention to recount the depths to which Aunty Bar-Bar dragged me during those long evenings when we were left alone. I imagine her reading these words – fat, alone and unloved in some obscure home for dying nannies – and feel not the slightest temptation to add to her shame by reciting a catalogue of her pet perversions. Suffice it to say that, by the age of twelve and a half, I had a fair idea of what rampant desire can do to a woman and I was less than impressed. To this day, I can hardly recall those dread words, 'Give it all to Bar-Bar,' without a shudder of dread and embarrassment.

After playing along with her for a while, out of curiosity and a certain old world *politesse* (someone at Elm Tree Drive had to keep up standards), I decided that enough was enough. I was tired of my nanny's tricks. My homework was suffering. I wanted my childhood back. Delicately, carefully, I engineered her departure.

'My nanny's a perv. She makes me give her climaxes.'

At first, there was scepticism in the schoolyard when I made this announcement. What was a perv? What was a climax? Could Fixx (who had gained a quite unjustifiable reputation as a bit of a romancer) be believed? None of the grimy, eager-faced lads who were soon pressing me for details had the firm grounding in rhymes for the modern nursery that I had.

So I educated them in the weekly adventures of Wee Willie Winkie – every rub-a-dub-dub, every hey-diddle-diddle, every come blow your horn and ride a cock-horse, from hooray and up she rises to when the pie was opened.

Naturally, Aunty Bar-Bar's accomplishments spread like wildfire through the school, becoming more exaggerated and bizarre as they were passed from one clueless youth to another and, children being what they are, it was not long before the hooligan element in the senior forms subjected her to a certain amount of raucous *badinage* as she collected me from school.

'Naughty Jon-Jon,' she said, looking unsmilingly ahead of her, as we walked home one day. A couple of boys from Class One had winked lasciviously and leered, ''Ullo, Aunty Climax,' as we walked past.

'Who's been telling tales?' she said a minute or so later, after several other boys had pointed at us and run away giggling.

'Sorry, Aunty Bar-Bar,' I replied, in my most appealing, hangdog tone. 'They made me. It just slipped out.'

'Of course it did.'

You'd think that someone as experienced with children as Aunty Bar-Bar claimed to be would have taken this sort of ribbing in good part, but the truth is that the bounce seemed to have gone out of her recently. Once she had been fun, fat and fruity; now she was moody and tearful, mooching about the house in an uncharacteristically distracted way. Even our Bedfordshire evenings together had become peculiarly joyless, with Aunty Bar-Bar frequently bursting into tears as she achieved lift-off. It was certainly not the last time this was to happen to me – in my experience, members of the fair sex frequently go off the rails at the *point sublime*, and are as likely to cackle with unrestrained laughter as they are to break down in sobs (why they can't just get on with it, like men do, I've never understood) – but all the same, it was disconcerting for a lad of twelve, doing his best under difficult circumstances.

'If only I could talk to you,' she used to wail, as if I were some kind of dumb animal. Unable to think of a suitable answer, I would adopt the kind of soppy, sympathetic expression which, I had already discovered, is the only way to handle tearful scenes when there's nothing useful to say.

It was a difficult time for everyone, particularly for me. There I was, on the very cusp of puberty, my young mind aswarm with plans, my young body a mess of confused desires. The very last thing I needed was a dumpy gloomy-drawers, sighing and casting doleful looks in my direction at every opportunity.

I had a life to lead, a future to attend to, just as she had a job to do and a household to keep tidy. If for some reason she was falling disastrously behind with her duties – on one memorable occasion I was obliged to iron my own trousers – there was really no need for me to suffer with her.

'Mother,' I said late one evening. 'I want to leave home as soon as possible.'

My mother looked up in surprise from her typewriter as I stood, pale and dejected, before her.

'Darling,' she said. 'What on earth is the matter?'

'I want to go to boarding-school.'

'That's rather too expensive for us, Jonathan. You know that.'

My little face puckered with distress.

'I can't stand it any more,' I sniffed. 'The way she looks at me.'

'Who looks at you? What are you talking about?'

'Aunty Bar-Bar. She's always pestering me. When I'm trying to do my homework. She wants to . . . '

'Yes?'

'Mother, she always wants to bath me. It's so embarrassing. All that dropping the soap and fishing round for it. Do I smell or something?'

There was a moment of silence.

'I'll speak to her.'

'I want her to go, Mother,' I said, warming to my theme. 'Either that or boarding-school.'

The showdown was spectacular. It was after I had retired to bed that Aunty Bar-Bar was summoned to the Snug. I could hear their voices – Mother's firm and authoritative, Aunty Bar-Bar's increasingly hysterical, Father's gruff and largely uncomprehending. After about half an hour, there was some sustained caterwauling from Aunty Bar-Bar, followed by the sound of slamming doors and sobs.

I was almost asleep when the bedroom door opened. It was Aunty Bar-Bar, and she was carrying a suitcase.

'You little bastard,' she hissed melodramatically across the room, her face blotchy and streaked with mascara. 'I hope you grow up to be a better man than you were a child.'

She snuffled noisily before turning on her heel and clomping heavily down the stairs. I heard the front door slam. Within seconds, I was in the Land of Nod.

– She never replied to the letter I sent to her mother's address.

– Typical. She always took more than she gave.

–Maybe she was suspicious of the postbox number I gave. A lot of them are, you know. We still haven't heard from Lord Talbot. Nor your friend Mr Collin.

–You can't trust people like Aunty Bar-Bar. If she knew where I was she would have grassed me up as soon as look at me.

–Still it would have been interesting to hear her story.

–A child molester? What on earth could she contribute to the memoirs of an achiever?

–I would have liked to have heard from her anyway. After all, we do have something in common.

–Of course. You didn't tell her–

–Would I do that?

–Perhaps not. You never know who to trust these days.

–You can trust me.

–I hope so.

'Miss Whiting has gone,' said Mother over breakfast the next morning. Both she and Father looked pale and short of sleep. It was, I supposed, something of a blow losing the woman who had made their life so easy. I felt almost sorry for them.

'I'll do my best to help,' I said. 'About the house, I mean.'

'You won't have to,' said my father with a surprising harshness in his voice. 'Your mother and I have decided to send you to boarding-school. Don't know how we'll pay. Army might help out. Sell a few things. We'll get by somehow. But you're off, sonny-me-lad. Public school will–' Father paused at the end of this astonishingly coherent speech '–sort you out.'

'It'll help you meet new people,' said Mother, almost sympathetically.

'Make a man of you,' said Father gruffly. As Mother looked at him sharply, he blushed, possibly aware that my manliness was hardly the problem. 'A *team* man of you.'

This was not at all what I had expected. In fact, it was a bolt from the blue.

'I'm not sure I want–'

'No, it was your idea, darling,' said Mother firmly, 'and you were quite right. We'll get in touch with the army school today. I'm sure they'll find a place for you, what with Father's war record.'

‘Army school?’ I said weakly. My little world was crashing about my ears.

‘Melton Hall,’ said my father. ‘First-class place. Bit rough and tough, but sound on sport and discipline. It’ll give you – ’ he looked at me, rather nastily, I thought ‘ – a sense of values.’

3
A rounded education

– Now we did hear from them.

– A particularly unhelpful communication, I thought.

– Yes, not very informative. 'Dear Mr Fixx,

'Thank you for your letter requesting information about your career at Melton for your autobiography. It is always a great pleasure to hear from Old Meltonians, particularly those who have made such a success of their lives as you appear to have done.

'Unfortunately, we have no record of your time at Melton Hall that will be of much use. You were a promising bat, I see, appearing once in the Colts Second XI and were briefly a member of the school drama group but, since you left school rather earlier than normal, in 1956 (the year of the legendary Planetarium fire – perhaps you remember it?), your name does not figure largely on the Prefect, First XI or Scholarship boards. Mr Crawley, the Latin master, who is still "in harness" recalls you distinctly but mysteriously claims that he has nothing to say that would be repeatable in an autobiography. His sharp wit is as lively as ever!

'You may be interested to hear that our next Old Meltonian Gaudy will be on 10th July. We hope to coax Major Fanshawe, who doubtless was Master in your day, out of retirement for the occasion.

'Yours sincerely,
'Bernard Dalton
'Master of Melton Hall'

– Dear God. Ferret Fanshawe, still alive. That'll be an occasion to avoid.

– So you were unhappy at boarding-school?

– Oh, I wouldn't say that.

As the lion runs with the warthog, so the achiever is obliged at times to keep the company of the also-rans, to be jostled by Mr Average,

Mrs Normal, Ms Ordinary. Looking back over the first half of my life, I can't help reflecting that I've been particularly unlucky in this regard, with losers flocking to me like moths candle-wise.

I picture them now, all those goofy, down-at-heel has-beens, scurrying to the bookshops as my memoirs are published to universal acclaim, 'Old Jon's gone public, eh, wonder what he has to say about me?', leafing eagerly through the index in search of their names – in vain! They stumble incredulously out of the shop . . . Ah. Without the book. A phoney index, perhaps? (Check with Mr Publisher.) Those whose dull little stories are amusing, or who complement in an interesting way my own development, I may possibly mention, but frankly I'll be keeping what I call the dross quotient down to a minimum.

This little detour down Dud Avenue was prompted by memories of Melton Hall. Seldom have I been surrounded by quite so many irredeemable mediocrities as I was at that inglorious establishment. Warthogs? They were more like lumps of mud. At times they made the folks back home in Biggleswade look almost interesting.

True, Melton has had its minor celebrities. Archer, the scribbler. Heseltine, the politician. Rice, the songsmith. Collin, the pinko sewer rat. Hunt, the racing driver. They were all, at some time or another, part of my set at college, they were Fixx men; I provided them with something to which to aspire during their formative years. Would they have achieved their modest success in later life without my benign influence? It is not for me to say. But I'll vouch that there are more than a few minor-league achievers all over the world who, as they go about their daily, profitable business, say to themselves, 'Thank God for Fixx!'

Because, in a very real and meaningful way, my necessarily brief public-school career can be said to have revolutionised the place.

In those days (and in these, for all I know or care) Melton Hall stood as living proof that private education is not always a passport to privilege. Indeed there were times when I and my contemporaries (in the main, the sort of edgy, underfed adolescents you'd expect to find in a bargain basement boarding-school) would have given a term's tuck for the privations often associated with the more squalid comprehensives. Muggings in the schoolyard? Five pupils to a book? Drugs sold openly in the classroom? That was nothing – the merest *rien* – to what we had to endure at Melton Hall.

Let me show you.

It is the first Sunday morning chapel of term. The Master, Major 'Ferret' Fanshawe, has announced the business of the week – a First XI match against Sheringham (any boy not cheering will run round the pitch twenty times), the opening of the new Planetarium by an eminent Old Meltonian, now a Conservative MP, the usual warning about smoking in the rhododendrons. The English master (better known as O'Weally Weid) has struggled his way gamely through the lesson – 'God is our wefuge and stwength, a vewy pwesent help in twouble' – and the entire school has droned along a couple of beats behind 'As Pants the Hart', one of the five hymns that Fanny Wilson, the obese, alcoholic music master, can handle on the school organ. Against the sound of muttering from the boys, some of whom are reading pornographic paperbacks or doing last night's prep, the new chaplain, the Reverend Derek (soon to be Dippy) Ward, ascends to the pulpit.

'If there's one thing that the Good Lord cannot tolerate,' he warbles good-heartedly, his bifocals catching the sun which streams through one of the stained-glass windows, 'and I must say I go along with Him all the way here, it is insincerity. Lack of integrity. What I call, hum – ' he paused for effect, ' – buggery.'

There is a moment of stunned silence in the school chapel. We had only been half listening. Had we heard correctly? The new chaplain has, albeit briefly, captured his audience. To our delight we see that Ferret Fanshawe is turning a deep, angry shade of red, and is looking up at the pulpit in a way that is not entirely friendly.

'Because humbuggery helps no man, does it?'

Now this is dangerous stuff. Does Ward not realise that only last term most of Nelson House was expelled after a fire practice had revealed a daisy-chain of feverish after-lights-out activity stretching from the head boy to the newest new man. Or that his predecessor, Poncy Pringle, was, that very same term, removed from office after Jones and Spitteler found him, in an agitated and defrocked state, mud-wrestling with a local police constable at Gunner's Hole? Has Ward not been briefed?

Perhaps he has. For now, after its promising start, his sermon nosedives into the predictable. It's not just cleanliness that's next to godliness, it's goodliness, decency, what we used to call gentlemanliness.

'We don't hear so much about gentlemanliness these days, do we?' Ward looks at us challengingly. 'It's a bit old-fashioned, isn't it – a bit *square*? But the gentleman – the verray parfit gentil knight, to quote Chaucer – is none other than the prototype, the blueprint for the Christian . . . '

Ferret has returned to his normal colour now. This is more like it; he can relax. In fact, we can all relax. The boys sit back, revert to their porn or drift off once again into some confused, grubby adolescent fantasy. The masters (or 'ushers', as they were called) sit, hunched in sleepy, nose-picking boredom, on the staff pews.

Dear oh dear, what a collection of grey, scurfy, warped, insecure has-beens they were – the very dregs of middle-class mediocrity. Drag Watts, the chain-smoking head of the maths department. Fiddler Curtis, his hands sunk deep into his trouser pockets. The school sadist, Thwack Bailey, for once without his preferred educational tool, Cedric the Cane ('Bow for Cedric, boy, touch your toes'). Squidge, the Neanderthal, musclebound PT instructor. Creepy Crawley, a mustachioed bender whose method of correcting the younger boys' Latin unseens was to run his cold, well-manicured hands up the legs of their shorts, pinching their buttocks tenderly with every error. Pip-Pip Peters, O'Weally Weid, Bogey Borrodaile . . . you get the picture, I'm sure. Without suggesting that every member of staff at Melton Hall was a slave to alcohol, homosexuality, sado-masochism or senile dementia, it's fair to say that, as a team, they covered the scummy waterfront of human weakness and corruption pretty thoroughly.

Dippy Ward's sermon is reaching what, for want of a better word, I'll call its climax.

'I'm not saying – ' to everyone's relief, Ward starts gathering up his notes (he made notes for *this*?) ' – that when the Bible says "In my father's house, there are many mansions", the author of the Holy Writ was working along the lines of Raleigh, Drake, Churchill and – ' he gave a knowing little smile (bloody hell, he *did* know) ' – Nelson. Merely that if the Lamb of God was amongst us today, here in this chapel, if Jesus was a Meltonian, then you would see in Him the very essence of gentlemanliness, of leadership and team spirit.'

Ferret nods approvingly at this brilliant perception. He likes a sermon that puts College in a suitably biblical context.

'I'm not saying that He would be some kind of swot, what you might call a goody-goody. I'm not even saying He would be in the first XV. In many ways, the Son of God was essentially ordinary. No superman, He. There is little evidence in the Bible that he was particularly strong or fast or that he had a good kick. But we do know – ' Dippy looks down on us boys with as stern an expression as he can manage ' – that he played the game, and like a gentleman. Whichever team Jesus, were he a Meltonian, found Himself in, you can rest assured that He would be a credit to His house, to college and to His parents – ' For a moment, he seems confused. 'To His parent. That, whatever the score, Jesus would *get His tackles in*. Now to God the Father, God the Son . . . '

Those few of us who have bothered to half-tune in to Ward's first sermon are impressed. Poncy Pringle had been dull and distracted, his mind no doubt on Gunner's Hole, but this was really quite entertaining.

'Jolly good sermon, sir,' we chirrup at him as he stands, grinning stupidly, among his flock outside the chapel.

'Really interesting.'

'We're really going to lay off the humbuggery, sir.'

The Rev. Ward nods earnestly. 'You do that, Wingfield,' he says.

Unfortunately, Dippy's success went to his head. The following Sunday, he took the pulpit and declaimed, 'The tongue is an unruly member, the Bible tells us. Now, how many unruly members are here this morning?'

But no other sermon ever quite lived up to the promise of his dissertation on gentlemanliness. Jesus as a fly-half in the Second House XV! You can see why we called him 'Dippy'.

You're not going to believe this.

Collin and I were strolling to the tuck shop across the small field which passed for a cricket pitch. In the middle distance, we could see Nobby Henderson, the school handyman, sweeping up leaves like some dinky old gardener from a tale by Beatrix Potter (except this Mr McGregor was a dribbling moron who exposed himself to the boys as and when the mood took him). We were veterans of two years at Melton Hall and, largely thanks to my efforts, could more or less do what we liked. I may have been smoking at the time, for example; certainly the money we were about to spend on chocolate and wine gums was not our own.

'Try me,' I said. Already a competitive little creep, Collin was forever trying to present himself to the world as being rather more interesting than he was (or is).

'Binns tried to harrow me last night.'

'Binns? Harrow? Urgh, horrible.'

'And when I told him I didn't like harrowing, he went all moody and pathetic. Then he said, "What about a quick shrewsbury then?"'

'What did you tell him?'

'I told him to sod off. Which he did. With Caldecott Minor.'

'Marlborough?'

'What else?'

You'll be familiar with public-school slang, if not the precise Melton *patois*. Doys, scugs, nervies, boggers and tishfags were part of everyday life at the school, just as etons, shrewsburies, marlboroughs, harrows and wellingtons were part of our rather more active and original nightlife. The relentless perversity of the average British boarding-school for boys has been too well chronicled for me to tarry long here, but suffice it to say that never in my less than sheltered career – not even in the late sixties, when I was at the moist, throbbing epicentre of the rock industry – have I encountered bedhopping on the scale it took place at Melton Hall. We may not have been in the top ten (or twenty, or fifty) when it came to academic achievement or sport but, my God, if they had awarded points for rampant, organised promiscuity, we would have been right up there. *Right* up there. Generation after generation of Meltonians would take the specialities of other schools and add their own distinctive refinements. So far as I remember, sharing an eton with someone was regarded as the highest compliment a chap could pay to a chap, while offering to wellington someone was as near to an insult you could get without an out-and-out rejection, which at Melton was almost unknown.

I was no doubt regarded as something of an oddity since, with a few rare and forgettable lapses – I developed a brief partiality for dulwiching with the younger Forester-Jones, as I recall – I preferred to save my energies for more worthwhile school activities, such as making money.

Of course I had my chances: I was passably attractive, popular and a damn sight more developed in every sense than most boys in the school. Yet I preferred to stay on the sidelines. Perhaps I was still suffering from a sort of delayed reaction – severe withdrawal symptoms, if you like – following my traumatic experiences under Aunty Bar-Bar.

'There must be a way we can cash in on this craze for sexual experimentation,' I said, as Collin and I watched with only mild curiosity as Nobby Henderson, a toothless grin on his face, unbuttoned himself and fished out his weatherbeaten old turnip in greeting as we passed.

'Hardly,' said Collin, nodding a crisp 'Morning' to Henderson. 'There's no money in something when all around it's free.'

'Ah, yes. Eton, shrewsbury and marlborough. But that's not all there is in life.'

'No?' Collin was puzzled. Then the penny dropped.

'You don't mean – ?'

'I do.'

'D'you think we could? I mean, it's brilliant. But how?'

I pushed aside a group of younger boys as we reached the Tucker.

'I'll tell you.'

Girls. That's what I had in mind. Not in the same way as my contemporaries, of course. Not as some sort of unattainable promised land, wondrous yet full of snares. I knew girls and, for the moment, I was steering clear of them, such was the effectiveness of my nursery training. No, what I had in mind was not girls as an end in themselves, but as a means.

It was like this. As with any isolated single-sex community, Melton Hall had its currencies. Tobacco, alcohol, sweets, favourable introductions to the more attractive and amenable of the younger scugs – all these important items could be bought at a price, but it's fair to say that administratively the place was a shambles until yours truly brought his precocious entrepreneurial talent to bear. The result of my input was a streamlined system of bartering controlled by a commodity brokerage system – me, basically – and a set-up that suited everyone. The punters knew where to score, the school authorities were untroubled by messy scandals and I became the recognised and even slightly feared Mr Big of the Melton Hall underworld. (The scugs used to whine about exploitation now and then but, by the time they had learnt what 'exploitation' meant, they were too old to be of use anyway.)

For a while, it was enough: the power, the influence, the knowledge that there were few, if any, of my contemporaries (not to mention several masters) whom I did not have in a carrot-and-stick stranglehold of dependency and useful information. It all made for a remarkably smooth passage through college. In exams, my marks were high, the prefect invigilator turning a blind eye to the casual mid-paper consultations that were frequently necessary. In sport, opponents fell away when I was in possession of the ball ('*Tackle* him,' Squidge would scream as an opposing rugger team parted like the Red Sea to allow me to make my majestic way to the base-line for another try). And, of course, I was popular. That charisma, the personal magnetism with which it appears I was born, stood me in good stead during the turbulent years of adolescence.

'Can I get you anything, Fixx?'

'Will you be needing your hot-water bottle yet, Fixx?'

'I've warmed the seat for you, Fixx.'

The happiest years of my life? No, there were better days to come. But Melton Hall was not a bad start. Not at all.

Yet there was something missing. It was not what I would call a total, rounded education. Unworldly as I was, I had become aware that, despite my efforts on behalf of my fellow Meltonians, the rewards were somewhat intangible. Power and pleasure are all very well but, for true, lasting independence, a man needs something else – a basic financial grounding. I was damned if I was going to leave school without the wherewithal to live a decent life by dint of careful investment of capital. What I had put in, I now wanted to take out in the form of solid earnings.

That was why girls were on my mind.

Collin was half-hearted about the scheme, to tell the truth, but there again Collin would be. Happy enough to play along when the stakes were low, he was the type to duck out when true commitment and character were required.

'Isn't that going a bit too far?' was his pained reaction when I broadbrushed my plan, cleverly named Operation Venus.

'Not at all,' I smiled disarmingly. 'You just do your bit. Leave the rest to me.'

Collin nodded miserably.

I needed him, you see. The Brian Collin of then was not the grey, owlish, stooped creature of now. He was – in an utterly superficial way, of course – quite a looker. The crooked, appealing smile, the thick black hair, the tall, athletic gait, the easygoing manner – he could charm the birds out of the trees, old Collers, and a bird-charmer was precisely what I needed at this moment.

Not that our relationship was based entirely on self-interest. We were quite close, Collin and I. In fact, before he contracted his bad dose of scruples (which, with complications post-Melton Hall, developed into a terminal case of social conscience), I used to row him in on many of my better schemes.

'I mean, it's sort of like a brothel, isn't it?' he whined, sharp as a whip, even then.

I looked pained.

'You're so crude sometimes, Brian,' I said. 'It's merely answering a need, and providing apt rewards to the suppliers. A bit like a corner shop for goods not readily available at the Tucker.'

'Why don't you do it yourself, if you're so keen?'

'Ah – '

Ah. I was sixteen now and, if my school career was going swimmingly enough, the same could not be said of my home life. Shortly after my arrival at Melton Hall, I had received a bombshell from 32 Elm Tree Drive that frankly knocked me for a loop during much of my adolescence. My parents had adopted a child. A little girl. They were lonely, they said. They felt they had something to offer (cue hollow laughter from their natural son, virtually abandoned at boarding-school). Her name was Catherine. I'd love her, said Mother. They already did. Of course, one day I *would* love her, in my own way, but for the moment this cruel act of parental desertion played havoc with my deeper feelings. On the surface, I was the same jovial, good-hearted Fixx as ever but underneath, I was deeply disturbed. The cauldron of confused, misdirected feelings within me bubbled to the surface when I was sixteen and played havoc with my complexion. Yes, I place the responsibility for my unfortunate skin during puberty fairly and squarely at my parents' (and their darling little Catherine's) door.

Not being quite as good-looking as I was later to become (also rather short for my age, I admit it), I needed a bait.

'Ah . . . I will go myself,' I reassured Collin. 'Just make the introductions and you need have nothing more to do with the whole business.'

– So that's it, is it?

– Now what?

– The arrival of Catherine. The extending of the Fixx family. Your little sister. Neatly dismissed as the cause of a teenage zit rash.

– It was more than a rash. It lasted for quite a long time. It was very traumatic.

– All the same. Talk about tunnel vision.

– Perhaps it's simply that events in my particular tunnel are rather more interesting than what was going on outside.

– Perhaps.

As it happens, Collin did me proud.

I knew that he had been seeing a local girl called Sandra, a trainee hairdresser of passable looks and negligible moral character, for a month or so, having – an enterprising touch this, by his standards – picked her up at a local sweet shop.

Needless to say, not much had happened beyond a few slobbering kisses and a spot of hit-and-miss light petting – I swear that man's epitaph will be 'HE NEVER WENT TOO FAR' – but it was clear to me that Sandra was not likely to be content with *hors-d'oeuvres* when she discovered that the main meal was available all around her.

She was suspicious of me when one afternoon I joined the loving couple and Sandra's friend Mandy in a local coffee bar, her coarse 'Who's yer little friend?' speaking volumes for her social aptitude.

'This is Jonathan,' said Collin. 'He knows all about you.'

'Oh yeah?' said Sandra, cackling unappealingly in the general direction of Mandy.

'Charmed,' I said smoothly.

'And Mandy,' Collin continued, as if he were doing the honours at a suburban sherry party, 'this is my friend Jonathan.'

‘I know,’ spluttered Mandy, nudging Sandra in the ribs. ‘I could *spot* ’im a mile off.’

I stirred my coffee unsmilingly as the teenage harridans doubled up with hilarity. It was clear that this aspect of Operation Venus was going to be tiresome in the extreme. Having allowed the girls a couple of moments to recover from their little joke, I fixed them with my coollest stare.

‘Whoops,’ said Mandy, sitting to attention like a naughty schoolgirl. ‘ ’Scuse us, I’m sure.’

It was an unpromising beginning, yet later that term Mandy and I frequently found ourselves keeping Collin and Sandra company as they groped their way towards sexual knowledge. There were giggles. There was cider. There was dancing around handbags at the local dance hall. There was a certain amount of clammy rummaging about in each other’s underwear. Day after day, we’d square it with the duty prefect and slip off to town, Collin to pursue his fumbling courtship of Sandra, me to set up my great enterprise. Mercifully, Mandy had even less interest in playing second fiddle to her friend than I had so, after a few moments’ dutiful groping, we would sit back on the settee, light a cigarette and make jokes about the starry-eyed couple going at it like blunted knives in the bedroom next door.

It was on one of these occasions that I mentioned, as casually as I could manage, that I had hit upon a foolproof way for local girls to pick up a bit of pocket money. Like £20 a week.

‘You mean hustling, I suppose,’ she said casually. Crude as it was, this frank, naked greed was, I confess, somewhat refreshing after Collin’s squeamishness.

‘No, no,’ I said, taking her hand and patting it reassuringly. ‘Not exactly hustling. Nothing as difficult as that. It would all be very straightforward.’

‘Go on,’ she said. She really was quite beady for someone of virtually no education.

‘In the woods at school, there’s a new building. It’s small, dark and warm. You can book it for half an hour. No one disturbs you. It’s very cosy.’

‘What’s it for?’

‘I’m coming to that. Its only disadvantage is that it has a hole in the roof with a telescope sticking through it. For looking at stars. That’s what it’s for. It’s the new Planetarium.’

'Seems a bit of a waste,' said Mandy thoughtfully. My God, I was beginning to like this girl more and more.

'Isn't it just? It's hardly ever used.'

'And where does the money come in?'

I gave her a brief lesson in free market economics. We had the demand and, thanks to the Planetarium, we had the means of production. All we needed now was the product.

'And what exactly would "the product" be required to do?' asked Mandy, a hint of harshness in her voice. It occurred to me that the economic argument might have been rather too sophisticated for her.

'Not that much, as it happens. Most Meltonians would shell out for the privilege of being alone with a girl for half an hour with no strings attached. It's largely a question of peer-group pressure, you see. Like marbles at an earlier age – you were no one in your set if you didn't have a few. Girls will be a craze like any other. And we'll cash in.'

I could see Mandy was sceptical.

'All right,' I said quickly. 'Maybe they would have to work now and then. We could arrange some kind of system – '

'A sliding scale?'

'Precisely.'

'And what's in it for me?'

'A fiver per girl and ten per cent of the profits.'

'Fifteen.'

'Done.'

'And no freebies, right?'

I smiled attractively.

'We'll see about that,' I said.

Personally, I found it surprising quite how many girls were prepared to give up their amateur status for a bit of spare cash to spend on a new hair-do, a hula-hoop or the latest Cliff Richard album. We were inundated with teenage hopefuls – and some of those weeded out by quality control (superintendent – J. P. Fixx) took optimism to the limit. There were even one or two tentative enquiries from mothers but, after consulting with Mandy, I ruled out anyone over nineteen on the grounds that the older generation might frighten the punters.

As boyish pranks go, it was enormously successful. For two terms astronomy enjoyed something of a boom at Melton Hall. One by one, trembling, eager adolescents would make their way through the wood to the Planetarium. There, waiting for them, would be one of Mandy's Maids.

Apart from a few minor hitches – the odd double booking, the rather more frequent loss of nerve by a punter – there was only one potentially serious setback to the glorious flowering of my first enterprise.

Never a great devotee of spectator sports, being by nature a hands-on sort of person, I nonetheless liked to keep a watching brief over Operation Venus with the help of a step-ladder left outside the Planetarium. Seen down the wrong end of a telescope in the semi-darkness, the clammy events taking place inside took on, I found, a soft-focus, filmic quality that made for most agreeable viewing of an evening.

'What exactly are you doing up there, Mr Fixx?'

I was observing the rather beautiful first meeting between Sandra, who despite her involvement with Collin had been one of Mandy's first recruits, and Brightwell, a shy, good-looking lad of sixteen summers.

Unusually for a punter, Brightwell had not lunged at his partner like an over-enthusiastic fox-terrier, but had stood, paralysed with fear and embarrassment, as Sandra, with a gentleness which I found both surprising and touching, unbuttoned his shirt. Soon, they stood naked before one another, oddly oblivious to the chill of the autumn night (even I was trembling slightly by now). It was Romeo and Juliet, Abélard and Héloise, Love's Young Dream – or rather it would have been had Brightwell's young body responded to Sandra's attentions with at least a small degree of polite interest.

Fascinated by this romantic scene, I failed to notice that I too was being observed. But it was getting interesting down there – more than interesting. Sandra had laid a blanket on the floor and, showing an involvement in her task which bordered on the unprofessional, was drawing Brightwell down to her. I was so caught up in their tender drama that it was all I could do to restrain myself from slipping down the ladder, bursting into the Planetarium and leaping into the fray with a cry of 'I don't care which one it is but I've got to have one of you!' But it was not to be.

'I said, what's going on, Mr Fixx?'

I kept icy calm.

'Who's that?'
'It's Mr Henderson, sir.'
'Thank God for that,' I muttered. 'Be a good fellow and bugger off, will you? Can't you see I'm busy?'
'That I can, sir,' said the flashing groundsman, with a hint of menace in his voice. 'Lot of busyness around here these days.'
Casting a reluctant last glance down the telescope (it looked as if Brightwell was unthawing at last), I climbed down the ladder. There was nothing for it but to deal with the old pervert.
'What exactly do you want, Nobby?' I asked wearily.
'What you got, sir?'
I sighed.
'Climb up the ladder,' I said. 'Look down the telescope – and don't fall off.'
Henderson mounted the steps unsteadily. He peered suspiciously into the lens and gasped.
'Gooooorrrrr.' It was a deep rumble of appreciation. 'They're . . . well, they're at it, sir.'
'Are they?' I said coolly. 'Well done, Brightwell.'
It took no genius of negotiation to finalise matters with Henderson as he stood at the top of the shaking ladder, his eye glued to the telescope. He had found his El Dorado. With as much good grace as I could muster under the circumstances (I had been looking forward to overseeing future meetings between Sandra and Brightwell), I granted the old man an open option on the step-ladder in exchange for his silence, adding as an afterthought that he would be expected to clean up the Planetarium at the end of every evening. In view of the messy way many of my punters shot off like two bob rockets, it was a thoroughly sensible arrangement.
The economics of Operation Venus worked out remarkably well. It turned out that most Meltonians, underprivileged as they were when it came to education, were adept at tapping their parents for cash, guilt being a great loosener of purse-strings. During the brief period before it folded so unfortunately, Mandy had made enough to put down a deposit on a hairdressing salon, which for all I know is still in business, many of her girls had acquired a considerable degree of financial independence, and a generation of Meltonians had been relieved, to a greater or lesser extent, of adolescence's greatest burden, virginity.
And me? Referring to my Melton Hall accounts (how nice it is

to keep a sentimental record of one's schooldays), I see that by thrift and shrewd economics (the sum from which Mandy drew her fifteen per cent was, of course, rather lower than that which I actually charged the punters), I emerged from the enterprise significantly in credit.

Yet at the end of the day, Operation Venus was more than a question of finance. I recall with a keen sense of satisfaction the moment, about a month after the business had begun to work at full capacity, when Collin, his handsome young face streaked with tears, confided in me that Sandra had left him.

'She's working for Mandy,' he wailed. 'She'll be up at the Planetarium tonight.'

'Oh, I knew that,' I said. 'I thought she had discussed it with you.'

'I said I'd have nothing to do with her if she cheapened herself like that,' he said, already quite the little prig.

'Not that cheap,' I smiled, choosing not to remind him that he had declined to be part of the enterprise that had lured his girlfriend away from him. 'Anyway,' I added, in a vain attempt to cheer him up, 'I'm sure we could do you a special rate.'

Collin was never much of a fighter and I easily parried the wild punch he threw in my direction. I left him sobbing quietly to himself in his room, pondering the day's lesson: love hurts. At that moment, I'm sure Collers felt that nothing could go worse for him.

How wrong he was.

4
A slip on the ladder

In retrospect, I can appreciate the lesson that the good Lord was instilling in me – Be Not Proud, Set Not Yourself Above Others, More Haste, Less Speed – but, at the time, I was crushed by the unfairness of it all.

Just as Operation Venus had overcome its teething problems and was working smoothly and profitably for all concerned, I was summoned to Ferret Fanshawe's study. I could tell that the news he bore was not the best from his expression, a ludicrously hangdog attempt at dignity usually only deployed for the Master's Remembrance Sunday address.

'It is my sad duty,' he intoned, fixing me with a watery eye, 'to inform you that your father passed over yesterday.'

My mind must have been elsewhere because I remember saying, 'Passed over, sir? Passed over what?'

'He's dead, Fixx. Your father has died. Go to your dormitory, pack a bag. Henderson will drive you to the station. Return to college when – ' Ferret treated me to one of his long pauses ' – the obsequies have been completed.'

He held out a cold hand which I shook in a suitably distracted manner.

'I'm very sorry, Fixx.'

'So am I, sir.'

And I was. This was a downer, and no mistake. I had a matter of minutes in which to put the running of Operation Venus into safe hands for the duration. Thinking with commendable speed, I took the red book, which contained all future bookings, and sprinted to the library where I knew I could find Collin.

'No no,' he said, recoiling in prissy horror as I thrust the book in front of him. 'Leave me out of this.'

'Brian,' I said quietly, managing to squeeze a few tears out, 'I've just heard that my father's dead. You're my only – the only person I can turn to.'

Reluctantly, he took the book.

'Just keep it running till I get back.' I thumped him gratefully on the back. 'You're a good man, Collin.'

I raced back to my room, threw a few clothes in a case and, pausing only to hide past Red Books and the addresses of all the girls under a carpet in the Planetarium, I made my sorry way to meet Henderson in the school Rover at the front gate.

The story of Father's demise can be briefly told.

He had not so much passed over, as Ferret had said, as passed under the wheels of an 89 bus on the Biggleswade High Street.

Mother, not unnaturally, was inconsolable and blamed herself for the tragedy – quite rightly, as it happens, although I was too sensitive to say so to her face. It appeared that it was she who had misguidedly encouraged Father to accept the job offered to him by some generous soul in a nearby solicitor's office. His duties were hardly onerous, being of the stamp-licking, making-the-tea variety, but, it was revealed at the inquest, the poor man had found even these tasks beyond him. During the fortnight before his death, Father had not been seen at the office and, delicate to a fault, his colleagues had covered for him. It emerged that he had left the house every morning with a cheery wave to return, feigning exhaustion, at five-thirty.

One morning, he stepped out on to the High Street and, as a double-decker bus bore down upon him, he was heard to cry, 'Hold your ground, men!' They were his last words.

To any sane person hearing the evidence, it was quite clear that Father had taken what under other circumstances I would have to describe as the coward's way out. Yet the coroner recorded a verdict of 'Death by misadventure' – exceptionally generous, I thought, since it had been revealed that the old boy had doubled his life insurance a few days before his death. By one of life's cruel ironies, Father dead was to be worth significantly more to his nearest and dearest than Father alive ever had been.

Now that I was head of the family (never actually spelt out but I was happy enough to take on the responsibility), I felt it right to tarry a while at Elm Tree Drive with Mother and Catherine. Destiny, in the form of my own intense sense of loyalty, was to dictate that at the very moment when Operation Venus went critical hundreds of miles away, I was in the bosom of my family, mourning for Father.

It was a time for tears, even for the odd regret. Would my life have been different had I been blessed with a normal father? Probably. Yet I was damned if I could find it in my heart to resent that great grey cloud of paternal dullness that all but blotted out the sunshine of my childhood days.

Even now, I find distant memories of Father are quite liable to ambush me at surprising moments. A butterfly fluttering against a window-pane. An old war film on television. A double-decker bus. Or, most poignant of all, a jumbo jet flying noisily overhead.

It all comes back. The both of us in the kitchen at Elm Tree Drive, him under the table, me trying pluckily to pretend that there was nothing odd about his behaviour. The sound of an aeroplane fades in the distance. I pull the table back and poke him, perhaps with a touch of childish impatience, as he crouches there, his hands over his head. 'Plane gone, Father,' I say with a brave little smile. 'Ah, yes.' Father stands up shakily and brushes the dust off his trousers. 'Yup. Right. Tea?' And he pushes the kitchen table back into place as if nothing had happened.

Ah, memories!

I returned to Melton Hall to find my business empire in ruins and my best friend expelled in disgrace. If management, as they say, is the art of delegation, I had clearly failed badly in entrusting Operation Venus to Collin. I cursed him for his ineptness – it was harsh, I know, particularly under the circumstances – but bear in mind that I was still in a state of emotional shock.

In retrospect, I can see that Collin, being Collin, could have done little to save the operation. Was he to know that Mandy had fallen in love with a car mechanic and had lost interest in the business? That her once scrupulous vetting procedures were now almost entirely ignored? That now virtually any local girl could make her way to the Planetarium of a Saturday night? No doubt, I would have headed trouble off at the pass but Collin never was much of a businessman.

With the reluctant help of one of my more regular punters, I was finally able to fill in the details of what had happened.

The first sign of trouble had been when the elder Caldecott boy reported to the Sanatorium in a state of some embarrassment. 'Pop down your trousers,' said Matron. (It was her favourite phrase. Cough? Measles? Bang on the head? 'Pop down your trousers.') But this time, although she was on the right track for a change, she was at a loss to explain Caldecott's condition. After all, she's reported to have said to Ferret when the news broke, you don't expect to have to deal with that sort of thing at a boys' boarding-school.

Later that day, Fortescue checked in. The next day, five more boys stood in an itchy, embarrassed queue outside Matron's door. Within a week a large proportion of the middle and upper school (including several prefects, I was later proud to note) had popped down their trousers. It was clearly some kind of epidemic. The doctor was called in, after all Matron's excited attempts to diagnose the disease had failed. A brief glance down a victim's Y-fronts was all he needed.

And there it was. As other schools have chicken-pox and measles, Melton Hall had copped a very nasty dose.

It was hushed up, of course. If there's one thing a traditional British institution, even of the second-rate tin-pot variety, knows how to handle, it's an internal scandal. Every generation has one, although I'm bound to say that a clap epidemic may have been something of a first in public-school history.

Ferret issued dire warnings in morning chapel. Nothing too explicit, of course – the last thing he needed was some idiot scug blowing the gaff in a letter home ('Dear Mummy. There are no games at the moment because most of the team have got something called the clap. Matron says it's like pink-eye, except not in the eye'). No, Ferret referred to it as a particularly virulent form of athlete's foot to be found in the lower abdomen, but then confused some of the younger boys by promising that no action would be taken against those reporting to the San. Naturally, he was lying. Every infected boy was lengthily interrogated in the Master's study within minutes of being injected by Matron, who had taken to wearing rubber gloves at all times.

For a while, the Melton spirit frustrated Ferret's investigations. I must have caught it from a lavatory, sir. In a rugby scrum, sir. (This last excuse caused the Melton XV v. Wellington 'B' XV to be cancelled for the first time in living memory – despite the doctor's reassurances, Ferret was damned if he was going to risk College's reputation.) Eventually a disloyal youth by the name of Spriggs revealed the truth about Operation Venus.

Or most of the truth. Spriggs was somewhat in awe of me following an incident the previous term involving some inadequately polished shoes and a cricket stump. Collin, on the other hand, he rather liked. Collin was everyone's friend. So Collin it was he shopped, and who was told to pack his bags.

This was the shattering news that greeted me on my return to college from compassionate leave.

Naturally, I was upset that my friend's school career – which had hitherto been rather promising, as it happens – should have ended so suddenly and ignominiously and I don't deny that there were moments when I blamed myself for his downfall. But then, if he had not introduced me to Mandy, Operation Venus would never have happened; if he had not been so sloppy in his caretaking role, the little business which I had nurtured so carefully would never have died prematurely. So really, he was as responsible as anyone for what took place.

It was some comfort that, even at a moment of crisis, the traditional values of honour and loyalty, which both Collin and I held so dear, the Melton spirit, still counted for something. It would have been so easy to lay the blame at my door. Yet, very decently, Collin left college without having mentioned my name in connection with the scandal. He had shielded his old friend from the slings and arrows of an outraged Ferret and had paid the price.

Naturally I would have done the same for him, had circumstances been different.

It's the mark of an achiever that, even at the very worst of times, his entrepreneurial faculties are still on red alert. His heart may be heavy, but his mind is as agile as ever.

While I was grieving for my lost friend, it occurred to me that enough evidence still existed to entangle me in the Operation Venus scandal. Under the carpet at the Planetarium, which was now locked and bolted, lay all my records and accounts, written in my handwriting and with my name prominent throughout.

Still dazed and confused by events, I crept out later that night, helped myself to some petrol from the shed where Henderson kept his mowing-machine and set light to the Planetarium. It made a good blaze.

Back in my bed by the time the fire alarm went off, I found it difficult to share the noisy excitement of my fellow pupils as we were herded into Great Squad in our dressing-gowns. While fire engines dashed hither and thither, I gazed at the bright sky above the woods in sombre, reflective mood. It was, after all, the end of an era.

Imagine my feelings of distress when, the next day, I heard that it had also been the end of Henderson, that the charred remains of his body had been found amongst the smoking ruins of the Planetarium.

My mind reeled. I hadn't wanted this. How could I have known? Perhaps, looking back on it, I might have checked that the old man was not in his favourite place at the top of the ladder but I was in a hurry at the time. Was there to be no end to my suffering?

Naturally, there was a certain amount of speculation as to what exactly Nobby had been up to on the Planetarium roof in the middle of the night, a mystery compounded by reports that the deceased had been found with the burnt traces of his old corduroys around his ankles. Only I knew the secret. Nobby Henderson had, in his own simple-minded way, been trying to relive some of the exciting and surprising scenes he had witnessed over the past two terms. He had died, as he had lived, a dirty old man. There was, I reflected sadly, some small comfort in the cruel symmetry of it all.

Not that Nobby's demise sat easily on my conscience. In a matter of a month, I had experienced more death and disaster than any young lad deserves. I grew moody and distant. My work suffered. My skin bubbled. I found it difficult to communicate with my schoolfriends. I slept badly. After all, to have taken a life, however minor, is a terrible burden for a seventeen year old to bear. Frankly, I felt really bad about it.

Thus it was that Operation Venus finally took its toll. Nobby Henderson's life. Brian Collin's school career. Mandy and her mucky friends' reputations. And now, like the wingèd Sisyphus of legend, I found that I had flown too close to the blazing sun of free enterprise and, feathers badly singed, I was plummeting earthwards.

To tell the truth, I'd rather not dwell on my last terms at Melton Hall. Today, all these years later, the sadness of a young lad turned on by his fellows, the victim of the kind of casual persecution the British public-school system has perfected over the centuries, is still with me. The deep psychological scars have yet to heal. Maybe they never will.

Following the collapse of Operation Venus, and Collin's hasty departure, I found myself without friends. Debts remained unpaid. Contacts failed to make contact. Punters ceased to punt. I was no longer regarded as College's premier commodity broker. Those I had once consulted during tests and exams now shielded their papers like girls playing poker. On the pitch, the very boys who had once given me a clear passage with the ball now tripped me with a curse. I was a hardy little chap, and quick with it, but many was the game I finished muddy and bruised, having been mercilessly flattened by both the opposing side and my own team-mates.

It was a confusing, unhappy time. I wrote home, begging Mother to take me away. With a harshness I have since found difficult to forgive, she insisted I stayed to take A levels. It was the final straw. I had managed a clutch of O levels when at the height of my influence at Melton Hall (Creepy Crawley, the invigilator for our form, very decently ignoring my swift and effective copying of Guy Chapman's answers) but A levels, unassisted and alone, were out of the question. It was not that I lacked brains or perseverance but simply that during my school years I had had better things to do than to swot. When it comes to achieving, book learning comes a bad second to real life, as any successful captain of industry will tell you.

These are painful memories. Indeed the extraordinary events in the weeks leading up to my departure are no more than a blur to me. I remember bursting into tears as the school sang 'To be a pilgrim' at morning chapel. I remember daubing my face with ink during History with Fiddler Curtis. I remember standing in the middle of the pitch singing the school anthem, '*Semper Domus Meltoniensis*', as the two teams scrummed down during a match. I remember wearing a pair of Fanny Wilson's voluminous camiknickers on my head for confirmation class. I remember answering Maths sums with bits of cod Latin, French unseens with long equations. I remember wandering the quads at night, wild-eyed and bollock-naked, like some ridiculous Shakespearian loony.

The school tried everything. I was spoken to severely, beaten, told to pull myself together, beaten, put in detention, beaten, thrown in cold showers, beaten, taken to the San and told to pop down my trousers, beaten again. But, under this onslaught, my condition only worsened.

After what seemed an age, Mother was asked to take me away.

'Thank you, sir,' I said to Ferret Fanshawe as, with barely disguised relief, he shook my hand. I sniffed miserably, 'And . . . sorry, sir.'

'Sorry, Jonathan?' he smarmed, putting on a fine display of avuncular concern for the benefit of Mother, on whose arm I was leaning. 'Why should you be sorry?'

'For . . . letting College down.'

'Now now. None of that. No one has let anyone down.'

(Dream on, you silly old sod, I was thinking to myself. I may not have failed Melton Hall but, sure as hell, Melton Hall has failed me.)

'Thank you, sir,' I said.

The three of us made our way slowly from the Master's Lodge to Mother's car, which was parked in front of the main gate. I fumbled my way into the front seat like one lost in a dream. As Mother put the car into gear, I lowered the window and allowed myself to slip out of character with a stagy, somewhat vulgar wink at the Master as he stood there stupidly, hands clasped in front of him, like a man at a funeral.

'See you, Ferret,' I said softly, with a revealingly chirpy grin.

He narrowed his eyes and, for a moment, I thought he was going to try to stop the car. But then he shrugged, turned on his heel and trudged across the gravel back into Melton Hall.

– So that was why they don't remember you there? You had to leave early.

– Only slightly early. And my achievements were not of the kind a school shouts about.

– Did you mind leaving like that? On Mother's arm? Without any exam results to speak of?

– But I never actually failed my exams, you notice. I simply declined to take them.

– What happened to all those boys who visited the Planetarium? Did they try and keep in touch with Mandy and the rest of them?

– Of course not. Within moments, they were back in the old routine. Eton, dulwich, shrewsbury, wellington. They had been raised to fear women and the Operation Venus débâcle merely confirmed their suspicions. Tricky chaps. Different from us. Always ends in tears. Best to

stick to rubbing each other down in the showers, eh? Least you know what you are there – playing on home ground, and all that.

– What happened to them after Melton?

– Got jobs, married, went mad, died. God knows, God cares. I don't.

– But you saw Collin again.

– Ah yes. We were to meet again.

After my recovery, which took a little under two days, I quickly came to the conclusion that Elm Tree Drive was no place for a young man of my energy and ambition.

There was an oppressive miasma of domestic contentment about the place: Mother in her study, tap-tap-tapping away at an early draft of the book which, years later, was going to cause me so much trouble; Catherine toddling about talking to her dolls, reading books to them, designing cute little cards (yellow, reds and blues, smiling faces, huge optimistic suns) for Mummy, Miss Brown at school, brother Jonathan. Had I been like this, so promiscuous in my affection, so happy, so bloody *childish*? Or did I – and this is the way I recall it – take on board the full complexity of life, together with a fair set of adult values, as soon as I could talk (which was remarkably early, so I'm told)? I'm not saying that Catherine should have been like me – being adopted, she was not blessed with the same genetic mix (ordinary ingredients, extraordinary result) – but there was something about her pervasive, gurgling presence that I found depressing.

For a while, it amused me to teach her a few tricks of the trade to help her gain a bit of extra pocket money, steal a march on her schoolfriends, but she was woefully backward in this department and afflicted by a sense of conventional decency that she had caught from her adoptive mother.

'But wouldn't that be lying, Jonathan?' she would say, her face a nest of confusion. 'Isn't that a bit unfair?'

Oh well, no one could say I didn't try. Abandoned by her natural parents, adopted by a couple of eccentrics, one of whom promptly died, the other hammering out bolshie propaganda when she should have been looking after the home, and the child was prattling on about fairness and the other person's point of view. Poor little Catherine. A loser even then.

Or maybe it was Mother who was bringing me down. As a committed feminist years before it became fashionable, I was never one to discourage the bored housewife from taking up a hobby but Mother's 'work', as she liked to call it, meant precious little took place in the Fixx abode vis-à-vis basic conversation and company, not to mention cooking, ironing and generally keeping the place spruced up.

'Be a love and give Catherine some fish fingers. I've just got to knock this chapter on the head,' she'd say with that distracted, I'm-in-the-magical-world-of-the-imagination look that writers like to adopt when they're 'working'. I made allowances – the menopause, Father's death, the fact that she was, at the end of the day, a member of the loony Williams family – but it wasn't on really, was it?

Here I was, a young achiever, betrayed by my school, trembling on the brink of manhood, badly in need of support and encouragement, and what did I get? Other people's happiness rammed down my throat.

I was allergic to suburbia, I discovered. Its tree-lined crescents, avenues and drives, its lawns and rose gardens, its haven't-we-all-done-terribly-well smugness. And this was no mere youthful rebellion. That familiar knot in the stomach, that restless anger, was to return years later when a certain ex-wife of cursed memory misguidedly tried to domesticate me. On both occasions, I was strong enough to tear out the bars and walk away free, a man that no woman, patio or sun-lounge extension could tame.

It would be nice to recall that my departure from the family home was attended by fond farewells, a packed lunch and clean hanky for the train, exhortations to eat at least one hot meal a day, the odd surreptitious tear maybe. It would be pleasant to report that my departure from the family home was attended by my family. But it was not.

The day that Jonathan Peter Fixx set out for London to seek his own way in the world, his mother and sister were otherwise engaged.

It was the early morning and I had packed a small case with a few essentials. As I tiptoed down the stairs, I could hear Mother hammering away selfishly in the room which had once been the Snug and was now (move over, Muriel Spark) 'the Study', and

Catherine was bossing her dolls about in her room.

I paused in the living-room. Small, untidy, decorated in execrable taste, it was still home to me. I glanced lingeringly about me, taking in Mother's favourite chair, the black and white photograph of her wedding day beside that of me, childishly serious in my school uniform, and one in colour of Catherine, dribbling in a cot, a hideous pair of china dogs on the reproduction dresser, Father's VC in its battered little framed case on the mantelpiece. That was what I was looking for.

You see, although I had saved a reasonable amount of money from my hard-earned Melton Hall account, I was still some way short of the kind of financial independence a lad needs to find his feet in the world. Career-wise, I was in a hurry; no one could possibly expect me to graft away in some lowly position for months, maybe years, before achieving a position of status. I wanted success, and I wanted it now. There was quite a premium on old medals, I knew, and a VC, in decent nick, could fetch upwards of £500. Mother might object but there again she was probably too self-absorbed to notice that the medal, which had cost her late husband so dear, was no longer there. As for Father, he had done little enough during his life to help me on my way; there seemed to me to be a sort of natural justice to this posthumous contribution to my finances. I felt sure he would have understood, had he been around, which he wasn't.

'What are you doing, Jonathan?'

The child Catherine, showing early signs of an unusual ability for being in the wrong place at the wrong time (a talent that she was to hone to a fine art as an adult), stood at the door. I turned, holding the medal case.

'Thinking of Daddy, Catherine. Can you remember Daddy?'

'Not really. I remember his blue eyes, that's all.'

'Yes. He had wonderful blue eyes.'

'Why are you holding his medal?'

'Because – ' I allowed a slight croak to enter my voice, 'because I like to hold his medal. Once a day I just hold it for a little while. Then sometimes I polish it . . . I think I'll polish it right now.'

'Can I polish it with you?'

'No. I like polishing it by myself. Why don't you go and tell your dolls all about the medal?'

'You tell them. My dollies like it when you talk to them.'

(See what I mean?)

'All right. I'll show them the medal when it's all nice and shiny. You go to your room, shut the door and line all the dollies up. Make sure they're all dressed in their nice clothes. Then I'll come up and talk to you all in ten minutes.'

'Promise?'

'Of course.'

Catherine came over to me and held up her little arms. 'Cuddle,' she said. (Was I ever going to get away?)

'Thank you, Jonathan,' she said seriously as she wandered out of the living-room.

Pocketing the medal, I scribbled a crisply worded note to Mother, which I left on the kitchen table.

Softly, I closed the front door and walked off purposefully down Elm Tree Drive.

I felt better already.

Two

'It's alright, ma,
I'm only bleeding.'

Bob Dylan

5
Streetlife

Soho in the late fifties. Hard, fast, wild, corrupt.

The world in which the young Jonathan Peter Fixx now found himself provided him with a crash course in the facts of life power-wise, women-wise, money-wise that his fellow Meltonians, drifting their way into the professions, serving dull apprenticeships for even duller careers, floating aimlessly down a river on a punt at Poncyface College, University of Cantab (which was where Collin ended up), would have envied if they had had the nous.

I left them there, trudging along the straight and narrow, while I ducked and dived around Chinatown's darkest alleyways, never knowing where the next tenner was coming from. They've been languishing in my slipstream ever since.

Dirty my hands? Sure I did. At the end of the day, it's what Hard Knocks College, University of Life is all about.

It was a time when the clouds of post-war gloom had rolled away, when the country had awoken from its mid-century slumber to find itself reborn, a teenager with spots, an overdeveloped sex drive and a phoney American accent. Dion and the Belmonts blared from every jukebox; outside coffee bars, attractive young girls with the wholesome, unsullied beauty of the early Doris Day were expertly practising with hula-hoops; inside, their boyfriends sipped frothy coffee and worked on their James Dean scowls and Marlon Brando pouts. The streets echoed to the sounds of young people high on the intoxication of youth, rock-'n'-roll and Benzedrine. It was no longer enough simply to be young. You had to be an outsider, a contender, an angry young man, a rebel without a cause. You had to have a girlfriend who wore pink lipstick, polka dots and a silly hairstyle, who didn't mind flashing her knickers on the dance-floor as you executed superbly accomplished jive routines, who was ready and eager to try the heavy petting that was suddenly all the rage.

Personally, I was an existentialist. Being and nothingness. Psychology is action. Rebellion as nostalgia for innocence. You are what you eat. I knew it all.

Better, I lived it all. Unlike the pale, whiffy beatniks with their earnest little beards and resentful eyes to be found on park benches all over London, deep in some bloody *carnet* or other, I was actually a practical existentialist, putting the Camusian action-not-words-life-is-a-cabaret ethic into positive, profitable action. Lacking the time to swot up on the detail, I discovered the truth of what I call 'entrepreneurial existentialism' through heady, first-hand experience. I was an intellectual, *c'est vrai*, but an intellectual who dispensed with dry-as-dust theorising. A hands-on intellectual.

Now is neither the time nor the place to divulge the full whys and wherefores of my early business career. Suffice it to say that, as one of London's unofficial movers and shakers, I rapidly became known among the live-now-pay-later set as a sophisticated sort of odd-job man, a lad who got things done, no mess, no bother, no questions asked.

'Get Fixx,' they'd say. 'Jon'll sort it out.'

True, I was never too fussy about the commissions I accepted – who they came from, what they were for, how the cash with which I was amply paid had been acquired. The entrepreneurial existentialist is not one to delve into the hidden subtext of a course of action; *l'action, c'est l'homme*. And, frankly, how refreshing my brisk, 'anything legal considered' attitude seems today in this age of droopy dole-drawers and spoon-fed scroungers! There was no easy signing on for the young Fixx; 'social security' meant nothing more than staying close to the exit door when in company – for, as a result of the occasional misunderstanding, the odd broken egg vis-à-vis the satisfactory completion of an omelette, I was not always surrounded by those who wished me well. No need to cross the 'i's' here. Go-getters will catch my drift.

Within three years of arriving in London, an unworldly public schoolboy from the outskirts of Biggleswade with nothing but his hard-earned savings and an old war medal, I owned a small bedsitter off Wardour Street, a Triumph motorcycle, a Jaguar with white wall tyres and a wardrobe of zoot suits that were the envy of Soho.

It had taken no more than a matter of weeks for me to learn that dealing in things, the buying and selling of product, is not the way to earn financial independence. Things require investment, work.

They take up space. Things are unreliable. Some twenty years before Great Britain Limited followed my example, I abandoned product in favour of the service industries. Insurance was my bread and butter, information my jam.

It was while paying one of my weekly visits to a trattoria in Dean Street – a believer in the importance of little acorns as regards the growth of mighty oaks, I was starting small – that I first encountered the man who was to become one of my closest friends during this period.

'Step aside, Shortarse,' I said to a tall, skinny youth who was chatting to Luigi at the bar as I walked in with my colleagues, Griff, Pete and Sharpie. 'I got business with Luigi. Confidential business.'

The young man looked at the four of us, smiled weakly and, with a weedy 'Some other time, Luigi', left the shop.

'Of course, Mr Kray,' said Luigi.

It was only as Luigi was in the back office collecting our premium that the penny dropped.

'The beanstalk who was just in,' I said amiably to the pasta pusher when he returned. 'Close friend, is he?'

'He wanna do business,' Luigi said moodily (in my experience, the sunny disposition of your average Italian is a myth). 'Suddenly everyone wanna do business with me.'

'Would he be Reggie or Ronnie?' asked Griff uneasily.

'He Dominic. Twins' little brother.' Luigi allowed himself a grin. 'Very interested in new Italian fast food. He like pizzas, Dominic. Nice boy.'

This was serious. Inexperienced as I was, I understood the insurance game well enough to know that interest from the Krays was rarely good news. A lesser man would have moved his operation elsewhere (sweet shops were relatively unexploited) but the young Jon Fixx was never one to shirk a challenge. I discovered through the grapevine the pub where Dominic Kray was to be found, met him there, bought him a Babycham and by the end of the evening we were playing Push Halfpenny together like the best of old mates. There may have been a few raised eyebrows in the Bull and Bush as we burst into a refrain of 'Lipstick on Your Collar', but then they were used to the Krays. On the legendary occasion when Ronnie Kray sank twelve pints wearing sequins and a cocktail dress, the vulgar lout who had criticised his colour co-ordination needed a new face after the boys had finished with him. No one laughed at the Krays in these parts.

Thus it was that I became one of the tight, friendly family circle known to outsiders and Fleet Street sewer rats as 'the Kray gang'.

Dominic, it turned out, was the problem child in the family. With his Babychams, his shy, unworldly charm, his collection of antique Dinky toys (unrivalled in the East End, he claimed), he was causing Ronnie and Reggie no end of aggravation.

'What we going to do about him, Jon?' Reggie asked me at a family tea party to celebrate the birthday of his dear old mum Violet.

'What's that then, Reggie?'

'I mean, *look* at him.' Dominic was sitting on the edge of his seat, daintily dunking his biscuit into a mug of tea. 'Talk about the white sheep of the family.'

'He's all right, Reg,' I said. 'He's very serious about his business.'

'Yes, but pizza containers, Jon. It's not on, is it? D. Kray, the Pizza-Pot King. We have our reputation to think of.'

It was true that Dominic's ambitions seemed, at the time, alarmingly conventional. He had worked it out. Fast food was on its way. Pizzas were going to be big. No one was making the little silver trays for the said pizzas. Get in quick and he could make a killing. Far from putting the frighteners on Luigi when we first met, he had been earnestly discussing pizza trays.

'But where's the angle, Dom?' we had asked, almost as one.

'No angle,' he had said with his innocent little smile. 'Just a nice little business. Making and selling. All above board.'

'Oh dear, oh dear, oh dear,' said Ronnie.

'Streuth!' said Reggie.

'He always was a pillock,' said Violet, her eyes twinkling dangerously.

'Sort him out, Jon,' said Reggie, biting deep into a bacon sandwich and wiping the grease off his chin with the palm of his hand. 'Use some of them words of yours on him. He listens to you.'

For months, Dominic and I worked together. I helped him with his tedious little business; he accompanied me on the various jobs I did for his brothers. Even then, I was something of an all-rounder, ready to turn my hand to any new craft that would stand me in good stead in later life. If Ron and Reggie needed a Jockey – described in

Jonathon Green's *Dictionary of Underworld Slang* as 'one who "rides" a "Punter" (q.v.), regarded by the firm as "Tote Double" (q.v.) or a "Banker" (q.v.)' – I was their man. If they needed a Butler – 'one who looks after the "Silver" (q.v.)' – or a Milkman – 'one employed to "milk" a "Punter"' – not to mention a Teacher, Doctor or Solicitor, they knew who to call.

'See, Dom,' I'd say as we drove away from another successfully accomplished mission in the Jaguar the twins had given me, 'it's so simple. No worries, no liquidity problems, no staying up all night trying to make the books balance, no tax.'

'No security,' Dom would sigh wearily. 'I'm telling you, Jon, my future's in fast-food accessories.'

Maybe I could have converted him, given a clear run at it. There are few people who can withstand the party political broadcast on behalf of untrammelled free enterprise, as delivered by J. P. Fixx. Unfortunately my relationship with the Krays was upset before I was able to coax Dominic into the fast lane.

It was 1961. We were in Newmarket, Dom, his girlfriend Muriel and I, staying at the cottage where Ronnie used to entertain his favoured stable lads. My brief, as I recall, was to do a spot of vetting. The twins were dabbling in the undercover bookmaking line – unwisely, as it happens – and some nag was down to lose them a lot of money if it won the Derby, which it surely would if we were unable to reach it first. Pinturischio, I think it was called.

While I was working out how to penetrate the country's most secure racing stable with enough laxative to send the nag in question into orbit, Dom was covering East Anglia's pasta parlours. Virgin territory, he called it, but full of potential vis-à-vis his little containers.

And Muriel? Well, she was virgin territory as well, so far as Dom knew – which, according to Muriel, wasn't very far. She stayed at a nearby bed and breakfast. She hung about the cottage. She read. She got bored.

As it happens, Muriel was not quite the little mouse you'd have expected to be hanging out with Dominic. It was true that, in her flat shoes, grey cashmere and sensible make-up, she was hardly *dolce vita* material, but there had been times – a risqué joke after a couple of port and lemons, the way she touched my arm while asking me something utterly dull – when I was tempted to forget that she was almost a Kray and move in, if only out of curiosity.

Dom and Muriel had been courting for almost a year. He was building up slowly to the moment when he would ask her to marry him. There would then follow, we all assumed, a lengthy engagement before Muriel was finally put out of her misery, and became Mrs Kray ('If neither of us die of old age first,' she once said to me in a moment of uncharacteristic frankness). During their courtship, there was much hand-holding and general mooning about, but precious little else.

It was a slow week for me, too. I had put the bite on one of the stable lads and now it was merely a question of waiting for the night when the trainer's head man took his wife out to the flicks and I could make with the Ex-Lax concentrate.

Months later, it suited Muriel's purpose to claim that it was I who had made the first move, that I had jumped her. *Quelle blague!* If there was an element of coercion – 'rape' is perhaps too strong a word – in the events of that week, I was more victim than perpetrator.

What an innocent I was then, how unaware of the powerful physical needs that can assail the most unlikely of women! It took all of thirty-six hours for the true Muriel to show her colours.

We were reading in the sitting-room, I remember. She was possibly a shade more restless than usual as she lay on the sofa, stretching extravagantly now and then while making intimate, sleepy-little-me noises.

'How long before Dom gets back?' she asked casually, kicking off her sensible shoes and rubbing her feet together.

I turned a page on my book.

'Another couple of hours.'

'Boring, isn't it?'

'Mmm.'

'Yes, I'm very, very bored.'

I glanced up. There was something about the voice. Muriel was looking at me, eyes glittering, a high flush to her normally pale features. Young as I was, I could tell the signs.

I put the book aside and smiled.

'Muriel,' I said in my soft, I-need-it-now voice. 'Take off your cardigan.'

Without a trace of embarrassment, she stood up and unbuttoned her Marks and Spencer's best. Then, for good measure, she stepped out of her grey skirt.

'That's better,' I said.

And it was. Today the black underwear, complete with suspender belt and frilly garters, that Muriel was wearing would be dismissed as vulgar, banal even. Then it was the ultimate in sexual sophistication.

She looked at me as if I were expected to make the next move.

'Well,' I said, perhaps a little nervously. 'You're a deep one and no mistake.'

Without taking her eyes off me, Muriel kicked aside the pile of clothes at her feet, expertly clearing a space on the floor.

'Then plumb my depths,' she said, stretching out languidly on the carpet. 'You can do . . . anything.'

Bloody hell. Anything? What on earth did 'anything' entail? Was something out of the way expected? In the early days, I favoured the straightforward meat-and-two-veg approach to physical relations. Departures from the standard menu confused me.

'Right,' I said briskly, standing up and unbuttoning my shirt. 'Anything coming up.'

It turned out that little Muriel wasn't one of those 'You can do anything . . . but not that!' girls. When she said 'anything', she meant it. So the rest of the week passed in an agreeable haze. Muriel played boudoir Jekyll and Hyde. I nobbled the nag. Dom wrote endlessly in his notebooks, apparently oblivious to the various items of evidence (broken table, torn sheets, scratchmarks up the wall) that were all around him.

That's how I remember it anyway.

– I'm afraid the list of literary agents turning you down is getting longer every day. They keep asking what you've written before.

– Idiots. I told them I'm a doer not a writer. What's happened to this country? Where's the spirit of enterprise?

– One of them said she was prepared to meet you – 'without prejudice', she said.

– Pompous cow. Doesn't she know that I can't be seen in public for the moment?

– She said that the only way of publishing your book would be as an 'oddball personality event'. She wanted to see if you're what they call promotable. It's surprising, isn't it?

– The stupidity of people connected with books? Not at all. If they had any brains, they'd be in a decent profession.

– I meant it's surprising that none of these people has actually heard of you.

– The secret of my success. Backroom boy. Shark under the water. Tiger prowling through the jungle's dappled twilight. You don't have to be yak-yakking on television every day to be an achiever, you know. The truly powerful are never famous.

– Agents don't seem to understand that.

– They'll understand when my story's completed. They'll see. They'll be kicking themselves.

– One of them suggested that you might like to write your story as a novel.

– What?

– Fiction.

– Do me a favour.

In these days of safety-valve sex, when the routine trading of orgasms is no more than a brisk, mutual servicing that scarcely interrupts the well-organised run of daily life, it's difficult to remember the heart-stopping excitement of romance thirty years ago.

Then, it meant something, that first date; the eyes meeting across the table at a modest bistro, hands held in back seats of a cinema, the tremulous, tentative kiss on a park bench. There was none of today's worldweary 'How-do-you-do-which-side-of-the-bed-do-you-like-to-sleep-on?' Indeed it often took two, maybe three dates before one reached that stage.

Young, relatively innocent, I spent much of the late fifties and early sixties in search of romance, pursuing what the Bard once so memorably described as 'the elusive butterfly of love'.

And what a chase it was! They loved me, the Ritas, the Doreens, the Mariannes. Although I was never good-looking in the conventional sense, there was a raffish charm about me. I was something of a name in certain circles. I could take them to the clubs they had read about in the papers, where MPs drank champagne with stars of stage and screen, where Barbara Windsor hung out with her latest beau, where Kenny Lynch was quite likely to take the stage and lead the revellers in an impromptu rendition of 'Down at the Old Bull and Bush'. They loved it and if, back at the bedsit, now and then one of them was reluctant to contribute her perfect end to my perfect evening, there were always others.

It was a time-consuming exercise, this quest for love, but even in my active and over-generous youth I never regarded hours spent with a member of the fair sex as entirely wasted, so long as the pay-off ratio vis-à-vis the elusive butterfly was reasonably healthy. In that way, I suppose I'm unchanged to this day.

Muriel never really understood. I had thrown open the gates to the Garden of Eden, in that little cottage on Newmarket Heath, and now, damn me, it was the devil's own job to prise her away from the Tree of Knowledge. Guzzle, guzzle, guzzle it was, whenever Dom's back was turned. Even after he astonished us all by proposing to her and actually fixing a wedding day some three months ahead, Muriel's obsession with me endured. There was less black underwear and more alarming talk of 'us'.

Then, one Sunday, she rang me in something of a state. She needed to see me. Dom was visiting old Ma Kray. It couldn't wait. Wearily, perhaps irritably (I had an amusing afternoon mapped out with an actress, as it happened), I agreed to meet her in a pub in Leytonstone, near her flat.

'I think I'm going to leave Dom,' she said in a stupid, wobbly voice after I had bought her a whisky (things had to be bad when Muriel was on spirits). 'It's all wrong between us.'

I was momentarily confused. Dom and Muriel were so good together: quiet, sincere, dull. It was true that Muriel's riotous sex drive was something of a fly in the ointment but doubtless Dom would learn to live with that. Anyway, I was damned if I knew what all this had to do with me.

'That's terrible news,' I said in my soft, sympathetic voice. 'I don't know what to say.'

'Don't you? I thought you were the one with words.'

'Don't joke, Muriel. This is serious.'

'I had rather hoped,' Muriel's chin was trembling ominously, 'that you might actually be pleased.'

It just slipped out. 'Good Lord,' I said. 'Why?'

Tears welled. I was experienced enough in affairs of the heart to know that this was the tricky part. The catch in the voice, the reddening nose, the trembly little hands fumbling in the handbag for a tissue, heads turning curiously from nearby tables. It could be embarrassing, but I had discovered that it was not a bad idea to terminate the average affair in public. Objects were less likely to fly across the room. A certain decorum is observed.

'Because of *us*, that's why.'

So the moment had arrived. If Muriel had been thinking of ditching Johnny Next-Door at this point, I would have been glancing over my shoulder in the direction of the nearest Exit sign. What with her being engaged to marry a Kray, albeit Dominic Kray, I was already in my walking shoes and halfway round the block, metaphorically at least.

'Muriel,' I searched for the right words. This was no casual dumping, after all – it required careful handling. 'Don't you realise – '

God, it was tempting. Don't you realise you were never more than a way of passing the time, that I'm in a different league from you, that in order to keep my over-active libido in check, I need to have at least three or four girls on the bubble, that you wouldn't be one of them anyway, that it – in so far as it ever was an 'it' – is over? But no, that was the wrong approach.

' – that I'm very involved with my work at present? I've no time for a romantic attachment, however precious. You're simply too important to me for second place to be enough.'

It was rather good, I thought, but Muriel, whose face was getting blotchier by the minute, seemed unwilling to accept the truth of the matter.

'We wouldn't have to live together, necessarily.'

I decided to use a line which I've always found particularly effective on these painful occasions.

'Muriel, I love you – you know that – but I'm not *in* love with you.'

That, as everybody knows, is the ultimate kiss-off line but, since she was none too bright, I added a final finesse.

'I respect you too much as a person to want to mislead you. I think it's over, Muriel.'

'There's something else you should know,' said Muriel, raising her voice. By now conversation at the tables around us had almost completely stopped. 'I'm late.'

'Late for what?'

'*Late*, you fool. I'm three months pregnant.'

The mature, worldly Jonathan Peter Fixx *de nos jours* can look back with benign amusement on the feelings of distress, amounting almost to panic, that this news provoked in me. Today my reaction would have been one of mild disappointment, annoyance even, that the girl in question had seen fit to share her secret with me. Quite rightly, the liberated modern woman accepts the occasional slip-up in the downstairs department to be solely her responsibility, to be solved as quickly and tidily as possible. It's what feminism is all about – independence.

But in the early sixties, it was all very different. Pregnancy for a man in my position and with my prospects was a major disaster.

'How much d'you need?' I asked tenderly.

'What for?'

She really was very slow. 'To . . . straighten it out.'

There was more blubbing and nose-blowing.

'I don't want anything straightened out. I just want . . . us.'

This was every bit as bad as I had feared. I was much too young to be tied down and, in any case, I was damned if I was going to be tied down with Muriel, who would clearly be out of her depth, both socially and intellectually, as Mrs Jonathan Peter Fixx. The idea was absurd.

I stood up and drained my drink.

'I need to think things over,' I said. 'I'll be in touch.'

How this tiresome, but essentially insignificant domestic scene came to spark off the most spectacular outbreak of gang warfare London has seen since the late twenties remains a mystery. I was, not for the last time in my life, the catalyst, the spark of whom historians are so fond.

It's odd. Something happens to the average person – you, for example; you act; life goes on as before. Something happens to me; I act; the world shifts ever so slightly on its axis. Why? Search me. Sometimes I wish I *was* ordinary like you, but I'm not.

The next day Muriel telephoned me, with the less than interesting news that she had been 'mulling things over'. I could tell from the unnervingly calm way she spoke that the mulling had done me no good at all.

'So,' she said. 'Are you going to do the decent thing?'

'I was going to ask you the same thing,' I replied light-heartedly.

From her reaction, I was made to understand that our concepts of decency differed significantly, mine tending towards a tidy resolution of the problem (visit to a clinic, a nominal outlay of readies, no one any the wiser), hers towards wedding-bells, the alienation of the Kray family and the eventual addition of one small individual to an already overcrowded planet.

Alienation of the Kray family! Christ, I had to move fast.

'So you'll be telling Dominic, then?' I asked, as coolly as I could manage.

'Of course.'

'Well well. I never knew you had a death wish.'

'It's only Dom.'

'– who'll tell Mummy who'll tell Ronnie who hates you and off we go – machete time in the Old Kent Road.'

'Oh Jonathan!'

I thought quickly. 'Here's what we do,' I said. 'I'll tell the twins – there's just a chance that they'll buy it from me. You take Dom off to the country and I'll let you know when you can break the news to him. Don't, under any circumstances, make contact with me or with them – it could spoil everything.'

'You mean – ' Muriel sounded more cheerful already ' – you're going to act like a man after all.'

'I'm a Fixx.'

'Oh Jon. I knew you were all right.'

'Good,' I said more briskly. 'Then just do what I tell you to. Whatever happens.'

'What did you just say, Jon?'

Something very strange happened to Ronnie Kray's face when he was angry. Normally a good-looking lad with fine natural colouring, he would turn sheet-white like a death mask when angry. His eyes sank back into his head, dark and glittering with excitement – not unlike Muriel's, funnily enough, during that fateful week in Newmarket.

'I thought you should know,' I said nervously. 'It's common knowledge in Soho. They've been seeing each other for some time now – Muriel and this Richardson bloke.'

It was a stroke of genius, though I say it myself. Relations between the twins and the Richardson gang had been somewhat sour for a while. There had been skirmishes, the occasional territorial dispute vis-à-vis insurance collection in the East Ham district, but until now the unpleasantness had been restricted to the odd rumble in the local snooker hall. Once the Krays had moved into psychopathic mode, reason went out of the window. Within days, they would have forgotten exactly why they were fighting the Richardsons. Even if Muriel grassed me up at a later date, she would be ignored.

'Well, that's it,' said Violet, pouring me another cup of tea. 'It's war, boys. It's them or us.'

'Come on, Mum,' said Reggie, who was looking distinctly uneasy. 'It's only Dom. You never liked Muriel anyway.'

'That's as may be,' said Violet, stirring her tea with a face like thunder, 'but Muriel's almost family. If anyone has laid a finger on her, well . . . that's not very nice, is it, Ron?'

'He's dogmeat,' said Ronnie.

I looked down at my own well-manicured fingers, and sighed.

'I'm just sorry it had to be me that told you,' I said. 'But I thought you should know.'

'You did right, son,' said Violet. 'It's a family matter now. We'll sort it in our own way. Have another rock cake.'

During the six months that followed there were moments when I wondered whether it would have been easier to marry Muriel, and have done. There was arson, there was violence, there was much belabouring of cropped, greasy heads with the business end of snooker cues. The police wrung their hands and shipped in spare noddies from the provinces, the sewer rats on Fleet Street had a field day. Reluctantly, I played a part in the occasional raid but, by concentrating on the administrative side, I kept my nose clean. As time went on and it became clear that the police would eventually have to do something about the carnage, I followed the instruction of my legal adviser (the youthful Tadeusz Jankic, also known as Henry Talbot) and distanced myself from the whole unsavoury business. After all, I had done my bit.

Fortune favours the brave, they say. The Muriel and Dom problem resolved itself unexpectedly. Back in Newmarket, love bloomed once more and, as all hell was breaking loose in London, they took off to the Channel Islands, where they married. By the time the baby was born, they had changed their name and, as Muriel put it in an angry little letter to me, 'started a new life'. Dom's obsession with pizza trays finally paid off and today he's said to be worth a fortune. I see from the papers that he donates millions to the Liberal Party. I've no idea what happened to his son but I wish him every happiness.

When the law finally caught up with the Krays, I had already bidden farewell to the rough and rowdy ways of my youth. There was talk of my being subpoenaed as a witness but eventually the police agreed that my off-the-record briefings were more useful than the limited amount of information I could have provided at the trial itself. As it happens, I had been keeping them informed of developments for some time so that, in my own way, I played my part in making the streets of London safe again for the law-abiding citizen.

– Did you keep in touch with them?

– What, those thugs? I thought about it, but my people felt it was rash to be associated with rough elements. I never actually visited the boys in prison.

– So that was your education at Hard Knocks College, University of Life.

– Yes, my crash course in the real world. Of course, qualitatively, there was hardly much difference between my life with the Krays and what privileged ninnies like Collin got up to as they drank their way through university. Arson and a spot of GBH at one end; jumping off bridges, removing policemen's helmets, boot-blacking each other's genitals at the other – it was just the exuberance of youth, taking different forms.

– But while their behaviour was regarded as boyish high spirits, your friends were collared as thugs and lawbreakers.

– Funny old world, isn't it?

6

Cherchez la femme

At this moment when, wild oats sown, finances secure, I stood, confidently surveying the future (the sixties, I just knew it, were going to be a *very* good decade), let us step back to glance momentarily at the wider picture, the *tabula rasa*.

Revolution was in the air. Or, to be more precise, revolutions.

There was the property revolution, first of all. We were all getting into it, the bricks and mortar game, the shift-the-sitting-tenant-bung-the-local-councillor-a-monkey-and-clean-up lark. With a combination of shrewdness, determination and hard work, Glentabbot Property Corporation Ltd, a firm I set up with my legal adviser Henry Talbot, had quickly gained a small but significant foothold on the changing face of London. We saw the gaps and we capitalised on them. An old-fashioned firm of bakers in Dean Street, somewhat weakened by the insurance premium demanded by the Krays, made way for a 24-hour massage parlour. A damp and under-utilised warehouse in Tower Hamlets was converted at minimal expense into a number of quite serviceable short-let bedsits. A so-called 'community garden' in Seven Sisters was bought up to help the local populace in more contemporary fashion with a swiftly built tower block. Industry, people, communities – Glentabbot served them all and, like other small, dynamic firms of the time, made its own meaningful contribution to Britain's bright new future.

Henry Talbot and I had worked out a certain management style vis-à-vis the development of the company's interests in property, asset-stripping and the loans sector – a style which cleverly capitalised on the individual talents of our partnership.

Despite his shrewdness as an entrepreneur, Talbot was an unprepossessing character, with his slicked-back hair, ill-fitting suits and phoney upper-class accent.

'We're in the image business,' I told him, soon after we had taken up residence in a cramped, smoky office off the Tottenham Court Road. 'And you don't quite fit the bill yet.'

'No worry, Jon,' he said. 'I'll get the suit. Savile Street. I take language lessons every night. Soon Tadeusz Jankic will be past. Henry Talbot, gentleman, will be present.' He straightened his tie self-importantly. 'Move up, David Niven.'

'But for the moment,' I said, putting it as tactfully as I could, 'you're the engine, the power behind the good ship Glentabbot. Pulsating, vital, below decks.'

'And you?' he said. 'You are captain?'

'I'm on deck. Equal partners, but slightly more visible than you.'

For a while, this bizarre double-act was irresistible. Fixx, hard, fast, impulsive, the attractive man of action, and Talbot, grey, cautious, dull, the restraining influence. While I was at the sharp end, fizzing about London in my open-topped Spitfire, making connections, sniffing out opportunities, Talbot would stay behind the desk, crossing the 't's', filling in the tedious detail on my broadbrush agreements, massaging the figures if necessary, Mr Nobody to my Sunshine Superman, Nowhere Man to my Jumping Jack Flash.

On particularly important deals, I'd field Talbot as a sort of stooge, a man so dull that those punters unnerved by the sheer I-Want-It-Now effervescence of Jonathan Fixx would be reassured by his quiet, lugubrious presence.

'Surely you could retain a small number of my existing staff,' some ashen-faced loser would intone, pen poised over an agreement to sell off his ailing family firm to us at a knockdown price. 'Some of them have been with me for years.'

'Forget it,' I'd say. 'We're doing you a favour already. We're not in the market for giving a load of clapped-out ancient retainers a meal-ticket for life – '

Bang on cue, Talbot would raise his hand with quiet authority.

'What my colleague says is naturally true,' he'd say, smiling apologetically, 'but I am with the personal opinion here that it would be wrong to ignore, shall we say, the human dimension – ' My jaw would drop in a 'Whaaaa – ?' of amazement and disgust. 'Maybe we can take, what, a token ten personnel? If you are able to take some twenty thousand pounds off the asking price.'

'I don't believe this,' I'd gasp, throwing my pen on to the table. 'I'm not hearing this, am I, Henry?'

'All right, all right,' the punter would say, nervously glancing in my direction as he signed the agreement. 'Ten people for twenty thousand it is.'

'So,' Talbot would say as, within moments of the loser closing the door wearily behind him, we cracked open another bottle of Moet. 'It is yet again every time the coconut.'

'But what are we going to do with the old farts?' I'd ask, confident that the scheming Polack had worked something out.

'A job, I said.' Talbot shrugged. 'But did I say what job? Maybe visiting the pensioners in Tower Hamlets with eviction orders and Dobermanns will not suit them so well. Or toilet-cleaning in a factory. Two months, I'm giving them, maybe one.'

'You're a bastard, Talbot.' I'd smile approvingly.

'Pulsating, vital,' the little creep would say proudly, 'below decks.'

Then, to return to the overview, there was the entertainments revolution. A new generation was growing up. It had no time for the dull, cheese-paring austerity of the past. It wanted to be amused, to be taken to new frontiers of pleasure. It had the money to pay.

Coincidentally, I was becoming impatient with the buying and selling of property that so fascinated Talbot. Three hundred per cent profit in six months on a block of dodgy pre-stressed concrete is all well and good but, at the end of the day, it was trade, no more nor less. I was ready to move into the people business.

Unlike the seedy old entrepreneurs eager to get their cold, scaly hands on the new generation, I was young, attractive, credible. I spoke the right language, played the right chords. Never trust anyone over thirty? Right on, man. I could dig it.

Above all, there was the revolution that, in a myriad of mysterious and intriguing ways, was taking place between the sexes. It was a revolution that eventually touched all of us young folk.

I was, of course, something of a babe in arms regarding *la vie emotionelle*. My unfortunate home life, my early history of child abuse at the coarse, chapped hands of Aunty Bar-Bar, my years in the emotional wasteland of Melton Hall, had left me cruelly unprepared for the harsh, confusing world of adult relationships. My tussle with Muriel had proved that.

So how exactly did it stand between men and women in the year of 1962?

The situation was damned confusing, I can tell you that. At the time, we men thought it was our fault – the uncertainties, the tears, the misunderstandings. Today, we can see that we were victims, tiny vessels caught up in a flashtide upon the raging torrent of female hormonal change.

I say this in a spirit of open friendship and admiration. An unashamed feminist, I yield to none in my admiration of the fair sex. Okay, so I've had my moments of exasperation and frustration in my dealings with them – what man hasn't? – but, goodness me, these passing irritations are nothing, a mere *rien*, compared to the times of intense pleasure which I have shared with them. True, I have invested heavily in feminine company, sparing neither money nor time, and, yes, there have been years when the balance sheet has shown the odd deficit or unfulfilled liability. Yet, at the end of the day, my relations with the ladies have shown a positive balance, the state of my portfolio woman-wise is distinctly healthy.

Thus in no way can it be said that the Fixx overview regarding the state of womankind in the early sixties is that of a whining, gelded misogynist or of a crass Casanova. I've been there. I've supped at the well. I know whereof I speak.

Let's start with the basics. The average woman is, scientists now agree, something of a slave to her deep, inner biology. While a man might assess a problem cerebrally, his 'other half' will be guided, almost exclusively, by the deep and mysterious processes of her hormones, known to some as 'female intuition'. Just as a man's cool assessment of a difficulty may lead him to the wrong decision, the particular state of a woman's inner workings can on occasions help her 'hit the jackpot'. How many times, for instance, has Mr Average Husband set his face against donkey-brown curtains to go with flamingo-pink wallpaper in the lounge-diner only to find that, when the donkey-brown curtains are finally in place – as they inevitably will be – Mrs Average Wife was right and he was wrong? To take another example, how many Whitehall brainboxes, once loud in their condemnation of the Falklands adventure, later, when the Union Jack fluttered proudly over Port Stanley, were forced to admit that the tempestuous ebb and flow of Mrs Thatcher's hormones had led us to a famous victory?

So it was that, following the events of the Second World War, the biology of British women (and, for all I know or care, French, Belgian or even German women) led them in one direction: to the altar.

They had had their fun. The GIs had returned home, knock-kneed and cross-eyed from sexual exhaustion. Our own heroes – wounded, bedraggled, in some cases limbless – were returning in triumph from the field of battle.

Little did they know that they were marching into a campaign that, in sheer scale and organisation, matched any mounted by Rommel and his famous 'Desert Rats'. Whether it was because the menfolk were in a dazed and vulnerable condition, or because the other side's biology was in such a state of frenzy, remains unclear, but the facts are not in dispute. During the three years following the Armistice, the free-life expectancy of the average bachelor was less than that of a subaltern in the trenches during the First World War.

The lads had no chance. If they had survived with more or less the right number of limbs and the wherewithal to 'start a family', as the popular phrase went, they became a victim to the womenfolk's rampant biology. Within less time than it took to defeat the might of the Third Reich, an entire generation of heroes had been married off, quite often to women at whom, in normal circumstances, they would never have given a second glance.

It is not for me to speculate on the effect that the many thousands of miserable, unsuitable marriages made in those years have had on post-war Britain. Would there have been the decadent hippies of the sixties? What about the shocking craze for lesbianism and group sex during the seventies? Could this be why, today, we are generally accepted as being the most irredeemably lazy nation in Europe? I leave such questions to the historians.

Yet one thing is clear. Between 1945 and 1956, the British woman was involved to the exclusion of all else in the full-time business of trapping husbands, reproducing and preparing their children for the 'brave new world' about which so much was being written.

Then, as the fifties wore on, the hormonal tide changed once more. The proud hero of ten years ago was now a broken man, worn down by the daily grind of dull, ill-rewarded employment and the grim, joyless reality of matrimonial life. Women, on the other hand, were enjoying the fruits of their victory. Now that the children were at school and rationing had ended, they were gathering their strength for another mighty leap forward.

The more mature of them satisfied themselves with drink, bingo and the odd extramarital fling, on occasions trawling the streets in twos and threes in their quest for young male flesh to slake their newly rekindled lusts.

For the new generation of womenfolk, it was a time of confusion and self-discovery. While their hormones were sweeping them towards new and exotic experiences, a dying morality still held them, but only just, in its ever-weakening grasp. As the new, unmarried male generation rode its mighty Harley-Davisons hard and fast through the dark hours to meet a bright new dawn – tousled, ill-shaven but free – their women rode pillion and had to be home by midnight. While angry, acned beatniks slept under bushes on Hampstead Heath and wrote pretentious, self-pitying twaddle about alienation and ennui, their girlfriends were weekend existentialists, bringing them cups of tea and taking their clothes to the launderette. While we were bug-eyed and wild on purple hearts and rock-'n'-roll, they were bug-eyed and giggly from the sheer terror of new, unapproved experience. The more honest of them would admit that they enjoyed more physical release from bouncing on a pogo stick or watching Cliff Richard wiggling his hips on *Six Five Special* than they did from the heavy petting which was virtually the only kind of sexual expression on offer.

Yet, with the sixties, a new age of feminine independence dawned. Pet Clark was on *Sunday Night at the London Palladium*. Helen Shapiro, a rather plain schoolgirl with a fine tenor voice, was top of the charts. Christine Keeler had proved that, with passable looks and the right telephone numbers in her little red book, a girl could take a well-respected public figure and toss him effortlessly on to the unreclaimed slagheap of history.

At first, those of us on the front line of contemporary mores welcomed the change. The days when the only outlet for amorous enthusiasms were scruffy street-girls with hard, mercenary eyes, of the Mandy and Sandra type, had given way to something of a free-for-all. The Pill was now widely available, with the result that a modest investment of an evening at the flicks, followed by lasagne and Chianti for two at the local bistro, rarely failed to pay dividends.

True, the beginnings of the new permissiveness had released an army of enthusiastic but inept novices on to the market – there were occasions, as I joined in a spot of hand-to-hand with the first wave to climb the barricades, when I felt more like an instructor than a lover – but to us dogged foot-soldiers the excess in quantity usually made up for the shortfall in quality.

Forgive the brief excursion into social history but it's relevant, you see. Because, in 1965, there was yet another major sea-change in the evolution of late-twentieth-century woman, and one for which none of us on the other side was prepared.

The basic proprieties went by the board. Overnight what had once been jokily known as the 'war between the sexes' turned into the toughest dog-fight imaginable. Girls no longer played by the rules. Some of them – contemporary *belles dames sans merci* – had torn the rule-book up and were throwing the pieces into our astonished faces. They had once refused to play. Then they played hard to get. Now they were playing, all right, but very, very rough.

Belle dame sans merci. How aptly that phrase, plucked at random from my extensive knowledge of the *lingua franca*, describes the woman who took the fragile dreams of Jonathan Peter Fixx, held them for an instant in her small, almost childlike hands before letting them fall, grinding them to dust with a turn of a sharp, stiletto heel. Yes, she was, quite literally, 'the beautiful lady without thank yous'.

I gave, she took. These are painful memories.

It had all started so well: a tidy little business venture, dovetailing satisfactorily into a spot of after-hours amusement. Even now, I find it hard to believe that something beautiful, uncomplicated and essentially minor could, in a matter of months, become such an ugly, tangled, emotional mess.

I blame Talbot. To my surprise, he had begun to take an interest in my diversification into the glitzy world of entertainment. Underneath that neat, spivvy exterior, I now realise, a showman was trying to get out. Money was nice but, like many of his fellow Slavs who at this time were moving in and taking over – the Maxwells, the Weidenfelds, the Kagans – Talbot needed more. He wanted to be noticed, to be at the centre of things.

'It so happens I have an act that might be of interest,' he said to me one day.

‘Oh yes,’ I said coolly. ‘The result of one of your forays into the social world, is it?’

This was something of a low blow, I admit. Talbot had taken to throwing (his word, not mine) a monthly ‘soirée’, to which he invited like-minded dullards from the world of politics and business. I attended just the one in the misguided hope that I would run into a fellow member of the new youthocracy – a record producer, perhaps, or a model, even a hairdresser – but within moments I could see I was wasting my time.

There were, as I recall, a few more semi-public figures than I had anticipated. Several of the beady, bri-nyloned types with their flat, classless accents and outspoken, ill-dressed wives, I took at first to be bank managers on the make or jumped-up bought-ledger clerks but turned out to be what Talbot described as ‘coming men’ – new Labour MPs, fastbuck merchants from the City, publishers, the odd egghead sewer rat.

Who cared anyway? Having searched in vain for someone young, amusing and available, I left the ‘soirée’ after ten minutes, vowing to give any future image-building events organised by my partner a wide berth.

How naive I was in those days.

‘In fact, nothing to do with my parties,’ Talbot continued. ‘An artiste of my acquaintance is looking for a personal manager. A singer.’ He gave me a card bearing the name of a rowdy, downmarket Knightsbridge restaurant.

‘Singing chef, is he?’ I quipped.

‘He is resident there. He has a big following. Great voice, great looks.’ Talbot wrote on the card. ‘See him, please – for me, old chum.’

I read the card, and sighed. ‘Jess Lawson. *Very* showbiz. He’s Polish, I suppose.’

‘A little bit. But good.’

He was terrible. The restaurant smelt of last week’s vegetable soup. It was full of jostling idiots in mod regalia who threw bread rolls and puked over one another. On a small, raised stage sat ‘Jess Lawson’, strumming ‘The Times They Are A-Changin’’ – or, rather, a tortured Polish version of the same dirge.

Just as I was making to leave, cursing Talbot for a fool, Jess shambled to his feet and announced, 'Now opportunity knock time for little Magdalena – ladies and gentleman, my sister, Magdalena Bobrowski.'

A nondescript, mousy teenager was helped on to the stage, and took the microphone. She began to sing some ridiculous traditional song – 'In an English Country Garden', I think it was.

Did a hush fall upon the room as the girl began to sing? Did the sweet, pure tone of her innocent young voice still the clamour of the crowd? Was a star born?

As it happens, no. She sang nervously, and off-key. The bread rolls continued to whistle through the air. She was almost completely ignored. Had I not been there that night, Miss Bobrowski would today be a fat, loud housewife surrounded by grubby children in a dingy flat in Gdansk. But I was, and there was something about this girl that set my pulse racing.

As I say, I had thought it was strictly business. I was wrong.

Damn damn damn.

– What about the home life?

– I'd moved into a flat off the Fulham Road by now. 'Busy' would be the best way to describe it.

– No, I meant your real home. Mother, Catherine, the rose garden – all that.

– Strange, that. The sixties, all those revolutions, seemed to pass Biggleswade by. I'd return to Elm Tree Drive now and then. The antimacassars were still on the cheap furniture in the living-room. The kitchen smelt of plum crumble. The hall needed dusting. The yellow dog-rose outside the front door was all over the shop. The new curtains in Mother's bedroom looked exactly like the old ones. Catherine was still growing, Mother was still writing. She fussed about me. Was I eating enough? Did I steer clear of these drugs she kept reading about? Was there anyone special in my life? How was I earning a living? There may even have been one or two tears when I left. It was every bit as depressing as it ever was.

– And what about Catherine?

– As I say, she was growing.

7
Talkin' 'bout my generation

There are those – perhaps you're one of them – who say, 'Ah yes, the late sixties. Pot, permissiveness, let it all hang out, take time to smell the flowers, Dave Dee Dozy, kill a pig for freedom – we heard about that. We read about it every day in our *Daily Mail*. But it was a myth, wasn't it? Okay, so Richard Neville was pulling teenagers behind his private barricade, Marianne What's-her-name was putting herself about a bit. But the rest of us? Swinging? Forget it.'

You're probably right. Those of us who spent five, six years lost in the heady nectar of the flower revolution were a small minority. We tried to turn the world on, but the world failed to tune in.

What exactly was the problem with you straights? Was the alternative we offered you too much, too adventurous? Did we place too much emphasis on pleasure, forgetting that for the average lamebrain pleasure means danger, pleasure means pain? Those who play must pay. Where's the catch, you were thinking, and, by the time you realised that there was no catch, that for some pleasure means profit, it was too late.

You thought we were out of our heads, destroying our bodies, upsetting our parents, blowing our savings, didn't you?

Wrong again. For us, excess meant success. We were bloody coining it.

I have experienced some heady and exciting moments during my life at the top but few can compare with the six months I spent grooming Magdalena Bobrowski for stardom.

Our professional needs meshed perfectly. She wanted her student visa exchanged for a work permit; she longed to sing; maybe, although she always denied it, she dreamt of stardom. I, an achiever now well on the way to his first million, was looking for a decent share of the new consumerism.

It was necessary for both of us to make sacrifices. She had to change her name (out went Magdalena Bobrowski, in came Mila), put on some weight, change her hairstyle, cap her teeth, improve her English, get her nose slightly straightened, and learn how to sound rather stupider than in fact she was. I had to allow her to share my flat and my bed.

At the time, it seemed fair to me. Now I can see that it was an arrangement heavily weighted in Mila's favour.

But, in the short term at least, it worked. Within six months, the homely lass from the back streets of Gdansk had been transformed into Mila, model, 'In-Girl', darling of the gossip columns, one of the flower generation's more glorious blooms.

In those days, when the public relations business was in its infancy, creating a star was relatively easy. She had a style to her, so Snowdon and Bailey were happy to use her on modelling assignments. She had, thanks to me, the right contacts and became a necessary decoration at the best showbiz parties. And she had, I admit, a certain unforced charm of her own. (It was Mila, you'll recall, who when asked whether she liked the Sergeant Pepper album set the BBC switchboards flashing with her casually innocent 'I am having something like a prolonged intercourse with this record, it is so delightful.')

Above all, Mila had the look. The slim, waif-like body, the pale victim face, the eyes that were guileless and yet promisingly knowing. Today her face would be that of a pretty nonentity; then a generation looked on her and saw what it wanted to see: innocence, corruption, perversity, courage, fear, youth, experience, decadence, freedom, honesty, dependence, the girl next door, the star, one of them, one of us. The nose job helped, of course.

Who was Mila? The question was asked a thousand times. Where did she come from? The line dreamt up by my publicity people – that she was a young Polish nurse discovered singing to a group of London children while on holiday – was hardly going to keep the media satisfied for long. Mila, the Singing Nurse, yes, but what was the secret behind the extraordinary aura of sensuality and charm that surrounded her? Now that we can be honest about that dishonest decade, was it all a question of grooming and shrewd personal management?

Of course not.

This is not the time for the boudoir indiscretions of which your average bookish voyeur, your literary sheet-sniffer, is so fond. Suffice it to say that few, if any, *femmes* became *fatales* without as it were being primed to their full erotic potential by a firm, knowing masculine hand. Where would the legendary Joséphine have been without Emperor Boney? Would Mata Hari have been the effortless seductress she was, had there not been a Monsieur Hari, skulking glinty-eyed in the background? *Non*.

And so it was with Mila. It was I who stoked the coals within her that later set Swinging London on fire. That inner glow, that silky understated sexuality, belonged to a girl who had become a woman in the deepest, most intimate sense, who had quite simply found herself, having experienced an ecstatic physical awakening at the hands of a master.

Not that it was achieved without personal effort. I read the books. I studied the techniques. I learnt the tricks. *The Sensuous Woman*, *The Perfumed Garden*, Kinsey. We took our sex seriously in those days.

As for homework, there were times when I forsook the office for days as I sensitively yet firmly led Mila ever deeper into the dark jungle of secret desire. Sometimes when we emerged, blinking in the sunlight after an intense period of practical work, we would smile pityingly at the dull, safe lives of the folks in the real world. Poor fools. If only they knew what they were missing.

Mila was an adept pupil, frequently surprising me by the enthusiasm and originality she brought to the project.

'You think I am too extreme in my behaviours?' she asked once, as we lay together during one of our brief respites. 'Am I too heavy in my desires?'

'No.' I sat up in bed and lit a cigarillo. 'I like that.'

She turned away from me and held a pillow close to her as if it were some damned teddy bear. Her pale, slight body looked strangely vulnerable in the half-light of the bedroom.

'It has deep beginnings, this desire,' she said, almost to herself. 'I'm thinking, if I do this, will Johnny like me? If my habits are a little bendy, is that interesting to him? Perhaps he will be less stingy with his affections. I scorn myself for it sometimes.'

'Don't,' I said, allowing a hint of harshness to enter my voice. Easygoing in so many ways, I found these maudlin confessionals tiresome, even in the early days.

'You are not so intensive, I think, as me. All the time, with me in bed, your eyes are open. Sometimes I find you are mechanic when we love.'

'Mechanical,' I said, slapping her jovially across the buttocks. 'Get it right, for Christ's sake.'

She pulled the pillow closer to her.

'Again,' she said.

It was a demanding time and, thrown oddly off kilter by Project Mila, I almost lost control. I would find excuses to skip business engagements. My mind would wander homewards during the most important financial meetings. I became a smiling fool, treating everyone – even Talbot, for heaven's sake – with a quiet generosity and warmth. I crashed three cars in six months.

When I was not putting her through her paces in the bedroom, Mila and I would spend hour after hour listening to tapes and demo discs in the hope of finding a hit number for her. We were looking for a song – as I explained a million times to the rat-faced denizens of Denmark Street – that had something of the touching, little-girl-lost feel of Twinkle's 'Terry' but with a more open and honest sensuality. They said I was searching for the impossible but, as my rivals would confirm, there's no place for impossible in the world of Jonathan Peter Fixx.

'This one, Johnny,' Mila would say as we listened to the efforts of yet another warbling songsmith. 'In my mind, I feel it suits the rhythm of my abilities.'

I smiled tolerantly.

'Crass,' I said. 'Derivative. Not good enough for you.'

'But what is good, Johnny?' she wailed. 'I begin to have a well-planted suspicion that it is me that is not good. I have done my humble studies of English. I have changed my face. I have some personal successes with these famous photographers with their not-so-good brains and wicked ways. It has been a very intensive time for me – '

'And for me.'

'– but, on the other way, I do not sing. It is all I want. I am not so much a useless person that you can imagine.'

'It's a matter of the right song.'

'I will be already dead before you find this song.'

I sighed, as I put on another record.

'Darling – ' I said reasonably.

'Tell me, the king of my heart.'

'There are people out there who are waiting for you to fail. You see them, the journalists, the photographers, the TV producers, the hangers-on. They smile, they build you up, they make you feel good about yourself, they give you fame. Why?'

'It is a bullshit, I know. That is my sad discovery already.'

'They want to see you fall. They've given you success. Now what they need is failure. They can't stand all this perfection and happiness. Mila,' I may have touched her cheek, 'they're waiting for you to lay an egg.'

She laughed. 'An egg?' How was it that only Mila could laugh at me without making me angry?

'They're determined your first record will be a dog.'

'Egg, dog. I didn't suspect singing a song was such problems.'

'Trust me.'

Mila got up and padded barefoot over to the record-player.

'Enough,' she said, taking the record off. 'Now tell me, my Mr Romeo. This dog. How am I laying it?'

Young as I was, I could see the danger signs looming. Instead of scaling the heights of show-business success, we were careering down the mountainside on a bob-sleigh of desire, heading full-tilt for a snowdrift of sickening self-indulgent mutual dependence. I had to put our relationship back on a business footing before it was too late. One way, domestic bliss; the other, the showbiz jungle. We needed a song, and fast.

In the end, I had to write it myself.

Maybe 'adapt it' would be more accurate.

I was paying one of the periodical visits to Elm Tree Drive which, as head of the family, I felt were my duty. Mother was growing scattier by the minute and Catherine was trembling, rather attractively I have to admit, on the brink of womanhood. Although she was not a true member of the Fixx family (indeed a less generous person might have regarded her as something of a cuckoo in the nest), a certain bond had developed between us. In a world of pop, pills and promiscuity, Catherine needed some sort of moral guidance and Mother, the past had shown and the future would confirm, was unlikely to provide it. Fortunately for Catherine I was there to keep her on the straight and narrow.

Mother, it transpired, was suffering from one of her creative attacks. The book she had been worrying away at for as long as I could remember had reached what she described, with characteristic self-importance, as 'final-draft stage'. Naturally, she turned to me for advice on what to do with it.

'There it is, Jonathan,' she pointed to a pillar of typed paper on the dining-room table, '*The Second Front*.'

'Goodness,' I remarked pleasantly. 'How many forests were destroyed to create this little masterpiece?'

Mother laughed lightly, with a fine show of embarrassment. Whenever her writing was under discussion, she assumed a thoroughly unconvincing air of girlish modesty. To an outsider, it would have been faintly nauseating.

'So,' I said, picking up the vast manuscript and leafing through it with a determined show of interest. 'What's it all about then?'

'It's principally about Father, the war and what it did to him. Then at another level it's about the women left behind at home during the war years and, I suppose, the shift of perceptions of the role of men that followed the war years, attitudes to the home, work and all that. There's obviously a strong element of autobiography particularly in the last part of the book – '

I confess that, with the word 'autobiography', I tuned out. Why is it that women can only think, talk, write about themselves? I, me, *moi* – that's all it is with them. No wonder Mother was, for a short period, regarded as 'important'. When it came to female self-regard, she was a champion in the making. Catherine was not like that yet but, from the way she was listening to Mother as she sat on the rug by the fire, I could tell her independence was likely to be short-lived. Goodness, what an enchanting creature she was, with those wide, serious eyes and long dark hair. I watched her, as she gazed in admiration at her garrulous adopted mother, and felt a sharp pang of brotherly affection.

My mother's lengthy summary had droned to a close. 'Perhaps you'd care to read it, Jonathan,' she said.

My heart sank. Frankly, I've never had much time for reading. A column of figures, yes; a tightly worded memo, of course. But I've always believed that if it can't be said on two sides of the paper, it's not worth saying. As for the so-called 'creative', the 'fictional', you can forget it. I'm a busy man.

'It seems to me, Mother,' I said as tactfully as I could manage, 'that you've summarised so well that reading it would be rather superfluous.'

I noticed Catherine looked rather disappointed.

'I think you should look at it, Jonathan,' she said. 'It's good. And it does rather affect you.'

This was a turn-up. Affect me? Had I missed something in Mother's turgid summary?

'I suppose I could glance through it tonight.'

'Read it carefully, Jonathan,' said my mother. 'I need your advice on how much to ask for it.'

'Ask for it?'

'From a publisher.'

Only then did the truth emerge. On close questioning, Mother revealed that she had shown *The Second Front* to a neighbour, Martin something-or-other, who claimed to be some sort of ex-publisher.

'Martin thinks it will be published,' said Catherine with touching pride. 'He thinks it's important.'

'Good for Martin,' I said coolly. 'I'll read it tonight.'

As it turned out, I was unable to get to Mother's masterwork until late that night, having spent the evening in considerable discomfort listening to The Cavemen, a local pop group which, according to Catherine, was about to put Biggleswade on the map. Normally I would have politely declined Catherine's invitation but, since the boys went to her school, and I was after all concerned for her moral welfare, I agreed to tag along to their rehearsal in a local church hall.

Funnily enough, they were almost talented in a drippy, second-hand sort of way. The lead singer, a scruff called Pete who wrote the band's songs, had a certain style and, at the end of the evening, I agreed to see them at Elm Tree Drive the next day.

Later, my ears still ringing from The Cavemen's musical efforts (a song called 'Take Me' was particularly hard to shift), I lugged *The Second Front* on to my bed and attempted to skim through it.

Let me try to be fair to Mother. She had worked hard. She had almost succeeded in making her banal life sound interesting. If the final result was undeniably boring, there were moments – her description of Father's return home from the military funny farm – that were quite moving. Mother had certainly tried.

But it wasn't enough. *The Second Front*, at the end of the day (and it was almost two in the morning by the time I had finally leafed through to the end of it), was no more nor less than a whinge, a book-length moan, the sort of poor-little-me confessional you could find in any women's magazine, topped up with lashings of the pseudo-intellectualism that passes for serious writing among lightweights.

In no way was I biased. As one of the first feminists, a New Man before his time, I have always supported the right of the fair sex to have its say. But, really, did it have to be so shrill, so vituperative, so unattractive? I was as left-wing as anyone in those days, having voted for Wilson and the white heat of his technological revolution both in 1964 and 1966, but mine was a gentle, inner revolution that had more to do with liberating the self than with liberating mankind. First liberate yourself, we believed – the rest of the world will follow. Our way was with the body, not the barricade. While others screamed for liberation on the street, we were putting it into practice in the bedroom. History will judge which revolution was the more successful.

It was not that I objected to Mother indulging in a spot of writing. Any sensible woman will have her thoughts about life and love and, in my experience, will express them at the slightest excuse. Some might actually commit their worthy thoughts to paper – the chatty letter to a girlfriend, the intimate diary with little asterisks to show when the next period's due – nothing wrong with that. Mother's problem was that, encouraged by Martin, her so-called literary adviser (whose interest in exciting the hopes of a lonely, gullible widow can only be guessed at), she had decided to wash her dirty linen in public. Now she was standing back triumphantly in expectation of a standing ovation.

It was too much. Or so I felt at the time. For Mother to make a fool of herself was all very well. There was even a case for giving Father the full loony-tunes-of-glory treatment. But how would it look if Jon Fixx, young meteor, were stripped bare for the public gaze by his own mother? This, *The Second Front* was saying, is the future; the war generation was confused and bigoted, but look what we're bringing up.

Personally, of course, I could take it but, as it happened, my career was at a particularly critical stage. If I fell, others would go down with me: Mila, Talbot, the various employees of Glentabbot Properties whose names I forget. Then the whole thing would be thoroughly embarrassing for Catherine.

No, taking the brave, broader view, I decided that, as head of the family, I had no alternative but to stay Mother's poison pen before she did irreparable damage to the family name. To save her from herself, if you like.

'You think so?'

Mother reacted to my carefully worded critique of *The Second Front* with predictable coolness.

'Publishers don't want pain, Mother,' I said. 'They want glamour. Girls. Spies with hairy chests. Sports cars.'

'This has nothing to do with your own feelings about the book?'

'About the manuscript?' I shrugged. 'I might question one or two of your conclusions. My memory of certain events differs from yours. But it's fine – of its type.'

'Martin was rather more optimistic.'

'Ah. Martin,' I smiled affectionately at Mother and sighed. 'He knows, does he?' I asked. 'I mean, he's some sort of expert?'

'Well, he was a publisher.'

'Was, Mother, was. There's no place for "was" today. "Was" is out.'

It was clear that I had no chance of persuading Mother to abandon her hopes of publishing *The Second Front* and that I had to adopt Plan B.

'Tell you what,' I said. 'Maybe I could arrange for one of my contacts in the publishing world to give you a first-hand view.'

'Publishing? You don't know any publishers. Anyway, I thought they were only interested in girls and spies with hairy chests.'

'I could be wrong. Fashions change fast in the book world.'

It was a bit of a struggle, but Mother finally agreed to let me return to London with excess baggage.

That was the end of *The Second Front*, or so I believed.

On the journey, I reflected on life's little paradoxes. During a dull family weekend, which cost-effectiveness-wise should have been something of a write-off, I had by sheer diligence managed to knock a couple of my more irritating problems on the head. First Mother's literary yearnings and then Mila's need for a hit song.

The deal I struck with The Cavemen seemed eminently fair. I couldn't guarantee a recording contract, I told them, after they had appeared the obligatory thirty minutes late at Elm Tree Drive, but I had contacts in Tin Pan Alley. I was prepared to put my reputation on the line and give them a leg-up.

That was true, incidentally. While The Cavemen were much like any other group at the time, they had a sound (not a nice sound, I grant), they wrote their own material and looked like neanderthals, all of which was in their favour. I gave them the benefit of my advice: get a few photographs together, if possible of the band in bear-fur loincloths scowling like a gang of prehistoric rapists, give me a demo tape, and leave the rest to me. The alleged 'rip-offs' and 'legal hassles' that were given a certain amount of coverage in the music press after Pete's sad end could hardly be laid at my door, unless passing over the contract to a well-known heavyweight pop manager could be considered somehow immoral. He was a specialist. Changing their name to Purple Turnip and encouraging them to dabble in psychedelic drugs was clearly a mistake, but it was his mistake, not mine.

The original letter of agreement I offered Pete and his friends was generous to a fault. I did all the work. They took all the money. My only stipulation was that the song 'Take Me' should become my copyright and that I should be credited as co-writer (Pete: 'But it's me best number.' Me: 'Good luck, boys, you're on your own'; collapse of scrofulous party).

Was I to know that, like so many groups at that time, Pete and his Cavemen (or Purple Turnips) were nothing more than one-hit wonders? It was tough luck, admittedly, that, as it turned out, they had no involvement whatsoever in that one success, but then rock and roll always was a hit and miss business.

– You'll be needing footnotes, perhaps.

– You think?

– Who's Richard Neville? What's Twinkle?

– You're joking.

– No. And who on earth was the Sensuous Woman?

– She's not relevant any more, sad to say.

8
Dreams and schemes

Doubtless you remember the fuss there was with the release of Mila's first single 'Break Me' (the subtle adaptation of the original, moronic lyrics was entirely my idea). Disgusting, they said, depraved. A shameful example to the young.

It was an excellent start.

When Mila appeared on *Top of the Pops*, all leather and little-girl-lost, causing spasms of male (and, less publicised, female) desire throughout the country, the Number One spot was assured. Belatedly the BBC banned it, the Controller of Radio One expressing the opinion that 'Break Me' was no less than an anthem for sado-masochism and, as such, was potentially harmful to the kids. There were questions in the House. Probed impertinently about her private life by lip-smacking sewer rats, Mila behaved with wide-eyed dignity. 'Sometimes, I am being lusty, like any girl, sometimes no. Is it interesting to the people? It is not.'

'Break Me', which was now played incessantly on pirate radio, came to symbolise the new freedom, rebellion, sexual originality. Overnight, Mila was a heroine of the counter-culture. She grew famous; I, her manager and copyright holder in her hit song, became rather rich.

For a while, the press were content to dwell on any titbit of Milabilia that my PR people fed them – 'POUTING POLE HITS BIG TIME' (*Daily Mirror*), 'WHY MILA BACKS BRITAIN' (*News Chronicle*), '"TWISTED UP WITH A WILD DESIRE" – THE SEXY SECRETS OF LUSTY GIRL STAR' (*News of the World*), 'PRIMP ME – MILA'S HAIRSTYLE SECRETS' (*Jackie*), 'THE SACHER-MASOCH IT TO ME GIRL' (*Guardian*), 'CONTROVERSIAL SINGER SUPPORTS LEGALISATION OF "POT"' (*The Times*), and so on.

Then, predictably, the sewer rats' gutter patrol began to dig for

Ugly Truth stories: 'The Making of Mila – The Ugly Truth', 'Mila's Nose – The Ugly Truth', '"Break Me" Was My Song – The Ugly Truth' (a libel, Pete's last bid for fame, which was strangled at birth by a cohort of lawyers flourishing my carefully worded letter of agreement). Finally, spurred on to greater efforts by their circulation-crazed editors, the desperate journalists happened on the only truly interesting story in the whole amusing saga, my own: Mila's Svengali, The Man Behind Mila, Mila's Mr Fixx-It. But it wasn't ugly, and it wasn't really the truth.

Unlike many prominent men, I am not afraid of publicity. I don't court it, neither do I shun it. In my book, there's absolutely nothing wrong with a spot of self-marketing, so long as the image presented to the mugs on the street is generally fair and positive.

'Boys, boys,' I said, as the scurfy, balding idiots with their notebooks and tape-recorders beat a path to my door. 'This is 1967, Swinging London. The public wants beauty, not truth. It wants up-beat stories about another great British success story. Go smear someone else. Preferably a foreigner.'

'Who?' they asked.

Well, Talbot had been asking for it.

The fact is, the little chap's attempts to worm his way into the ranks of the establishment had actually paid off, in the short term at least.

The plump East European wide-boy of yesteryear was suddenly the thinking person's capitalist. Rich, yes, but caring with it, a man of the people. Stylish, of course, but also modishly classless. Once he started running with the class of '64, the new technocrats with their dead eyes and cheap suits, he travelled everywhere by taxi – his own taxi, as it happens, complete with chauffeur, but rather more acceptable, in the silly image-conscious sixties, than the old Daimler he had owned not so long ago.

Tailoring his past to suit the times, Talbot no longer bragged about his war years in the Polish Ukraine when he was a teenage profiteer on the black market but spoke reluctantly – always reluctantly – of hardship, starvation, acts of mindless heroism as part of the Resistance. His entire family, he sobbed during that famous interview with David Frost, was wiped out during the war. He arrived in England with nothing more than 7/6d, a copy of *Barchester Towers* and a spare pair of underpants ('and perhaps a few gold ingots in an old suitcase', he later told me in a rare unguarded moment). Astonishingly sensitive to the mood of the times, he discovered socialism in 1963, semitism shortly after the Six Day War. Only I knew that he was one of life's most dedicated capitalists, and would do anything to avoid paying his taxes. In fact he was not – despite his Oy Vey mannerisms and passionate support of Israel – even Jewish. As for his sickening attempt to present himself as a family man ('For my darling Brenda' went the hilarious dedication to his autobiography *Tomorrow the Stars*), there are countless women today who, having been on the receiving end of his loathsome, oily attentions when they were young and looking for work, could present an altogether less affecting portrait. Ugly he may have been, but Henry Talbot could never be accused of lacking energy, nerve or, as he would have put it post-1967, 'chutzpah'.

No sour grapes here, mind. He's down. I'm up. *C'est la vie*.

Influence, sucking up to your betters, can only take you so far. That was what Talbot never understood. As a small-time entrepreneur at the spivvy end of the property market, he had effectively used a succession of clapped-out aristos and bent MPs to provide much credit and credibility. It was a fair swap: he (or, to be more precise, we) fed their habit (pills, tarts, boys, whatever); they allowed their names to be used on the notepaper of the particular shell company we were using at the time.

Once we became legitimate members of booming Britain, we dropped the losers, the yesterday men, and ran with the true movers and shakers. While I became one of the beautiful people in the entertainments sector, Talbot cultivated the grey men who now ruled the roost at Westminster.

Hence the 'soirées'. In what seemed no more than a matter of months, Talbot was one of the new élite. At his parties the new establishment paraded their social consciences and traded gossip. He developed an interest in the opera, in literature. He sat on various reasonably influential quangos.

I was surprised, but what did I care? I was moving effortlessly among the ranks of the beautiful people. If my partner chose to mix with a particularly dull bunch of arriviste politicians and pseudo-intellectuals, that was entirely up to him.

Until September 1966, when Henry Talbot, formerly Tadeuzc Jankic, became Lord Talbot of Sonning.

It was too much, you'll agree.

There were certain aspects of Glentabbot Properties that were somewhat irregular, that were perhaps – as a squirming Lord Talbot of Sonning later confessed to the greaseball probe-merchant Frost – 'not quite tickety-boo'. Local planning officers being straightened with briefcases packed with used fivers, rent-collectors whose rough-and-ready manner and skilful deployment of the firm's Dobermann Pinscher gave certain recalcitrant tenants the brown-trouser treatment, custom-built high-rise buildings that toppled over within a year of construction, that sort of thing.

My nose was clean, vis-à-vis the evidence at least. I was Glentabbot's man on the move, remember; it was the paperwork that gave the game away. And, rather sensibly in retrospect, I had left all that to my colleague.

Once certain documents found their way into the hands of journalists (with the help of some disgruntled employee, no doubt), Lord Talbot, magnate, millionaire, man of conscience, was up to his fat little neck in it.

Stories about Talbot started appearing in the press. Lawyers were alerted, writs issued, editors warned by the little man's friends in government.

He might have survived, had it not been for the Save-a-Saigon-Child scheme. That, and the reappearance in my life of Brian Collin.

It was a busy and exciting time for me. Mila's record. The need to keep her on the bubble publicity-wise (not helped by a new moodiness which frequently afflicted her). Outwardly supporting Talbot through his troubles while laying a few mines in his path. Interviewing, entertaining, comprehensively auditioning the scores of empty-headed Mandys eager to be handled by Mr Success.

It was hardly surprising that it was a good three months before I found time to deliver Mother's manuscript to the man I trusted to do the decent thing.

Once, you might recall, publishers used to look like history teachers. Between that golden age and today, when they look, think and behave like bank managers, there was a brief period – ten or fifteen years, perhaps – when they tried to be fashionable. Producing books, they believed, was no longer a backwater, where particularly dull toads flopped about idly in the still, brackish waters, but was now part of the media mainstream. They became trendy, over-excited and silly.

There may have been sillier publishers than Marc Shelley – greedier publishers, more self-obsessed publishers – but in 1968 I had yet to meet them. A passing fling with a semi-successful model had enabled Marc to run with the tail end of the King's Road crowd for a while and it was at some minor show-business function that I first came across him. Was it possible that this beanstalk in outmoded mod gear, Zapata moustache, granny glasses and shoulder-length hair actually dealt with books? It was. Marc had just landed a job with the paperback division of a large London publisher anxious to jack up its credibility with the younger reader.

His interest in the written word was easily summarised. Was the book about drugs or sex? Would its content outrage the *Daily Mail* and guarantee him frequent mentions in the underground press? Could he pull the skinny model his art director had chosen for the inevitably lurid cover?

'Marc, me old mate,' I said, having allowed him to buy me lunch and explain drunkenly for three hours why Mila should allow her no-holds-barred autobiography to be written for her, 'one small favour.'

'Shoot,' said Shelley, trying unsuccessfully to focus his eyes on me.

I reached under my chair and took *The Second Front* out of my briefcase. With some difficulty, I found space on the table for the vast manuscript.

'A *small* favour?' said Marc, with a weary, sulky pout. This was going to be easy. No publisher likes reading, and five hundred pages of middle-aged blather when he was expecting a pageless, high-glam deal with Mila would be as welcome as a toothache. 'I'm really not sure – '

'Fine,' I said briskly. 'If you don't want to meet Mila.'

Marc sighed and reached for the title-page. '*The Second Front* by Mary Fixx. How old is she?'

'Fifty.'

He groaned.

'Don't worry,' I smiled. 'It's not as bad as it seems. You don't have to read it. Market-wise, it's a no-no. But you know how it is, Marc. Member of the family writes semi-literate memoirs. I'd give the old biddy the bad news myself but, call me soft, I don't want to hurt her feelings. Anyway, she wants a real publisher to look at it.'

'That lets me out.'

'No hurry, Marc,' I continued, ignoring his rather percipient jest. 'In your own time. A curt rejection letter in a couple of months will do the trick.'

Marc shrugged and moodily pushed the manuscript into his shoulder-bag, tearing some of the pages. With a bit of luck, his annoyance would be reflected in the tone of the rejection letter.

At least, I would be able to tell Mother, I had tried.

The achiever ignores what I like to call 'the human dimension' at his peril. I was in the people business and, as I had already discovered, there's a problem with people. They let you down.

It was 1968. I could be excused perhaps a moment of satisfaction at the way things were going. In addition to Mila's singing and modelling royalties and personal appearance money, which continued to pour in at an astonishing rate, the other branches of my business were flourishing.

It would be churlish of me to deny that Talbot's ennoblement (before the Fall) contributed to our success. He was a high-flyer in the straight establishment; I had the 'alternative' world at my fingertips. No wonder the activities of Glentabbot Properties and its sister companies, particularly in the property and so-called 'asset-stripping' line, reached an astonishing 530 per cent annual growth rate during this period.

Such was the aura of success which enveloped us that we hardly had to leave our large new offices in Kensington to make a killing every day of the week. One after another, in they would totter, the halt, the lame, the overextended, the red-nosed, pin-striped chairmen desperate to offload their tottering businesses on to Talbot and Fixx; indeed, if their shareholders had permitted them, they would probably have given them away.

Selling was never a problem, either. The new generation of City spivs fell over themselves in their efforts to overpay for virtually any two-bit firm which had passed through our hands. They liked celebrity in those days; they thought it was catching.

Because, by now, I was really quite famous. You might not have heard of me, but I was. Famous to the people who mattered.

Was that the problem with Mila? Was that why her success, unlike mine, was so transitory? Or was the problem some flaw which I, in my weakness, had overlooked? Who knows? We were both working hard during this period but, whereas I thrived under pressure, she buckled.

People, as I say, let you down.

'Out, out, out. Always it is out.'

Mila was wandering about the flat in a dressing-gown, like a bad actress about to be nixed by the Bard in Act III.

'Why is it never in these days? You are out one way, I am out another way. It is a hell to live like this.'

It was early evening, always the low point in Mila's day. After several hours of so-called work (warbling in a recording studio, interviewed by a tame journo, opening a boutique, snapped by a lensman), it was sometimes all I could do to get her on her feet, out of the door and back into the limelight.

'Mila,' I said patiently. 'All you have to do is appear, and smile a bit for the cameras.'

'Who is Mila?' she murmured, almost to herself. 'She is marching doll. The premières, the parties, the charities, here is Mila, all nice and wound up. Look, she smiles. Look, she talks. Look, she is with the pop star who likes the men but is not owning to it. Maybe he swings both sides. Maybe Mila swings both sides. Maybe it doesn't matter if everyone swings, everyone smiles, everyone is just clever and pretty and a beautiful people. Look, here she is, snap snap, nice face, nice dress, nice legs. She is excellent girl, Mila.'

How strange women can be, I reflected. When I had provided her with security and a home, Mila had wanted fame and success. Now, thanks entirely to my efforts, she had been given more fame and success than her distinctly fragile talent deserved, and what did she want? Security and a home.

'We'll take a break soon,' I said. 'Remember I'm working too.'

'And who is she, this work tonight?' Mila replied with the spite that had become all too evident recently.

It was true that, with the development of my personal management firm Magic Mushroom Ltd (no hippy connotations here, merely a witty reflection of the overnight growth of my enterprise), I was obliged to spend more and more of my time with some of my younger artistes. But, as I explained to Mila, it was my duty to look to the future, to develop tomorrow's stars, to give my other clients the kind of benefits which she had enjoyed so fully. Not by nature a selfish person, she was nonetheless curiously slow to grasp this point.

'At the bottom of my heart I caress this dream,' she burbled on, as I anxiously glanced at my watch – unless she was in the white, chauffeur-driven Rolls within forty-five minutes, a well-known film star (and undeclared gay) who had paid me handsomely for a highly publicised date with the In-Girl would be holding his own hand tonight. 'I am once more solitarist, no longer a prisoner in my own life, and you – '

I allowed my eyes to narrow in a way that, had her confused, addled brain been receiving messages, would have reminded her that even my patience was not inexhaustible.

' – you have escaped your devils.'

Resisting the temptation to tell her a few home truths (that if she didn't play her part, she'd be 'solitarist' sooner than she planned, for instance), I smiled wanly and, with a sigh, adjourned to the bathroom to fetch a couple of Dr Feelgood's gaily coloured pills which had become so much a part of Mila's life in recent weeks.

'These will make it better,' I said, giving them to her with a glass of wine. She really didn't look too good these days although, to be fair, the dark rings under her eyes and Marilyn Monroe pallor were high fashion at the time.

She looked up at me, mournfully.

'The life, it is not smashing, Johnny.'

'Take the pills.'

And within the hour, thanks to my patience and Dr Feelgood's medication, she was dressed in her skimpy leather outfit and ready, if somewhat wide-eyed and wobbly, for the social merry-go-round.

'Smile, Mila,' shouted the photographers who camped on the doorstep during this period. The flashlights popped as, zombie-like, she made her way to the Rolls. 'Who's the lucky guy tonight, Mila?'

Having watched from behind lace curtains, as the In-Girl departed unsteadily for the bright lights, I returned to prepare for my own less public night out.

I made mistakes. I'm a big enough man to admit it.

I was too ambitious for her. I wanted too much on her behalf, and too fast. I forgot that, not so long ago, Mila had been plain Magdalena Bobrowski, with a dull brother and ordinary, girlishly modest plans for the future. I was blind to the side-effects of Dr Feelgood's evil potions. I underestimated the genetic effects of insanity among the Bobrowskis ('In my family,' she said, 'the threat of history is always appearing. My grandmother was often historical, my mother even is a little bit screamy').

Above all, I failed to understand that for Mila I was not just a personal manager and, rather more seriously, that Mila for me was not just a chart-topping cutie providing 85 per cent of all net receipts. Years later, I am still likely to be ambushed by Mila fantasies as I lie in bed in the early morning, startled by a girl passing on the street with Mila eyes, mouth or hair. Now I can see it; then all I could sense was a certain lack of equilibrium, an incompleteness, when Mila wasn't there.

It was in Paris, where I was spending a weekend trying to land one of my newer clients a part in a Vadim film, that I first became fully aware of my new vulnerability.

There had been something of a row, with maybe even a few tears shed, when I told Mila that I needed to take the actress – whose name (if I could recall it) is not relevant to this account – for a few days abroad. Various accusations went one way, various virulent denials went the other but, in the end, I left, vowing fidelity, everlasting love, virtually anything that would get me out of the door and en route to the airport.

Later, as I gazed over the Seine from my room in the Hôtel des Anglais, I found myself reminiscing over the times Mila and I had spent together, our public and private successes. I had helped her grow – of course I had – but she had also changed me; I had become a more complete person, able to see that wealth, deals, the petty rivalries of commercial life were only part of the story. Without heart, passion, *l'amour*, they are almost completely worthless.

Sighing, I turned back to the bed where my actress lay in the deep, untroubled sleep of the child which, give or take a couple of years, she still was.

I had even, at one point, considered booking us into separate rooms but she was of Indian extraction, which was to be something of a first for me, and anyway it was important that she was fully relaxed and self-confident for her audition with Roger the next day.

What is it about the first time? Why is it that, for all the guff you read in the agony columns, it's the sweetest moment of all?

I compare it to the management lark. Assessing, valuing, laying siege to a firm you wish to acquire is all very well; retrenching, rationalising, consolidating after the event have their satisfactions. But there's nothing quite like the actual takeover for pure, uncomplicated pleasure.

So it is with *la femme*. The joys of a shared lifetime, two armchairs in front of the telly, the pleasures of a so-called 'long-term relationship', naturally have their supporters among life's joggers and slowcoaches. But for the true achiever in the noble art of love, domestic contentment can never compare to that magical moment when the paltry feminine defences (respectability, shyness, self-control, first-night nerves, what would Mummy say?) crumble, the little army of resistance meekly lays down its arms, and the last citadel, the conqueror's prize, is his. Call me a romantic fool, if you wish, but for me there's nothing like it.

And yet damn me if, sharing this sweetest moment of all with my young actress an hour or so back, I hadn't heard a voice crying out the name of Mila, to discover to my surprise (and hers, not that it mattered) that the voice was my own. Damn me, if I wouldn't have given a month's royalties to have Mila slumbering in the vastness of that double bed, rather than an anonymous (if attractive) nobody who, in a matter of days, would be no more than a hazy memory. Damn me, if the heart of Jonathan Peter Fixx was not assailed by unfamiliar feelings of, what, guilt? Surely not.

The thought of Mila unsettled me, stirred me even. Perhaps if I woke my teenager, she would make me feel better.

Probably not, but it was worth a try.

It is, I suppose, the mark of a man in control that he refuses to allow the stormy waters of personal concerns to deflect the speedboat of professional achievement from its course. I returned from Paris with a somewhat subdued actress (she had fluffed the screen test with Vadim and I had made it clear that ours was to be a don't-call-me-I'll-call-you relationship from here on), and the script for Mila's first film.

Written by one of Vadim's protégés, *Venus in Furs* was an imaginative and provocative interpretation of the classic work of erotica. The script had been touted around the various Julies, Judys and Mariannes who were taking their tops off for the right money, but all of them had backed away squeamishly. The film company was looking for a high-profile, controversial star; we needed to crank Mila's career up a notch or two. Perhaps naively, I believed that the contract I signed in Paris, subject to final legal confirmation, was in everyone's best interest.

I was not entirely displeased to find that, on my return to the flat on the Monday evening, Mila was out, presumably working. So often, when I was unable to be around to buoy her up with pills and a pep talk, she would sit at home sullenly watching television rather than advancing her career on the party circuit.

On the table in the hall, there was a note to call my mother. I dialled the number wearily – it had been a tiring weekend in one way and another.

'Jonathan!' There was an ecstatic trill to Mother's voice which, in my innocence, I attributed to the pleasure of talking to her only son. 'Have you heard the news?'

'What news is that, Mother?' I said coolly.

'From Marc. He wants it. He's going to publish *The Second Front*.'

My heart sank bootwards. Delegate, they say, encourage the next man to share the load of responsibility. But if the next man is Marc Shelley, what then? My instructions to the long-haired bimbo could hardly have been clearer: allow the manuscript to gather dust for a couple of months, do *not* read it, reject it as brutally as you like. So what does he do? Takes it home, reads it overnight, rushes dementedly into his boss's office the next morning screaming he's found the new Edna O'Drabble or whatever, and, within the week, he has an already unbalanced middle-aged woman dancing around the kitchen making hysterical, self-congratulatory telephone calls to all and sundry. That's where delegation gets you.

'He says he thinks it's a masterpiece.' Mother was gushing tearfully. 'He's paying me five thousand pounds for it.'

Bloody hell, I thought, what kind of doped-up stupor induced

Shelley to make that kind of offer? Not that I said that to Mother, naturally.

'Five thousand pounds? That sounds *very* low.'

'And it's all thanks to you, Jonathan. You were right, I was wrong . . . How d'you mean, low?'

'We'll put it on the block,' I said briskly. 'That's what we'll do. A literary auction. Five thousand,' I laughed like a man amazed that a publisher could pull such a stunt. 'Marc should be ashamed.'

'But, Jonathan, I've accepted it.'

'Ah.'

Muttering congratulations with as much grace as I could muster, I hung up. For the life of me I couldn't think of any way of preventing Shelley from publishing. Threats? Bribery? A shot across the bows from a libel lawyer? None seemed likely to deter a publisher greedy and unscrupulous enough to let down an old friend in order to make a quick buck. It was all devastatingly depressing.

Typically, just when I needed Mila (the cup of tea, the soothing tones, the mindless feminine chit-chat to take my mind off things), she was nowhere to be found. The girl on whose behalf I had been working much of the weekend, landing perhaps the biggest deal of her spoilt young life, had apparently elected to carouse the night away, rather than greet her lover's return with a spot of thoroughly old-fashioned loyalty and affection.

'Glad you could make it,' I said waspishly, when she finally tripped in some time after midnight. I was alone, nursing a malt whisky in front of the fire, reflecting on the ingratitude of women. 'No, I won't bother with a homecoming supper now, thank you very much.'

'I have news, Johnny,' she said, her eyes wide and unblinking. It was something, I reflected, that she was at least able to use the go-faster pills without my assistance these days.

'I've had enough news for one day.'

'But this is about your very good friend, who is working as journalist. He has conceived this idea of doing a big story about Henry and you. *Frost Programme* on TV is interested. Brian Collin. I like this man, with his smile and his thinking eyes. He took me Chez Victor.'

'Very touching, I'm sure,' I said like a man who has awakened from one nightmare to discover he's in another.

'He thinks you are good for *Frost Programme*. That is the climax.'

'Me?' I said weakly.

'He talks about his schooldays with you. I think you make an important impression on his life. As for me – ' Mila sat down heavily beside me ' – I stuff myself enormously when he takes me Chez Victor restaurant tonight. We speak of you all night.'

'How kind of you.'

'It was half a pleasure,' she trilled. 'I think maybe more than half. I was missing you. Your so sardonic eyes. Your grand machine, your – '

'Yeah, yeah,' I said, suddenly tired. What a cruel mistress *l'amour* can be! When in Paris, all I wanted was Mila; now I yearned for the quiet solitude of a single bed. Collin was on my case. For years, he had waited to pay me back for the small part I played in his departure from Melton Hall. Diverting him was likely to be difficult. Bloody hell, it was all I needed.

'They are my good news,' said Mila, fumbling with the buttons on my shirt. 'What are yours?'

It was time to clear the decks. Talbot, Shelley, Collin – why *was* it that I was obliged to deal with these people? Bad luck? A flaw of judgement? Over-generosity of spirit? They weren't exactly losers but, in making their way through life, each of them had managed to obstruct me, slow me down. I resented the time I would have to spend sorting them out and yet, at this moment, I had no choice but to descend to their level.

Talbot reacted rather badly to the news that Collin was after us (or rather, as I explained it, after him – a white lie told in the firm's best interest). There was much wringing of hands and wetting of knickers at the thought of appearing on *The Frost Programme*.

'But it's trial by television, everyone knows that,' he wailed, as he paced up and down in his office.

'Sometimes Frosty goes in a bit hard,' I admitted. 'We need to prepare your case very carefully.'

'*My* case! What about you?'

'It appears that Collin's particularly interested in your involvement. Peer of the realm, friend of government ministers, one of the great and the good – ' I paused for effect ' – unmasked.'

Talbot scurried over to a filing cabinet and started pulling out files.

'Peter Rachman. The Balham Point Disaster Enquiry. The Lichtenstein account. These must go. They must be shredded.'

'Don't forget the Kray Brothers file,' I said helpfully. 'And the Save-a-Saigon-Child Appeal.'

With an anguished sob, Talbot ran to his desk and, having fumbled with some keys, took another couple of files from the bottom drawer.

'What are we going to do, Jonathan? Think of something.'

'Do?' I said, enormously reassured by this total collapse. 'Personally, I'll be going about my business as usual.'

'What about me?'

'Leave this to me, Henry,' I said smoothly. 'I was at school with Collin. I might be able to straighten out some of the details that appear to be troubling him.'

For a moment I thought the little Pole was going to burst into tears.

'Yes yes,' he said eagerly. 'Old school tie. That will do the trick.'

'Maybe you should go on a lengthy business trip abroad for a few weeks. Somewhere communication with London is tricky. Check out some factories in deepest Korea, for example.'

'Excellent,' said Talbot, rubbing his hands, almost his old self.

'Leave a number for me. I'll call you when the coast is clear.'

'Jonathan, my partner, my chum.' For a moment he stared at me with the sincere man-of-the-people expression he had taken to adopting whenever photographers were about. 'I am eternally grateful to the bottom of my soul.'

'And leave those,' I said, as he started gathering up the files. 'I'll deal with them.'

When I put a call through to Shelley and suggested man-to-man that it might be worth his while to ditch *The Second Front*, he reacted as if I'd just goosed his grandmother.

'This is a book that deserves to be published, Jonathan,' he said, in all apparent seriousness. 'It speaks for the war generation unlike anything I've ever read.'

Hardly an impressive claim, I was about to remark, but checked myself.

'Since when has Marc Shelley been interested in yesterday?' I asked. 'I thought it was our generation you were meant to be publishing.'

'I guess I'm growing up.'

'So you wouldn't be interested in my substituting the authorised Mila story for *The Second Front* at the same price?'

'Mila? What's Mila got to do with this?'

It appeared that once again I had overestimated Marc's deductive powers.

'She wants to work with you, Marc. In fact – ' I allowed the suspicion of a you-lucky-dog chuckle to enter my voice, ' – she wants to work with you very much.'

'That's nice – '

'It is nice, Marc.' I could almost see the silly, vulpine smile spreading across his face as the penny dropped. 'And do you know what she likes?'

'I can't think.'

'A friend. She really likes to party in company. That's what she's into.'

'I see.'

'So she could probably bring a friend. If you . . . like the idea, that is.'

'I'm not sure I'm quite with you.'

Bloody hell, was I going to have to spell it out?

'Let me put it another way,' I said rather more briskly. 'Drop my mother's book and I'll fix you up with Mila.'

There was a silence from the other end of the phone.

'Oh all right,' I added crisply, 'I'll throw in the friend as well.'

There was another lengthy silence.

'Let me just get this right,' said Marc eventually. 'In exchange for my cancelling the contract for a book regarded by those who have read it as an important work of social observation, a potential classic, a *tour de force* even, you are offering me a group-sex session with a pop star.'

'Don't knock it, Marc,' I said jovially. 'I know which I'd choose.'

'Yes.' There was something about his goofily self-important tone that suggested I may have misread the situation.

'Hang on, you're not gay, are you? If so – '

But he had hung up. Like all publishers, I reflected gloomily, Marc had difficulty with the real world. He was used to living life at second-hand. Two years ago, the sexy thrillers he published had doubtless been substitutes for his own unthrilling, sexless everyday life. His interest last year in pseudo-radical, rabble-rousing pamphlets had presumably taken the place of genuine, first-hand political action. Now, he had elected to experience the harshness of life as an adult through Mother and her turgid confessional.

Marc Shelley, a grown-up? Stroll on.

Collin was more amenable. I bought him dinner that night. We reminisced about old times. He bragged about his piffling achievements (a First at Cambridge, traineeship at the BBC, chief researcher for Frost, etc., etc.). I mentioned some of the more interesting stepping-stones in my career, about which he appeared to know rather a lot. I ribbed him jokily about his dinner with Mila. He changed the subject and told me that he was about to blow the whistle on Glentabbot Properties Ltd and its sister firms. I invoked the old school spirit. '*Semper Domus Meltoniensis*, eh Collers?' We raised glasses. The subject was dropped.

As all-male evenings go, it was reasonably agreeable and entirely successful.

– Funnily enough, I came across a note to you from Brian Collin just the other day.

– Very relevant, I'm sure. Did I ask you to ransack my belongings for obscure correspondence?

– I was looking for love letters from Mila, as requested. This looked more interesting.

– When I require your literary judgement, you'll be the first to know.

– 'Fixx – You should know that I did this for Magdalena. If it weren't for her, you'd be finished and I can't say I would have shed too many tears for you. She saved your bacon, God knows why. Now that you no longer have her skirts to hide behind, I shall one day tell the true story even if it is, as I fear, too late for the luckless Talbot. Your time will come. Collin.' What on earth was all that about?

– Practical joke, probably. Marvellous sense of humour, Collin. He's had me in stitches on many an occasion.

– Doesn't sound like a joke to me.

– So you're hard to amuse. Don't bring me your problems.

9
Product crisis

All right, I suppose I had better tell you what happened.

Collin, the school goody-goody, had become Collin, the incorruptible, the crusading journalist, the friend of the underdog, Mr Social Conscience. Within a couple of years of emerging from the University of Cantab with passable honours, he had written a biography of that deeply misunderstood man, Peter Rachman, which, in its sneering, negative contempt for profit and enterprise, weakly caught the spirit of the times and earned him something of a reputation.

So while the rest of us were living dangerously on the front line, taking chances, throwing our weight behind Great Britain Ltd, wealth-creating, Collin had discovered his own vocation – sitting on the sidelines and complaining. We did; he commented. We achieved; he told the world what a terrible thing our achievement was. No doubt he earned a pretty penny as a professional whinger and naysayer but his public image – all faded denim and uncombed hair – somehow managed to conceal the fact.

Although I had little enough time for reading, rarely straying beyond the pages of the *Financial Times*, *New Musical Express* and *Playboy*, I was nonetheless vaguely aware of Collin's reputation, even before he unwisely elected to tangle with me in the twilight of the sixties.

'Collers!' I greeted my old friend with characteristic open-heartedness when we met one lunchtime at a noisy pub in Notting Hill Gate (the sanctimonious prig having declined my invitation to lunch at a decent restaurant in favour of what he described as 'm'local').

'How yer doin'?' he muttered as I clapped him warmly on the back.

'Your local, eh Collers?' I said, glancing around at its clientele of middle-class time-wasters, dressed up like brickies. 'Very smart. But perhaps we should move to the public bar – ' Collin looked confused. 'Bit up-market here, isn't it?'

'Eh?'

'Bit bourgeois,' I said, hoping to crack the atmosphere with a spot of light irony. 'People might think we've been to public school.'

'Here will do me fine,' Collin said, electing not to see the joke. 'Let's get a drink.'

I pushed my way through a crowd of scruffs who were standing near the bar.

'What's your poison, Collers?' I shouted over my shoulder. 'No, don't tell me. Pint of best bitter?'

'Right,' said Collin.

I waved a tenner in the general direction of a young girl in jeans who was behind the bar. 'When you're ready, my love,' I called out. 'Pint of best and a large g and t.'

The barmaid shot me an unpleasant you-talking-to-me? look and went to fetch the drinks.

'Tasty,' I said conversationally to some lout in jeans.

The man moved away.

'Thanks, darling,' I said, cheerfully giving her the tenner after she returned, still scowling.

'I'm not your darling,' she said.

'Dear oh dear.' I was still chortling as Collin and I sat down at a nearby table. 'They don't make 'em like they used to, eh Collers?'

My old pal was looking uneasy.

'Like Sandra,' I continued. 'Remember her? What a little cracker she was.'

Collin looked at me stonily. 'I'm not here to reminisce about m'schooldays,' he said in that odd, classless accent left-wing toffs had taken to affecting. M'schooldays, m'family, m'holiday house in the Dordogne. It fooled nobody.

'Of course you're not,' I said. 'What can I do you for?'

Collin pulled a notebook from his pocket and frowned self-importantly.

'We want to do a *Frost Programme* on charities,' he said. 'I've dug up a few interesting details about your so-called Save-a-Saigon-Child Appeal. Before we book you in for a studio appearance, you might like to comment on some of the information which we've unearthed.'

'Ah, you'll be wanting to see the person primarily responsible,' I said quickly. 'But, as it happens, Lord Talbot has just arranged a lengthy business trip for himself.'

'How very unfortunate.'

I winked at my old schoolfriend as he sat there, pencil poised over his pad. 'He never did have much stomach for a fight, our Mr Jankic.'

'Not to worry,' said Collin. 'It's you we want on the programme.'

'Waste of time,' I said coolly. 'You'd be chasing the wrong fox.' I pulled a thick envelope out of my briefcase. 'Take a look at these papers. They tell the whole story.'

Collin looked with an unconvincing display of indifference at the papers I had given him.

'Yes,' he said finally. 'I'd still like you to answer some questions.'

It occurs to me that I may have skimped over details of the Save-a-Saigon-Child Appeal. Until Collin started snooping around, it had seemed relatively unimportant, its bottom-line contribution to turnover being frankly neither here nor there. But since there was something of a fuss at the time, a few hysterical headlines, even a spot of blood on the carpet at the end of the day, I suppose some crossing of 'i's' is in order at this point.

As the sixties wore on, it became clear that there would be some sort of reaction to the fast, vulgar, fashion-obsessed times in which we lived, that a new mood of introspection was likely to set in. Like a group of teenagers awakening from a wild party and worrying in a vague, unfocused way about the schoolfriends who had never been invited – the fat, the spotty, the charmless, the unloved – the ageing sixties crowd would, sooner or later, step back from their revels, adjust their clothing, and wince. This is silly, they would say to themselves. There's more to it than this. Above all, what are we going to do about the people who weren't invited?

At that point, everyone would feel terribly guilty about the good time they had been having and, because it seemed the best way of proving that you did after all have a social conscience, there would then be a brief upsurge of modish sloganising and brick-lobbing.

This, because revolutionary activity tends to entail danger and discomfort and anyway plays havoc with nicely designed clothes, would not last long. The feeling that somehow things should be better, fairer, kinder, the sense of unease about those, as the phrase went, 'less fortunate than ourselves' endured.

That was the spiritual underpinning of those ill-tempered, hung-over days. Care. Concern. Guilt.

The Save-a-Saigon-Child Appeal was a remarkably simple scheme. The refugee problem in Vietnam was receiving a certain amount of bleating coverage from various pinko sewer rats. Homeless, parentless, victims of a war they cannot understand, the usual thing. Money was needed.

With very little difficulty, I acquired hundreds of photographs of Asian children with help-me eyes (snapped at a primary school in Thailand, as it happens, but no one could tell the difference) and with the help of certain image-conscious celebrities – they wouldn't thank me for spelling them out, you'll doubtless recall their names – we encouraged members of the great, concerned British public to 'sponsor' a child. So that our contributors' efforts were suitably promoted, we would now and then take a full-page advertisement in the *Guardian*, giving credit where it was due . . .

> DING HO SAYS 'THANK YOU' (cute picture). Aged five and the only survivor of the Ding family, Ho has been sponsored by Jeremy and Lucy Bleeding-Heart of Camden, the Goody-Two-Shoes family of Hartley Witney and everyone at the Tolcombe Square squat.

It was, in retrospect, unfortunate that when His Holiness Collin started poking around asking awkward questions, none of the money that had begun to pour in had actually been passed over to the charities concerned. There was frankly something of an administrative cock-up: the staff at the Fixx Talbot offices were particularly busy at the time, banking the many thousands of cheques that were sent to us.

Of course, with my hands full on the model and starlet front, I was rarely to be seen at home base, so much of what came out in the Frost interview was news to me.

Unfortunately for him, Talbot had no such excuse. He was in

the office when the cheques arrived; it was he who banked them, signing the payment slips with that unmistakable, show-off 'Talbot of Sonning' signature which he now affected.

There was no escaping the fact that the poor little fellow was up to his neck in it.

None of which – or no more than what I call the 'edited highlights' – I told Collin at our meeting. The way I saw it, I had been at the sharp end for long enough; it was time Talbot enjoyed some of the limelight for which he had once been so eager.

Considering the amount of information I was giving him, Collin was remarkably ungrateful. I even caught him glancing over my shoulder once or twice at my friend the barmaid.

Interesting, I thought. So Collers is not quite dead from the waist down, after all. I made a mental note. It's always useful to know where a chap keeps his Achilles' heel.

It was the Bard, was it not, who used to go on about troubles never coming in ones and twos but in a monstrous regiment of women? He might have been describing the life of Jonathan Peter Fixx at this time.

Mother was in a sickening flush of middle-aged excitement at the prospect of being published ('Charming boy. He *understands*'). The little Indian actress I had misguidedly tried to help in Paris had resorted to the old hysterical three a.m. phone calls routine. And Mila had gone into a serious decline, refusing to eat, failing to appear for appointments, frequently spending all day in bed with her head under the sheets.

Frankly, at this moment, it was all I needed – the number-one celebrity on my books going down with a case of the screaming abdabs. No wonder there were occasions when I allowed impatience to get the better of me.

If only we had known then what we all know now. I blame myself – in my determination to bring Mila success (and therefore happiness), I pushed the accelerator to the floor, cut corners and all but ran out of road. At the end of the day, achieving is all about pressure. Some of us can take it, some – Father, Aunty Bar-Bar, Talbot, Mila – can't. I confess that I've been slow to learn one of life's most important lessons – that not everyone is blessed with the same qualities as oneself.

Then there were Dr Feelgood's pills. With the wisdom of hindsight, I can see that the gaily coloured capsules with which, in innocence, I helped Mila out of her catatonic depressions were, in the long term, not entirely helpful. After a while she began to help herself. The moods blackened. She took some more. Eventually it became clear that I was living with two Milas, neither of them pleasant: one bug-eyed and crazy, the other sleepily suicidal. While I had the character and strength of will to avoid narcotics, she was found wanting. Not that I, as manager and companion, did not play my part – my over-generosity vis-à-vis Mila and her problem was clearly misguided in the long term – but the fact is, she was still at the top and, if a few pills could help her stay there, it seemed fair enough at the time. On camera, Mila, well wired, could just about hold her own; doing cold turkey, she'd be downright depressing.

One of the problems with drugs, as we now know, is that, for the dependant whose brains have been turned to scrambled egg, little things assume an exaggerated importance. So it was with Mila.

A few days after my meeting with Collin, I returned from a series of rigorous interviews with members of an all-girl singing group to find Mila staring glassy-eyed into space. Without a word, I went to the bathroom to fetch some pills. Rather to my surprise she refused to take them.

'Here are the news,' she intoned, holding up a copy of the evening paper. 'They are only little news. Another rock and roll suicide. The world is wide, it is a small thing.'

I looked at the newspaper. At the bottom of the page there was an item which read:

> SINGER DIES
>
> Services on the Metropolitan Line were disrupted this morning following the death of a man at Latimer Road Station. Witnesses remarked that the youth, who was said to be in a distressed state, threw himself in the path of a train shortly after 8.15 a.m. He was later named as Peter Harper, a singer and composer. Services are now said to be back to normal.

'Poor old Pete,' I said finally. 'I had no idea he was bonkers.'

'What is bonkers? To feel is bonkers? To discover that everything is just a nonsense in this world is bonkers? Myself, I feel a profound disgust.'

'You?' I said reasonably. 'What on earth has this to do with you? Or me for that matter.'

'You know,' she said, tears welling up in those famous eyes. '"Break Me", it is his song. When we rip it off him, that goes beyond the borders of human behaviour. It was I who was killing him, with my stolen success. It is a hell to think of it.'

For a moment, I watched her as she sobbed, the coloured capsules clutched in her hand. To tell the truth, Mila (or at least the zonked-out Mila) was one of those people who take the world's problems on to their shoulders. Vietnam, starvation, police horses who were roughed up a bit by demonstrators – she felt bad about them all. When one of my singers died in a plane crash, it was somehow our fault that the plane's fuel tanks were insufficiently full for the journey (the hat trick of posthumous number ones hardly helping my defence, I admit). Now Pete's early-morning dive looked set to take her one step further down the primrose path to Loony Lake.

'Mila. Darling,' I said, managing just about to control my impatience. 'None of this has anything to do with us. Neither of us had seen Pete for over a year. He fell in with a bad crowd – drugs, drink, the lot. It happens. Come on, take the pills – you'll feel better.'

She gulped down Dr Feelgood's bombers and stared into space, waiting for the hit.

'Now,' I said calmly. 'Have you read the *Venus in Furs* script?'

'No script. No film. Is absolutely foolish exploitation. I hate.'

I smiled affectionately.

'Controversial, yes, but I thought tasteful.'

She closed her eyes. 'How can you be in many things so clever and in others completely villain? It is a miserable discovery for me.'

I sighed. Pills or no pills, Mila was pushing my legendary tolerance to the limit.

'Was it villain to pluck you from obscurity, to train you and groom you as a star, the In-Girl?'

'Like prize poodle at the dog show, yes? All fluffy with round and so appealing eyes. Sit up and beg, Mila. Die for queen, Mila. Come here, Mila, roll over for master – '

'Not that there's been much of that recently.'

Mila looked away angrily. In a game attempt to bring her out of herself, I had introduced her to a circle of attractive celebrities who liked to check each other out at intimate private parties – not so much 'swap-ins', as the sewer rats later called them, as informal encounter groups where liberated friends were encouraged to share their assets in an uninhibited way.

Sharing, it turned out, was not part of Mila's nature. On the last occasion, she had declined to participate in the amusements, despite the earnest efforts of some really quite famous people, and had spent the evening darting pained, bemused looks in my direction as I tried to cover for her lack of social graces by mixing noisily with another group. Eventually I disappeared into a back room with my new friends to explore subjects of common interest, leaving Little Miss Moody to fend for herself among the middle-aged gropers and also-rans. It was a little harsh, I admit, but there's a limit to the amount of nannying a grown man can be expected to do.

'Yes,' I said, choosing not to risk more hysteria by going into detail. 'I could tell them a thing or two about the In-Girl.'

'And I have the idea that you will. Why not? Everything is for sale in the world of Jonathan Fixx.'

The chin was wobbling now and an odd, uneven flush had come to her face as she dabbed at her nose.

'Let me rest, Johnny,' she was saying, hugging her knees in a way faintly reminiscent of Father suffering one of his attacks. 'Let me be hausfrau, girlfriend, let me no longer be molested by horrible publicities.'

Wearily, I helped myself to a whisky and soda from the drinks cupboard, pouring Mila a stiff brandy at the same time.

'Darling,' I said, sitting down beside her and placing a consoling arm around her. 'The In-Girl is too important to be a hausfrau. In fact – ' a rather brilliant thought had occurred to me ' – she's too good to be a girlfriend. Why don't we get married? Soon – as soon as possible?'

The snuffles subsided. Mila turned to me, her eyes sparkling with an excitement for which the pills were only partially responsible.

'It a best idea you have ever conceived.'

'I'll get the ring, fix the date. You can start on the invitation list tomorrow. It will be the wedding of the year.'

'No,' she smiled. 'Why not small wedding? Chelsea Registration Office.'

'Of course. IN-GIRL IN SECRET WEDDING DRAMA. It's perfect. How does the end of October sound to you?'

'But we are May now. Why do we wait?'

I shrugged. 'I have to go to New York next week. You've got the film to do – '

'Film?'

'*Venus in Furs*. The public expect it of you, Mila. Then we'll get married.'

Wearily, she rose to her feet and walked to the bathroom. I heard the door locking.

'Don't worry about the sex scenes,' I called after her. 'I can arrange a stand-in.'

The fact is, I needed product – and fast.

The rumours in the press about Talbot, the new fashion for criticising wealth-creators, particularly in the asset-stripping and property lines, not to mention Mila's failure to build on the success that I had established for her, meant that my enterprises were going through something of a cashflow crisis. As my enemies gathered at the ramparts, those I had counted upon as friends and colleagues deserted me. Cast-iron deals fell through. Bills remained unpaid. I was rarely, if ever, invited out to lunch. Some of my own staff abandoned me with disdainful, self-righteous sneers on their faces. Various snoops and noddies began to take an unhelpful interest in some of my accounting procedures.

It was a shock to the system, suddenly to find myself an outsider in the very society to which I had contributed so much. One moment, Young Meteor (Aitken, Broackes, Fixx, Slater – we were role models to a generation); the next, a pariah.

Not that I was naive. I realised that the young man in a hurry can expect to stub a toe, crack a shin, take a tumble now and then, but I hardly expected the slowcoaches huffing and puffing in his slipstream to trample on him, raking their spikes down his back before blithely continuing on their boorish way. I suppose it should have come as no surprise; the classless sixties had, if the truth be known, welcomed some decidedly unsavoury characters into the business. The camaraderie was dead, the old loyalties that had once counted for something. So, the word went round among the jumped-up barrow boys, Fixx is in trouble;

let's kick him in the nuts. The facts of the matter – that I had frequently helped them on my way up, that I was a hard-working member of the business community, that I was the son of a war hero – were conveniently forgotten as the vultures gathered.

During one of her increasingly rare moments of lucidity, Mila agreed to see Collin again. Although I hadn't heard from him since our somewhat unproductive meeting, the way he had been sniffing around some of my less public contacts and business acquaintances suggested that I had failed to direct him on to the trail of the true guilty party. In many respects, fielding Mila was the last ace I had up my sleeve.

Was I right to use her in this way? It had been a difficult decision. In the brightly coloured wonderland where she spent most of her waking moments (and there appeared to be fewer and fewer sleeping moments these days) there was little room for reason. My clear instruction – 'Just get that bastard off my back and on to Talbot's' – was quite likely to be misunderstood, misinterpreted or clean forgotten. Then again, she was unbalanced enough to decide that I was somehow exploiting our relationship and throw yet another wobbly. Or simply not turn up. Or burst into tears in public. Anything could happen.

I'm in the gambling business. I've played the loaded dice. But the night Mila tottered off to dinner with Collin, the stakes could not have been higher (nor, come to think of it, could the dice have been more dangerously loaded). Frankly, I was uneasy about the whole thing.

When she returned to the flat at a ridiculously late hour, Mila was more subdued – a good sign since, fizzing like a firecracker, she would almost certainly have been unable to achieve the delicate task in hand.

'Well?' I could hardly contain my impatience.

Mila gave me an odd look.

'Debt repaid,' she said, slumping into a chair. 'Talbot is to be TV star.'

I felt a great surge of affection for this simple, confused girl who had, in her own small way, saved my career.

'There,' I said warmly. 'It wasn't that painful, was it?'

She looked up at me, and smiled, almost like she did in the old days.

'For Brian, it is painful. He saw this programme as his top achievement to date. For me, it is not so painful.'

Despite my excitement, there was something that troubled me. Something about the way she said 'Brian'. Bloody hell. 'Be nice to him,' I had said. She couldn't have misunderstood me and . . . ? Was that why she was behaving in this odd, superior fashion?

'What was the debt?' I asked lightly. 'The debt you've repaid.'

'To you.' She looked away. 'Until now, I was in a horrible debt to you. Now I experience a great relief.'

'There's more to us than debts.'

'Was.'

'Tomorrow we celebrate,' I said. 'It's been a great worry. Now I'm free at last.'

'And so am I.'

Losing. I don't like it. I never have. A deal goes down the tubes, I'm pissed off as hell. A game-plan goes into unscheduled turnaround, we're talking major short-term depression. I go a set down in the great game of love and I can feel bad about it for days.

It happens. You don't ride life's bucking bronco without taking tumbles.

So when Mila walked out on me, wearing (a predictably melodramatic touch) the drab, ill-fitting clothes of Magdalena Bobrowski, I could be excused for being more than a little piqued. After all, it was not just the company of a slightly spoilt Polish girl I was losing, not only deals and game-plans, but Mila herself.

Need I add that she moved in with Collin, that schoolfriend and lover had united to betray me? Probably not. Girls like Mila quickly lose the knack of living alone; there's something about single beds that seems oddly alien to them. The fact that I screwed a handsome settlement out of her and her new adviser (Collin proving to be rather better as a journalist than a negotiator) should have cheered me somewhat. Yet it didn't.

The loss of Mila nagged at me like a toothache for months. Forget her, I told myself. It was hardly the first time a woman has found herself out of her depth with a man intellectually and socially superior to her. In all affairs of the heart there's a giver and a taker. I would gain from my experience, learn to give less of myself in the future.

And yet, sentimental fool that I am, Mila is still with me today, part of what some poet called 'the tender baggage of the heart' (Mila, my hold-all, my overnight bag). Of course, the girl who invades my dreams, whose face I see in the face of strangers, is the Mila of the sixties, frozen in time and perfect; she has nothing to do with the Magdalena Collin, dumpy housewife, mother of three squalling children, suburban also-ran, of today. But she's still there.

– And so are her clothes. What are you going to do about them?

– If I could get back to the flat, I'd sell them off. It fetches quite a bit, relics from the sixties.

– Looks like rubbish to me.

– Of course, it's rubbish. But it's Mila-rubbish. She still has quite a following. She reminds the bald, the fat, the middle-aged of a time when they were still alive. I sold a signed Bailey of Mila for three hundred pounds at Sotheby's. Her notebooks would fetch a bomb.

– You'd sell them?

– The early ones, yes. The later ones I was obliged to burn. The drugs, you know – they turned her head. She thought everyone was against her.

– Even you?

– Crazy, isn't it?

The appearance of Lord Talbot on *The Frost Programme* caused a storm of protest at the time. You probably remember it.

Some claimed that it was television's coming of age, the final proof that it could be a force for good, casting the harsh, critical glare of public disapproval into society's murkier corners, isolating the rich, the privileged trickster, prising him away from his smart-ass lawyers and well-connected friends to face the Great Inquisitor himself, Frosty, probe-merchant *extraordinaire*.

There were others, and I count myself among them, who felt a twinge of sympathy for the little chap, as he squirmed and sweated under the studio lights, wide-eyed and toad-like beside his magisterially self-possessed inquisitor. He had, after all, returned from abroad to clear his name. But David was at his most forbidding;

Talbot his most cringing. Before long, the studio audience were baying for blood.

Poor old thing. He never stood a chance.

'*Cześć, dobry wieszór, witam pana, panie Tadeusz Jankic*,' was David's masterly opening to the programme. Talbot, of course, knew what he was saying – 'Hello, good evening and welcome, Tadeusz Jankic' in Polish – but he had made such an effort to appear thoroughly English (Huntsman suit, old school tie, brogues, Trumpers haircut) that he was momentarily caught out of character.

'I beg your pardon, David?' he said uncertainly.

'I said – ' and the phrases tripped off the tongue once more. 'It's Polish. You are Polish, aren't you, Mr Jankic?'

'*Tak*. Yes . . . '

And so it went. Talbot, smarmy and apologetic ('But, *David*, you misunderstand me . . . '), Frost, pumped up with a growing sense of outrage.

At one point, during a painful discussion about the Save-a-Saigon-Child Appeal, Talbot tried to introduce my name into the conversation.

'Mr Fixx?' said David, pointedly looking through the notes on his clipboard. Eventually he pulled out a slip of paper and, almost sympathetically, passed it over to his victim. 'But this payment slip, whose signature is on it? Speak up, Mr Jankic – sorry, Lord Talbot – I don't think our audience here quite caught your reply.'

Perhaps, had Henry been blessed with a more telegenic personality, he might have survived the onslaught. Maybe his foreignness let him down (Profumo, Rachman, Savundra, we liked our villains to sound exotic in those days). Either way, I felt sorry for the little bastard. He had asked for it, of course – it could even be said that I contributed to his downfall – but at the end of the day we had worked together over the years, through the bad times and the good. It afforded me no pleasure whatsoever to see him make such a complete and utter chump of himself in front of millions.

Talbot skipped the coop the next day, a take-the-money-and-sod-the-rest-of-you merchant to the last. A final farewell to his old colleague might have been nice but that was not Henry Talbot's way. Instead he left on my desk a tearful, abusive, ill-written note, containing various lunatic allegations. Not a man to bear grudges, I shredded it without delay.

Once it became clear that my partner had turned tail and was likely to remain in hiding on the Costa del Sol, I took steps to put Glentabbot Properties into my own name. Financially, I had gained from the Talbot débâcle but, there again, I was now shouldering the entire responsibility for the enterprises which had formerly been jointly owned and, by any standards, deserved the more than adequate profits that came my way.

Personally, I would have given up all that for the chance to shake my old friend by the hand and wish him good luck.

Years later, in the early eighties, he took to writing begging letters to me. He was bored with his boat construction business in Spain and wanted to come home – wealth-creation, he had heard, was back in fashion. But by then I had moved on and, frankly, had other fish to fry.

Besides, quaint as it may seem to some, the idea of consorting with a coward who had betrayed and abandoned the country which had once adopted and enriched him was morally repugnant to me.

It was a harsh decision, but one has to draw the line somewhere.

Three

'As a jewel in a swine's snout, so is a fair woman
which is without discretion.'

XI, Proverbs, 22

10

A surprise celebrity

– Personally, I think it's time to move.

– Move? Don't be ridiculous.

– We have no light, Jonathan. Winter's closing in. It's getting cold. I can't work like this.

– I know, I know. To tell the truth, I was wondering when the whining would start.

– It's all right for you, lying in bed, reminiscing into that machine. I have to type the thing, tapping away in the gloom and cold. It's not fair.

– Of course, it's not. Nothing ever is. Give up, then. Be off. I'll type 'the thing' myself. Frailty, thy name is woman.

– They'll find us here, you know that.

– Let them. So long as my masterwork is complete, they can do what they like. I'll be vindicated at last.

– I'll stay with you for the moment. But we'll have to go soon.

– When I'm good and ready.

– And remember I've got one or two points about what you've written.

– Points?

– Of fact. Corrections.

– Yes yes. We'll pick those up in the second draft.

Were I to dwell upon my every golden moment, my triumphs of the bedroom and the boardroom, this account would run to several volumes. It's tempting – heaven knows, today's young achiever needs reminding of the joy of winning – but time is against me.

You can take it as read that as the seventies, one of the century's duller decades, unfolded, all was well for Jonathan Peter Fixx.

Following the premature burn-out of Talbot's career, I resolved to build up my fortune and, for a couple of years, to shun the limelight. Did I want to manage a hot new band known as the

Bay City Rollers? No thank you, I'm moving out of showbiz. Was I interested in becoming a founder-director of London Weekend Television? Forget it, I'm a busy man. Would I be prepared to add my name to a list of prominent personalities in aid of this charity, that self-important letter to *The Times*? Not today, my friend, but here's a tenner for your pains.

There's a time for publicity, a time for keeping *schtum*.

These days I was virtually invisible as, from my suite of offices in the City, I controlled my various companies (property, investment, insurance, other in-and-out sudden-money operations the details of which I'll spare you) with a cool, softspoken maturity that belied my youth. My days of fizzing around London in a sports car drumming up business, doing deals, were over. Now that the outer reaches of the Fixx empire were robustly policed by my handpicked squadron of sharp-suited hooligans (the public school drop-out, the plausible spiv, the cash-hungry ex-secretary), I was busy enough with the broadbrush strategy, what I call 'the macro issues', to keep ennui at bay. My fellow Young Meteors – Blooms, Slaters, Bentleys – had burnt themselves out, plummeting into black holes of their own making. I had consolidated. Only just thirty, I was looking towards my second million.

And, as I worked hard, so did I play. Good God, I deserved it, didn't I? Now that I had dumped Mila, leaving her to breed in suburban mediocrity with Collin, my natural fun-loving propensities were well and truly off the leash.

You will have heard that power is the ultimate aphrodisiac. You will have noticed how the average woman in her prime is blind to age and ugliness in a man if the price is right. You will have seen the wizened financier with a lissom teenage beauty on his arm. Never mind the watery eye, the trembling hand, the brain atrophied by years of poring over balance sheets – if he has bulges in the right places (plastic next to the heart, serious bank notes in the pigskin wallet), the wealth-creator is never short of company.

Now. Imagine, instead of Lord Dodder of Dotage, a young man at his peak, a suave entrepreneur who, in addition to the aforesaid bulges in the right places, has bulges in the *right* places. A millionaire *sans* wrinkles, utterly contemporary, exuding an appreciation of life's bounty, whose very presence is seen by some to be a passport to pleasure. Can you wonder that, at a time when personal wealth was no longer a source of embarrassment, I was more popular and in demand than ever?

For me, it was amusing – of course, it was – but there were occasions, I must admit, when I felt ever so slightly used. What caused this restlessness among my many women friends? What were they looking for? Adventure? Pleasure? Excess? If so, I delivered on the button, awakening in them needs and hungers they never knew existed. Yet somehow a night out with me, inevitably ending in an intimate, breathtaking rollercoaster of the senses, was never quite enough. They wanted more, more, more. Perhaps I should have taken the time to explain that promiscuity, that angry search for love, solves absolutely nothing in the long term but by then I had moved on to the next in the queue and it was too late.

Wealth. Popularity. Pleasure. My life had achieved a sort of stability at last. I knew who I was, where I was going.

What could stop me now? Who could hold me back?

Enter stage extreme left, mad eyes rolling, uncombed hair bobbing like a bush in a gale, declaiming loudly from the works of Simone de Signoret and Rosa Klebb, followed adoringly by a rabble of angry lesbians keening for a bright new non-sexist dawn, feminism's brightest and most exotic flower – Mother!

You'll remember the fuss when *The Second Front* was published. At the time it was thought to be saying something significant – it was a statement, no less. With the benefit of hindsight, we can see that its passing success was simply a matter of fortuitous timing, but then it caused no end of a rumpus.

The furore surrounding the publication of Germaine Greer's *The Female Eunuch* (a sort of Highway Code for ballcrushers) had more or less died down. *Very* interesting, we had said, nervously eyeing the wild 6′6″ Australian hippy, *very* perceptive – in an odd, exotic, foreign, loud-mouthed exhibitionistic sort of way. But was it *entirely* relevant to those quieter members of the sisterhood, the suffering silent majority who, while Germaine had been taking her clothes off and trading expletives with rock and roll stars, were making their own way in the world as secretaries, shop assistants, Girl Fridays or average housewives? They needed perking up too – Miss Jones in the outer office, Tracy on the till, Mum gloomily sipping tea in the kitchen. They wanted to play the liberation game. It was time someone stood up for them, someone from their own ranks, someone who spoke their own simple language in their own long-suffering whine. Someone essentially very ordinary.

No wonder *The Second Front* rocketed to the top of the bestseller lists, guaranteeing its honest, plain-speaking, dowdy author a regular spot on the afternoon chat shows or in the pages of the middle-aged women's magazines. Reassuring yet concerned, radical yet somehow acceptable, Mother was an Everywoman for her time. She took the sting out of revolution, gentrified it, brought it down from the barricades and into kitchenettes and bedsitting-rooms throughout the country.

To tell the truth, the effect of Mother's warblings on my career was not as catastrophic as I had feared. The way she told it, the post-war male (me, in other words) was as much a victim of the times in which he lived as Father had been. If he was aggressive and over-competitive, then that was what was expected of him by society. If he was materialistic, grasping even, it was because his achievement as a person was judged by the way he dressed, where he lived, the size of his car. If, fundamentally, his problem was a lack of confidence (you're losing me, Mother), it was because deep down he knew he was uncomfortable in the part he was playing. If the only way he could deal with women was through a joyless bed-hopping routine, that was no more than a deep-seated fear of the female – perhaps even of the female within him. Of course, she avoided mentioning my name in interviews but it was the sub-text of her every public comment. It was never your fault you've grown up to be a bastard, dear, that your sexuality is a mess, that – and this was the final straw – you're like all the rest, just another confused post-war male in serious need of liberation.

No man, least of all a respected captain of industry and well-loved partygoer, likes to be patronised by his own mother, particularly in the form of a malicious fantasy version of his private life.

Joyless bed-hopping? Tell that to the hundreds of conquests noted in the little black book I now liked to keep.

Sexuality a mess? My score-sheet (complete with marks for effort, performance, originality) scarcely suggested a man with that sort of problem.

In need of liberation? That was rich – the usual complaint was that, if anything, I was rather *too* liberated.

Deep-seated fear of the female? Only certain females, Mother –

like those so self-absorbed that they were unable to recognise an irresistible, Grade A pistol between the sheets because he happened not to boast about it.

But it was not for me to speak up for my generation. Actions, in the private as well as the public arena, spoke louder than words. I had the proof, the vital statistics (would you believe seven different girls in one week?), but I was not prepared to divulge them.

For the moment, I was content to act the proud son, escorting Catherine (now, there *was* a showstopper) to several of Mother's public functions.

'You don't like this, do you?' Catherine said to me once, as we stood at the bar in some BBC hospitality suite. Mother had just completed another triumphant chat-show appearance, having made a monkey out of her lamebrain interviewer with a few well-practised verbal party tricks. Catherine and I were watching her as she held court among a group of media hangers-on.

'Mother having a good time?' I replied. 'Nothing could give me more pleasure.'

'You think you should be there, the centre of attention. Something's gone a bit wrong with the Jonathan master-plan, hasn't it? Mother in the limelight, you in the shadows?'

'I was made for the shadows,' I smiled. 'Some of the most interesting things happen in the shadows. Sometimes the action centre stage is no more than a diversion.'

I thought back to Mother's performance that evening. There was little doubt that her celebrity (not to mention that of Marc Shelley, now the toast of literary London) was a passing, fluky sort of thing.

Yet her continuing success as a public figure never ceased to amaze me. All right, so her book was essentially run-of-the-mill and depressing, and the average part-time feminist could relate to a message that was run-of-the-mill and depressing but, really, was the *author* obliged to look run-of-the-mill and depressing when she appeared on television? Was that part of the deal? I swear you could almost smell the boiled cabbage wafting about the studio as she droned on and on. Dull clothes, sloppy make-up, hair all over the shop – Mother may have done something for the suburban sisterhood, but she depressed the living shit out of the rest of us. Frankly, she was an affront to celebrity.

'I wonder,' I said. 'I'm concerned about the pressures on her. Not to mention the people she's mixing with.'

'What, the women in the movement?' Catherine laughed. 'Don't tell me – they're witches.'

'Some of them are lesbians, you know. It worries me, the way they hang around her, stay at the house.'

'You don't honestly think Mother's going to – '

'No. Not Mother. But – ' I paused, uncertain as to how far I should go ' – I've seen the way they look at you.'

'A lot of people look at me.'

It was true. Catherine at twenty was, in spite of her best efforts (torn, ill-fitting denims, uncombed dark curls, hairy armpits), unavoidably beautiful.

'I just ignore them.' And astonishingly cool for her age.

'Forgive me,' I said sincerely. 'I'm just concerned about you, Catherine. You matter to me.'

'Thank you, brother.'

Our eyes met briefly.

'Step-brother,' I smiled.

It was John F. Kennedy, was it not, who confided in Harold Macmillan, as the two statesmen took a midday constitutional along the beach during the Nassau summit conference, that, unless he made love to a woman at least once a day, he suffered from the most intolerable headaches? I'm like that. It's a physical thing with me. Not headaches, but a certain lack of concentration, a deep physiological restlessness.

Supermac's reply is not recorded, but I'm sure he understood.

In a sense, Catherine was right. I was not at ease with myself, not as happy as a man whose affairs (business, social, personal) were booming should be.

It had nothing to do with Mother and her ridiculous book. If Lady Luck had smiled on her and on Marc Shelley, who was I to begrudge them their moment of glory, however fleeting and superficial it may be? Life's but a walking shadow, as the old saying goes, and, if it was time for Marc to strut and Mother to fret their hour upon the stage, so what? At the end of the day, did the passing fad of a small, pseudo-literary clique matter – I mean, *matter* like a significant financial coup, a deal, a takeover?

Hardly. It was only a book. Personally, I didn't give a toss.

What was wrong then? During my more contemplative moments (like all philosopher-entrepreneurs, I like to put aside at least five minutes a day for what I call an internal concept session), I became increasingly aware of a gnawing dissatisfaction, a deep yearning within the soul – a *zeitgeist*, if you like.

Applying myself to the question as if it were an everyday business problem, I jotted down a lifestyle checklist on a memo pad.

Worldly goods?	OK
Prospects?	OK
Home comforts?	OK
Popularity with peer groups?	OK (?)
Overall state of investments	OK
Family relationships?	OK (??)
Romance?	OK (!!!)
General standing in society?	

Ah. General standing in society. That fell somewhat short of being OK.

In my own circle, of course, I was a giant, a lion, monarch of all the starlets and self-made spivs that I surveyed. Yet my name was rarely to be found in the right social columns of acceptable newspapers and, when it did, a certain disdain was evident: 'the upwardly mobile socialite', 'arriviste about-town', 'expense-account Lothario', that sort of thing.

Naturally the lies that some jealous scribbler cared to put about meant little to me, but the growing realisation that Jonathan Peter Fixx was 'Not Quite Our Class, Darling' had become something of an irritant. I'd been to public school, hadn't I? The David Bailey Cockney twang, which I had adopted during the classless sixties for purely professional reasons, had given way to the natural, well-bred tones to which I had been born. I had the right kind of car, bought clothes at the right boutiques, had my hair cut once a week at the right salon. What more did they want?

The fact is, snobbery was back in vogue. The old school tie, Boodles, the boat race, in-bred ninnies bouncing about at Queen Charlotte's Ball – all the old crap – mattered once more. Those of us modernists who found the concept of class pointless, tedious and old-fashioned, who cared not one jot about your parents' social position, your school or your accent, whose attitude was 'So long as you're my sort of person, that's all there is to be said', were suddenly out of step with the times.

As it happens, I was born to respectable parents, my father a war hero, my mother an authoress, and frankly my position in society's top drawer should have been unquestioned.

I'm not saying it mattered, or even that I minded finding myself below stairs, merely that, just when everything was going so swimmingly, it was irritating to find certain doors were closed to me.

Irritating. I put it no higher. Just damnably irritating.

By some odd coincidence, I found myself considering matters of the heart at this time. I had loved but, thanks to Mila, I had loved and lost. I had explored the byways of desire but, as the Bard has it, the road of excess had not led to the palace of wisdom.

It was time to put love on hold, lust on the back burner. I needed a wife.

11

Desperate measures

Picture the scene.

A glorious summer's evening. On the lawn in front of an imposing country house is a large marquee. It is full of noise and people in evening clothes. They are almost without exception flushed and unbeautiful. At one end of the marquee, an over-excited midget with excessive body hair and an imitation American accent is running a discothèque, playing records that normal people would travel a long way to avoid: 'Simple Simon Says', 'Tie a Yellow Ribbon', 'My Ding-a-Ling'. In front of him, red-faced youths, honking with delight, hurl their bulky, ill-dressed partners about the dance-floor. At the tables, parents drone inconsequentially at one another while drinking themselves into a stupor. The talk is of recent days' hunting, the City, the Common Market.

An attractive young man, slightly older than the dancing jackasses and considerably more dignified, sits on the perimeter of one such group. He is nearing his boredom threshold; revolting food, horrific music and a total lack of anyone worth talking to, much less seducing, have taken their toll. He had been warned that the Ponsonby dance was a waste of time; his source, damn her black, all-knowing heart, had been right. The young man would like to leave but, since he is with a weekend party, he's obliged to stay for at least another hour.

Two tables away, he sees the only other passably attractive person in the marquee, an Honourable Sarah Something. Pretty in a pink, dimpling English rose-ish sort of way, if somewhat pneumatic. She smiles at him. He, for reasons of politeness or curiosity, walks over to her table.

'You look as bored as I feel,' she says.

The young man, a sophisticate, senses what is expected of him – the raffish smile, the *sotto voce* 'Shall we go somewhere?', the discreet withdrawal to a distant bedroom in the West Wing – but for some reason holds back.

'I was, until now,' he says suavely. She blushes. It's lucky he has read the situation correctly.

They talk. She is impressed by his eventful and varied past, modestly but wittily expounded. He is interested by the facts she reveals about herself. Just left Benenden. Wants to go to art college, but Daddy insists she goes to finishing school. Daddy is a very determined man, very difficult to contradict. Does he know Daddy? Lord Harcourt – a genuine sigh here – *the* Lord Harcourt?

No, he does not know Daddy. But he knows of him.

Each generation, they say, is obliged to fight the battles of its immediate forebears, only in different forms. So it was with me and Father.

He had his war; I had my sustained struggle to join the ruling classes. He had to show courage, initiative and endurance on the battlefields of Normandy, I displayed much the same qualities in a bedroom in South Kensington; he had the Germans, I had Marjorie Taylor; we both emerged from our respective campaigns victorious but scarred. I was fortunate enough to have the strength of character to pick up the reins of everyday life after my ordeal, Father unfortunately did not.

Yet even before Marjorie Taylor blundered into my life, I had successfully made the first moves in my game-plan. Having correctly assumed that, in order to become a member of the landed gentry, it was useful to have a spot of land, I found myself in a position to buy Studley Grange, a rambling Georgian thing with parkland attached, staff included in the deal. It was a complicated business – charming old duffer who owned the place attempts to jump property gravy train, train unfortunately not in station at time, yours truly bales him out, yours truly finds himself a bit strapped, calls in debt, duffer obliged to lose the Grange to stay afloat, ends up in farm worker's cottage at the end of the drive, his passably attractive only daughter corralled into round-the-clock service by the new Lord of the Manor – I'll spare you the details.

I was man of the world enough to know that it takes more than a pile of antique bricks and a few fields with oak trees stuck in the middle to establish your credentials. We live in a world where Sid the local bookmaker can take his nan and the family for a boating trip on his own moat, where Harry the dodgy scrapmetal merchant can swagger about his own estate in a loud check suit, sucking a cigar, as he exercises his Alsatians and Dobermanns. I'm no snob; the decline in social standing of the average landowner is a matter of record.

I had my few hundred acres, my Grange. Now I needed to become known. Jonty Fixx (Jonty seemed somehow appropriate for this stage of my life) had to become a name without which any decent guest list would be incomplete.

It's not easy becoming a nob. They close ranks, you know. They can sniff you out at thirty paces if you don't belong. Search me how they do it, but you can tell. They talk to you in a different way, as if you're deaf or retarded. They say 'How do you do' with smiles on their faces, while transmitting 'Bugger off out of it' signals with their eyes. Frankly, without Marjorie, I would never have cracked it.

I had known her, on and off – mostly off, thank God – for almost ten years. Her husband, a nondescript individual with a nicotine-stained moustache and loser's eyes, had been put in touch with me during my apprenticeship in the East End. He had just set himself up as a supplier of game (only the best birds shot on the best estates) to butchers in the Home Counties, having discovered that a certain snobbery pertains even in the matter of dead birds. 'Old Phil the Greek's been busy up in Scotland, Mr Parrott,' he'd say. 'Nice one, Major, I'll have a dozen royal grouse.' Naturally, it was down to me to supplement the Major's stock with birds shipped in from the Med, where they shoot anything that moves, occasionally topped up by a few dozen exotic specimens snatched from wildlife parks around the country. Even after I moved into property, I ensured that one of my staff kept the Major supplied, for old times' sake. Don't ask me why, but it seemed amusing at the time.

The Major's wife Marjorie used to give me the eye on the rare occasions I visited them. There's optimism, I used to think as she fixed me with the gorgon glare I was clearly meant to find seductive. Fifty-five if she was a day and she was still on the pull.

But there was more to Marjorie than the odd menopausal yearning. She wrote a social column for a glossy monthly magazine, much read by the tweedy set. Over the years, she had become the first port of call for many a rookie hostess, anxious to set her unlovely daughter on the path to matrimony with an absolutely smashing coming-out ball. In fact, when it came to drawing up guest lists, weeding out the unsuitable (social climbers, rapists, people who were sick in taxis) in favour of a thoroughly acceptable mix of hearty, impeccably bred bores, she wielded considerable power. She was, I decided, my gateway to what was laughably known as 'polite society'.

My visits to the Taylor household became more frequent. 'The Major's out,' Marjorie would say. 'Perhaps you'd care to stay for a cup of tea.' Yes, that would be nice.

I tried charm, I tried discreet investment advice, but Marjorie had been flattered too often and regarded money as vulgar. I made polite conversation, choosing to ignore the predatory way my hostess would stare at me as she stirred her tea. She was flirtatious, coquettish, embarrassing. Finally, with sinking heart, I decided that there was no alternative. Having prepared myself with a fortnight of enforced celibacy in the hope that my ravening life-force would somehow carry me through the ordeal, I leapt in where no man had leapt for many a long moon.

On this occasion, when she leered over her teacup, I responded with a shy, appealing smile.

'It's so kind of you to spare me so much of your time,' I said.

Marjorie shifted in her armchair. She was wearing a low-slung paisley dress which was not going to make my task any easier.

'The pleasure's all mine,' she said.

'Life can get lonely, can't it?'

'For a good-looking boy like you?' Marjorie raised a sceptical eyebrow.

I shrugged modestly. 'I have one or two friends, of course. But somehow they're not quite the right kind.'

Marjorie smiled knowingly. 'Loneliness can be a terrible thing,' she said.

'I just don't seem to be mixing with the right set.' I shot her a disarming smile. 'Except for you, of course, Marjorie.'

'Of course.'

Marjorie ran her tongue over her top lip in a way that she doubtless thought was provocative. For a moment my determination wavered. I walked over to the window behind her and looked down at the street outside.

'If only – ' I said, searching for the right words.

'If only someone would give you a hand,' said Marjorie quietly. 'A leg-up, socially.'

I turned and stood behind her chair. It was the moment of truth.

'That would certainly help.'

'Yes.' Marjorie sighed. 'Life can get very lonely.'

In one swift decisive movement, I buried my face into the crook of her neck, while letting my hand wander down the front of her dress and paddle about a bit.

Marjorie whimpered as she put down her teacup.

'Down boy,' she said huskily, clasping my hand to her bosom. 'Feelies are for upstairs. Haven't you been house-trained?'

I let her go and she stood up, straightening her dress.

'Stay here,' she said, as she collected the teacups and put them on the tray. 'I'll be ready in three minutes.'

I was taken aback, to tell the truth, hurt even. Having taken the trouble to act the lovestruck suitor, I was insulted to be treated in such a cool, matter-of-fact way.

After the shortest three minutes in the history of time, there was a piercing whistle from upstairs. It was a professional, two-tone effort, which wavered chillingly on the second note. For a moment my courage failed me. Bloody hell, she was already treating me as if I were one of her damned pooches. Did she honestly believe that she was doing me a favour? The whistle rang out again. And yet, I needed those parties, those contacts. There was no going back.

'Woof,' I said quietly, making for the door. 'Woof sodding woof.'

Sensibly enough, Marjorie had drawn the curtains in the bedroom and had minimised the effects of the old enemy gravity by lying across her bed. Horizontal and in the semi-darkness, she looked almost desirable. Or maybe it was my fortnight of night starvation doing its work.

Smiling gamely, I stepped out of my clothes and walked towards the bed. As I leant to kiss her, Marjorie placed a hand on my chest. 'Now,' she said. 'Let me tell you what I like.'

She's different, the older woman – that I discovered very quickly. She knows what she wants and, damn me, she's going to get it. My memory of that afternoon, and indeed of all subsequent trysts chez Marjorie, consists largely of urgent, gasped imperatives. Not yet, Jonathan. Now. Lower. Higher. A bit to the left. Talk to me. That's right, tell me what I am. Slow down. Faster. Rough.

Rougher. Not that rough. Keep talking. I'm a slut, what am I? Now, flip me over. Quick . . . yes . . . yes . . . *Good* boy . . . very good . . .

It was tough work. Your miner, your dustman, your sewage operative complain of their lot. Undignified? Tiring? Unhealthy? I tell you, working on Marjorie beat the lot.

The fact is, all those years of decorous restraint had played havoc with her hormones. Endowed, as I discovered to my cost, with an above-average bedroom appetite, she had until now been thwarted at every turn. The distant, prehistoric dawning of her womanhood had occurred at a time when a girl's virginity was regarded as a girl's most important asset, rather than an unfortunate liability. Along had come the Major to introduce her to what he called 'manoeuvres' with the subtlety of a sergeant-major drilling a recalcitrant squaddie. And that, apart from the occasional scruffy and ill-organised one-night stand, was that. The Major took to drink, Marjorie took to breeding King Charles spaniels.

No wonder that, by the time yours truly offered himself in that pink, perfumed boudoir with its portraits of prize dogs on the dressing-table, a certain tension, a head of steam, had built up. Heaven knows what would have happened had I not been there to attend to it – some sort of horrific, messy spontaneous combustion, no doubt.

Satisfied, for the moment at least, Marjorie lit a cigarette. Inhaling deeply, she looked across at my poor, used body with no more than mild curiosity.

'What,' she said, reverting to her familiar *grande dame* tone, 'did you call me just then?'

– I have to tell you that I'm finding this increasingly hard to take.

– So how do you think I felt? I'm sparing you the heavy stuff.

– It's just not plausible. I don't believe any of it.

– I'm a liar now?

– Maybe not a liar. More a romancer, a fantasist.

– Fantasy had remarkably little to do with my arrangement with Marjorie, as did romance.

– Oh yeah?

– All right. I'll admit it. She wasn't that bad. For her age, she was pretty good. She taught me a few tricks. We had some laughs.

–Careful. You'll be saying you liked her soon.

–No. Merely that I was able to enter into the spirit of the thing without too much pain and self-hatred.

–I see.

–Satisfied?

It was not long before Marjorie, the middle-aged frump, had been transformed into Marjorie, the perkiest King Charles breeder in town. Her tail was up, there was a spring in her step, a healthy dampness to the nose, a twinkle in the eye. You didn't have to be an expert to guess the cause. One look in the direction of Jonty, the lap-dog (dull coat, dry nose, no spring in his poor old step these days), would tell you all you needed to know.

To be fair, Marjorie was as good as her word: within a matter of weeks, the social renaissance of Jonty Fixx was under way. Invitations arrived from all over the country. Hunt balls, coming-out dances, twenty-firsts, charity thrashes – I attended them all, no matter how dull or distant.

'You wouldn't abandon your pooch now that she's made you so popular?' Marjorie said to me on one of our Wednesday afternoons together.

'Why on earth would I do that to my favourite poochy?' I replied with as much conviction as I could manage. The fact was, I had always assumed that, once you were in the house-party set, that was that. The grapevine would do the rest and Marjorie could go hang.

'Just remember,' she said, chucking me somewhat roughly under the chin, 'what Marjorie giveth, Marjorie can bloody taketh away.'

I smiled gamely. 'As long as I have poochy, who needs popularity?'

Frankly, spending up to thirty weekends a year in chilly country houses, shooting birds, riding horses, keeping the company of dull, brainless pinheads, afforded me almost as little pleasure as doing time with Marjorie. Naturally there were advantages – free investment advice, passable wine, the occasional invitation to Gstaad and Mustique, some amusing seductions, the acquisition of a wife – but, in all honesty, I have to admit that mingling with the upper classes is an overrated activity.

For a while, of course, the novelty of the thing kept boredom at bay. The crunch of gravel as my Porsche swept up to another vast country pile. Jonty, my dear chap, give Jones that bag and come and have a Scotch. The undemanding dinner-table chat. Father, this is Jonty Fixx, he's something rather grand in property. The Saturday spent shooting down friendly, overweight pheasants bred for the occasion (I turned out to be an excellent shot). The few elegant turns about the dance-floor of a Saturday evening. The inevitable three a.m. scratch-scratch on the bedroom door (debs now and then but I quickly discovered maids and mothers were a better bet). The occasional lucrative business deal after Sunday lunch (chinless yo-yos in their cups being, in my experience, even simpler to take than the fattest pheasant, the easiest debutante). The trip back to London, usually with a Celia or Venetia in the passenger seat – 'Chelsea? Oh Jonty, I s'pose you couldn't drop me off at Ennismore Gardens? You could? *Great!*' Then home, more often than not having given Celia or Venetia a brisk seeing-to back at her place. It was amusing for a while, but soon palled.

You know how it is after a rather pointless, embarrassing one-night stand? The sinking feeling as you remember what happened, the oppressive sense of time wasted? That was how I came to feel after my weekend parties.

All this, I thought one afternoon surveying Marjorie sprawled inelegantly across her bed, a silly satisfied grin on her face, for all that. If I don't get a wife within the year, I'll cut my losses and be off.

'You're not really going to the Ponsonby do,' said Marjorie, reaching for her cigarettes. 'It's hardly top-drawer stuff, you know.'

'Maybe I won't,' I said. 'I wouldn't mind a weekend at home.'

'The Major's away in Norfolk this weekend. We could spend Saturday night together. Croissants on Sunday morning, the papers. *Do* cancel, Jonty. Poochy loves her playtime.'

That clinched it. Playtime for Pooch meant overtime for Jonty. Anything was preferable to that.

'I don't know. I hear the Ponsonbys are rather fun.'

'You heard wrong,' said Marjorie, rather harshly. 'A few generations ago, they mattered but not any more. They're on the skids.'

'Why the dance then? Three hundred people have been invited.'

Marjorie stubbed out her cigarette.

'It's their last throw,' she said. 'All the Ponsonbys have left to show for themselves is a few hundred acres of second-rate land, a couple of tired hunters, the obligatory labrador and a dumpy eighteen-year-old daughter. If she doesn't find a husband, they're finished.'

'Hence the party.'

'Precisely.'

'I think I should go. After all, I did accept.'

'Bastard,' said Marjorie, moving in on me. 'Darling, darling bastard.'

Thus it was that I found myself, that balmy summer's evening in Gloucestershire, entwined on the dance-floor with the Harcourt heiress, the richest and probably the most attractive (this was before she let herself go) item on the Ponsonbys' otherwise unimpressive guest list. The evening was drawing to a close. The older generation had drifted off to bed; their offspring were tugging away at one another in distant bedrooms or being sick in the kitchen garden. The hairy midget was playing 'Strangers in the Night' to a marquee that was now almost empty.

'What happens next?' she murmured.

I was sophisticated enough to sense that this was not the come-on it might have appeared.

'I take your telephone number. We make a date. Very soon, I hope.'

'A date. How romantic. And tonight?'

'Tonight, I kiss you goodnight. Like this.'

We kissed in a brief, chaste, old-fashioned sort of way.

'That's strange,' Sarah said finally. 'Someone told me you were a bit of a rake. That – ' she blushed becomingly ' – you were a bit fast.'

'Not me. Must be someone else. Sorry to disappoint you.'

'No,' she said. 'It's good. I can't stand rakes.'

12
Project Harcourt

– Is something wrong?

– What could possibly be wrong with me? Holed up in London's fashionable East End. Unable to go out. Attended to by the lovely Katrina. If they could see me now. Hah.

– You haven't spoken into your machine for almost a week. You stare out of the window. You lock yourself in the lavatory for hours. You sleep badly. What's the problem? Can I help?

– I'm a writer. Sometimes the words don't come. The toiler in the literary vineyard may be allowed to lean on his spade now and then, surely.

– Very pretty. The fact is, you dictate, I write.

– Now you're trying to upset me.

– You don't believe me. Wait till you read it.

– Would it be noticed if I just skipped the Sarah bit? 'My marriage to Sarah Harcourt safely over, I resumed my life?' What d'you think?

– It was hardly a passing phase. Eight years. And she gave you a child.

– She extracted a child from me.

– Try to remember how it was. The good times. The springtime of your relationship.

– Which led to the dullest, chilliest summer on record. I re-run life's video in search of a Juliet and all I find is a Lady Macbeth, an untamed shrew.

– Kid yourself along then. Pretend that it all ended happily, amicably.

– If only she had died. Stylishly, prematurely. A hunting accident, perhaps. A car crash would be nice, if a bit banal. A mysterious, romantic wasting disease. That would be good.

– I think Sarah's lawyers might have something to say about that.

– They have something to say about everything.

– You'll just have to tell it like it was.

–I suppose so.
–And what was it?
–Just another marriage.

So we dated. Pretty soon Sarah was in love with me. At the time, I thought she fitted the bill pretty well. After a couple of months of hand-holding and soppy talk, we became engaged.

There was, in certain quarters, something of a fuss.

What on earth is going on here? they said. The only child of Lord Harcourt, respected City magnate of glorious lineage, pillar of the Conservative Party, throwing herself (not to mention her considerable fortune) away on some wide-boy from Biggleswade? Surely not. Surely old Christy Harcourt would never agree. And we always thought Sarah was so sensible. Look at this photograph of her, taken by Lichfield on the occasion of her twenty-first birthday: the whipped-cream complexion, the hint of a maidenly blush about the cheek, the tremulous half-smile, the eyes as clear and untroubled as the future that surely awaited her.

And what a future, if she played the game. Dances, dinner parties, perhaps an undemanding job in one of Daddy's firms to show she didn't think the world owed her a living, weekends with chums in the country, point-to-points, bit of stalking in Scotland, perhaps the odd, harmless romance with someone suitable (Jimmy's boy at Sandhurst maybe, or the younger Thick-Richey who's doing so well at Lloyd's), a winter in Verbier, summer mucking about on the Baroness de Jongle's yacht in the Med, improving her French and learning how to sail. The normal sort of things a girl of her age likes to do. How could she throw all that up? She wasn't *enceinte*, by any chance? No? Why the marriage then?

So the talk went among the country-house set. What about her responsibility to the family home? Does the word 'duty' mean nothing these days? Wild oats discreetly sown (so important for the young to be slightly wild in their twenties), she could easily find the right, sensible young chap, earning a solid income, a bit of land in the family. Slap-up wedding, three or four children in quick succession, ship 'em off to boarding-school as soon as they're house-trained and, by the age of forty, she will have done her bit for class and country. *Then* she could go mad, collect lovers, fall for her bit of rough. Then it was expected, a bit of amiable eccentricity in the older woman.

Showed character, gave the young folk something to talk about. But not now. No, she's let the side down very badly. It's poor old Christy I feel sorry for.

Such was the birthright of the Honourable Sarah Harcourt, as perceived by her friends and contemporaries; such were her expectations before, at the age of twenty-two, she met me. Or rather they would have been, had the bright blue spring sky under which she walked been troubled by the occasional wispy cloud of introspection. That it was not, brainwork of any kind being seen as unfeminine and a waste of time, was in my view one of her most endearing features.

My God, how she changed over the years.

During what may be loosely described as our courtship, I came to know the man you will know of as Lord Harcourt (Christy, I called him) passably well.

Frankly, he was not as frightening a character as the sewer rats would have you believe. Of course, he was tall, imposing, with the beady patrician air of one of our saner field-marshals, inscrutable, cold, shrewd, ruthless, but underneath, once you got to know him, he was a pussy-cat. Like many Englishmen of his age and class, he clearly found public life somewhat easier to handle than private life. His wife had run off with a Spanish groom when Sarah was only eight and, since then, his romantic life had been something of a grey area.

On the other hand, the family business that he inherited – biscuits, jam, soup – expanded so rapidly that, by the time I became his son-in-law, it was an international corporation with an annual turnover that ran into millions. Old Harcourt was the very model of establishment businessmen. To the world, he presented himself as an old-fashioned paternalist type, maybe a little out of his depth in modern business but a decent, solid boss who looked after his staff and put basic human values before purely financial ones. Underneath he was the toughest corporate ballplayer I had met since Talbot defected to the Costa del Sol. No wonder he was a power within the Conservative Party, speaking up – sanely, coherently, firm but fair – on moral and economic questions. Combining old Tory style with new Tory savvy, he was tipped as a future cabinet minister. Lord Harcourt, the thinking-man's aristocrat, the golden boy of the Upper House, the entirely acceptable face of capitalism.

So it was a matter of some regret that, in spite of my quite serious efforts vis-à-vis charm, wit and general amiability, the old boy and I never really hit it off. His attitude towards me showed a certain wary respect, but it fell some way short of affection, even when I became a member of his family.

Yet, heaven knows, he could hardly complain of my behaviour during the weekends I spent at Colevile Hall with Sarah. Impeccably dressed in country-squire mode, I merged effortlessly into the social scenery. In fact, far from being out of my depth among the City big-shots and political power-brokers Harcourt liked to invite for the weekend, I rapidly became the focus of attention, riding, shooting and drinking in hearty, roustabout fashion with the best of them. Time and again I would reduce the table to a respectful silence with amusing anecdotes of financial coups from my past. I earned quite a reputation with the old twelve-bore, on one occasion bringing down more birds (including, to Harcourt's surprise, a heron and a brace of barn owls) than any other gun. No one could claim that Jonty Fixx failed to make an impression among the country-house set.

Naturally my future father-in-law's somewhat frosty attitude towards me was a personal disappointment. I had hoped, I suppose, that we might become close in a gruff, manly sort of way, that Harcourt would be the father figure my own father had failed to be: strong, stable, a winner by birth and nature, a man to look up to. After all, how much more straightforward my life would have been had I lived among the cool certainties of Colevile Hall rather than in the seething cesspit of undirected emotion at 32 Elm Tree Drive. The world of Lord Harcourt may have been a wasteland but at least it had a map.

On only one occasion did I attempt to express such feelings. It was one Sunday evening, the other guests had departed and Sarah, her father and I had eaten modestly well in the small dining-room. As the port appeared, Sarah, who knew her place in those days, excused herself, leaving the two of us alone.

'Excellent weekend, Christy,' I said, snipping off the end of one of his large cigars. 'I feel quite like one of the family.'

'So I've noticed,' he said.

To tell the truth, the old boy never appeared to be entirely at ease in my presence. A certain restlessness was evident, which I put down to the fact that he was rarely confronted by achievers from the younger generation. He had even gone so far as to leave the table on a couple of occasions as I regaled his guests with tales from business life, a gesture which, in a lesser man, would have appeared rude. Doubtless, his shyness would disappear once I had joined the family.

For a while that evening, I chatted to him about the weekend's sport. A jowly merchant-banker friend of Harcourt's had become unduly exercised when, in a moment of excitement, I narrowly missed shooting his gundog, an incident which I recounted with my usual good humour.

As I told the story, Harcourt smiled thinly. Encouraged, I did a rather amusing impression of the banker advancing on me, his bemused dog at his heels.

'Why can't people train their dogs properly, Christy?' I concluded. 'The bloody animal completely spoilt my shot.'

Harcourt passed the port.

'You're not planning to marry Sarah, are you?' he said in that quiet voice which, had I known him less well, I might have taken to be threatening.

Somewhat surprised at the turn of direction the conversation had taken, I adjusted my expression to one of appropriate sincerity.

'We are,' I said, 'jolly fond of one another.'

'*Jolly* fond, are you? You see, Sarah's *jolly* fond of her Pekinese. It doesn't mean she plans to marry it. Sometimes she doesn't even feed it.'

'I have no complaints on that score, Christy,' I smiled and patted my stomach. 'Anyway, I'm not a Pekinese.'

'No, you're not. More like a bloody pye-dog. On the scrounge.'

I chuckled good-naturedly. How lucky it was that I had become so attuned to the old boy's sense of humour. A less sophisticated person might so easily have taken offence.

'What I really want to know,' I parried wittily, 'is whether the husband of an Honourable becomes Honourable too. Where does Debrett stand on that?'

'You'll never be honourable. You'll be as common as ever.'

'Pity. The Honourable Jonathan Fixx has a certain ring to it. Eh, Christy?'

It was at this moment I noticed that the port had brought a vivid flush to Harcourt's normally pale cheeks.

'No,' I said, sensing that a degree of seriousness was now in order. 'I do believe that this could be the big one, Christy.' I puffed at my cigar. 'I'm financially secure, Sarah's crazy about me. I have a feeling that we'll be personally . . . compatible, if you know what I mean.'

'I'm not sure I do.'

'Upstairs?' I winked chummily. 'I know, father and only daughter, special relationship. This must be difficult for you but, as they say, you would not so much be losing a daughter . . . '

Harcourt was staring stonily at the fireplace, so I decided to press home my advantage.

'I dare to hope,' I said, 'that one day I shall be able to call you Father.'

Harcourt made a sudden grunting sound, like an old labrador that has just been poked hard with a shooting stick. 'Bugger off, Fixx,' he said as he stabbed out his cigar and rose from the table, somewhat red-faced. He put the decanter of port on the sideboard and stumped out of the room without another word.

So much for the man-to-man approach, I thought to myself as I brought the port back to the table and poured myself another glass. So much for honesty and plain-speaking. Of course, I could marry Sarah anyway but frankly the exercise would lose much of its point if she were cut off from her inheritance and we were banned from Colevile Hall, where I had begun to feel so at home. I would doubtless have to come in on another tack.

Despite the evening's setback, it felt good to be sitting alone sipping His Lordship's excellent port and smoking one of his cigars. I would just have to be patient.

Doubtless love would find a way.

It was General Monty, was it not, who opined that no commander with his wits about him would attempt to win a battle with a simple, frontal assault? You need diversions, wings, flanking attacks. So it was with Operation Harcourt. On my left, well dug in and as yet unyielding, was Daddy; on my right, pliant and all too yielding, was little Sarah. It was a classic pincer movement, which never looked like failing.

There were flowers, there were baubles from Cartier, there were endless evenings of clammy togetherness at the theatre, the opera or at some nobby West End eatery. There was much vapid chit-chat from her and charming badinage from me. We discussed our backgrounds: hers sheltered, privileged and dull; mine harsh, deprived and exciting. Having discovered that Sarah had a taste for life on the wrong side of the tracks, at second-hand at least, I astonished her with accounts of my past, cranking up anecdotes of Melton, the Krays, Mila and Talbot a few notches where the truth was somewhat prosaic. You may argue that it was unnecessary to embroider the truth in this way but who, in all honesty, can claim that they have not told the occasional porky to ease the path of true love? We were two young people embarking on a great adventure, or so I thought. There would be time enough for truth later.

I was naive, I admit it. I believed that finding a suitable wife was only slightly more difficult than landing a top-level executive secretary, that it was merely a question of establishing certain criteria (Is she reasonably attractive? Possess a passable brain? Languages? Does her face fit? Does she make you feel good about yourself?) and putting her through her paces. Now, with the benefit of painful experience, I see that there's more to the whole business than that. I blame myself. I should never have allowed my heart to rule my head. A cooling-off period was what was needed, a few months' calm appraisal of the situation. But my deep and heartfelt desire to *belong* once more, to be known as the future master of Colevile Hall, was such that reason flew out of the window.

There was a certain magic between Sarah and me, of course there was. I discovered an innocent pleasure in being reported in the gossip columns as 'the Harcourt heir's latest beau'; she, for her part, clearly found it increasingly difficult to keep her hands off me, in spite of my insistence that we should obey the proprieties incumbent upon members of the aristocracy. After all, if we were at it before we reached the altar, what kind of example would that be for the lower orders?

'Do you want to come up for coffee?' she once asked me after yet another night of hand-holding and small-talk.

I smiled like an indulgent uncle. 'There'll be time enough for all the coffee we want when the time is right,' I said.

It was no great sacrifice, to tell the truth, for my feelings towards Sarah were utterly untroubled by thoughts of a lascivious nature. I was curious, sure – one always is – but there was nothing here to keep me awake at night, which, in my view, was an entirely good thing.

I'm a great believer in playing by the rules when it comes to marriage. This sweet, unspoilt young thing was, after all, no mere bed-partner; she was destined to be my wife, the future Honourable Mrs Fixx. Lovers were two a penny; wives like Sarah Harcourt were not. Besides, mutual respect, so important in the successful marriage, rarely walks hand in hand with physical desire. You need to be able to look one another straight in the eye over the breakfast table, not shudder with embarrassment at the memory of some undignified excess of the night before.

Naturally I avoided spelling all this out to Sarah, assuming in my innocence that, bred as she was, she would somehow take it as read.

There was a time, I make no secret of it, when I regarded the older generation as strictly irrelevant to the life of a modern achiever. They were dead leaves on the pavement of life. Yet, as my matrimonial plans became clearer, I was to discover that the achiever takes for granted the tired, the spent, the saggy, at his peril. It would not have been difficult for Harcourt or Marjorie to smile benignly, cuff me playfully on the arm and, with a 'God bless you, me old scallywag', send me on my way to the altar. But no. Some people actually grow more selfish with the years, clinging to the diminishing resources of their lives with a total disregard for the dignity of age.

Harcourt and Marjorie. The old guard. They both stood in the way of true love, fate, *le destin*. What a couple of chumps they were.

Sex is power. Everybody knows that. As Project Harcourt achieved lift-off and Marjorie became a less essential part of my plans, our relationship changed subtly. For the moment, it was sensible to retain the Wednesday afternoon routine but, now I was no longer the supplicant, we played by my rules. The balance of power shifted.

To my dismay, Marjorie failed to pick up on my waning enthusiasm. I dropped hints, I made excuses, I performed in an absent-minded, perfunctory way. All to no avail.

My assumption that, if it came to it, I could end our arrangement by the simple expedient of grassing her up to her husband also turned out to be pathetically optimistic.

The Major must have had his suspicions even before the afternoon he stumbled drunkenly into the bedroom at a moment when, for reasons not relevant to this account, I was in the cupboard and Marjorie was pacing up and down, dressed in a nanny's uniform and carrying a cane.

'What on earth are you doing back at this time?' I heard her ask without a trace of embarrassment.

'Feeling a bit dicky,' said the Major. 'Thought I'd take half a day off.'

'Well, you might have rung first.'

'Sorry, dear.' I heard the Major sit heavily on the bed. He cleared his throat nervously.

'Marjorie,' he said. 'Why are you in that uniform?'

'Discipline,' Marjorie snapped back, as if insulted by the question. 'Disciplining the dogs. It's a new theory. They respect uniforms.'

'Ah.' The reply appeared to have satisfied the Major. 'Cane seems a bit tough on the little blighters, isn't it?'

'Cruel to be kind. They've got to learn,' Marjorie said in a tone that I knew only too well.

'Where are they?' The Major's voice was slurred but suspicious. 'Under the bed?'

'I'm practising, you old fool. Now leave me alone, will you.'

Muttering 'Poor little devils', the Major left the room.

He knew, of course. Gin-pickled and gaga as he was, he could hardly have failed to notice the difference in Marjorie, or indeed in me during this difficult time.

'Are you all right, old boy?' he asked me once when we met for a drink. 'You're looking a bit peaky these days.'

'I'm fine, Major.'

'It's all these tea parties,' he said gruffly. 'They must be wearing you out.'

'What? No, it's just the work.'

'Good show, old boy.' The Major patted me on the knee. 'Keep up the good work, you're doing a great job.'

The idea that the Major could be induced to bring his wife back into line had been pathetically misguided. I was actually doing the old fool a favour. The wife was happy. She slept better, smiled a lot and had given up waking him in the middle of the night with tiresome demands for manoeuvres. It was a damned good show all round.

The Major was no ally. Clearly, if I wanted to lose Marjorie, I was going to have to do it myself.

A word to the wise among my lady readers. If you're going to succumb to the heebie-jeebies, strafe the enemy camp with a take-no-prisoners screaming abdab attack, put your better half straight for once and for all, please remember this golden rule.

For heaven's sake, put your clothes on first.

Because no man, I don't care who he is, can take you seriously if you do it in the buff. It should work, I know – the primal force of nature and all that – but it doesn't. So throw something on first, take a deep breath – *then* open fire.

You'd think that Marjorie, being a woman of the world, might have understood this. But no. One moment, all was calm in the boudoir after the first bout of the afternoon (the lady in the pink corner running out an easy winner after two knockdowns and a submission), the next it was like an earthquake hitting the Naples Blancmange Festival.

There were screams, curses, objects flew across the room, a Cruft's Certificate whistled past my ear. I took refuge under the duvet and clung on for dear life as the mad old bat tugged and pulled to get at me, quite like Aunty Bar-Bar back in the old days. After what seemed an age, the storm relented somewhat and I peeped out nervously from the cover. Marjorie had lit a cigarette and, like an Amazonian grandma, was glaring at me, arms akimbo, from the centre of the room. It was at this moment, blotched and wobbly and heaving, that her body let her down so badly. By some miracle, I managed to keep a straight face but inside, I tell you, I was creased up.

'You little *shit*,' she said at last. 'You've used me, you little bastard, and now you're going to use her.'

'Marjorie,' I said as coolly as I could manage. 'This is all very difficult for me – '

'Not as difficult as it's going to be. You're finished. Your social-climbing days are over.'

I sighed. 'The parties meant nothing to me, to tell the truth. I just wanted to widen my circle of acquaintances.'

'You're a deceitful little toad. It was a fishing expedition, wasn't it? You wanted a wife – someone to bring a bit of much-needed respectability to your life.'

'Pooch,' I said seductively. 'Come back to bed. I hate to see you take on so. Let's . . . just remember the good times.'

'You're not going to get away with this. Nobody uses Marjorie Taylor as a stepping-stone.'

The fact is, my interface with Marjorie was not going at all as planned. I had expected a more sympathetic hearing, not this unseemly row.

'All right, you can see the little tart,' Marjorie said briskly, after a moment's silence. 'But just keep your Wednesday afternoons free, all right.'

'Marjorie,' I said reasonably. 'I'm engaged. I couldn't betray Sarah like that. It wouldn't be right.'

'*Now* he takes a moral stand,' she sneered. 'You make me sick.'

'And the Honourable Sarah Harcourt may be many things, but she's hardly a tart.'

'Poor child. If only she knew. D'you honestly think she'll know how to handle your little private fetishes? Nanny? House-training?' There followed an unpleasant litany of bedroom activities that Marjorie had somehow convinced herself appealed to me. 'Would she put up with that, like I have?'

'We'll work something out,' I said coldly.

'Anyway, her father's a wrong 'un. Everybody knows that.'

'Christy? But he's a Lord. He's a Conservative, for heaven's sake.'

'Precisely. He's got mistresses all over Maida Vale. And none too savoury personal habits, so I'm told.'

I allowed my jaw to sag dramatically.

'It's not true. Tell me it's just tittle-tattle. I couldn't marry into scandal. I have my reputation to consider.'

'I'll prove it to you,' said Marjorie, a note of triumph in her voice. 'My spies will get the evidence. Maybe then you'll see sense.'

'Maybe I will,' I said.

– Should I write to her?

– Old Marje? Forget it. Of course, she was knocked for a loop when I finally ditched her. Aged terribly. Major couldn't take the strain. Cashed in his chips – a fatal stroke, brought on by alcohol poison. She went to Ireland.

– Looking for new toy boys.

– As it happens, no. I believe her boudoir received no more young visitors from my departure until her death.

– She's dead?

– Hunting accident. Used to go out with the Galway Blazers. She had a sort of death wish on the hunting field, I heard. Went all glassy-eyed and odd. Jumped anything, rode her exhausted horses into the ground. It was some sort of escape, I suppose – a substitute for something or other. Then one day she took on one too many stone walls. Spurred her exhausted mount into it, the nag had a heart attack in

mid-air, landed on her, breaking her neck. She never recovered consciousness.

– Sad.

– Yes, poor old thing.

– So you did feel something for her then.

– Actually I was thinking of the horse. I know just how it felt.

13
Hitched!

Despite these promising beginnings (future wife helplessly in love, angry old lover steaming about the mucky end of Maida Vale in search of evidence against randy future father-in-law), Project Harcourt was finally to test my considerable strategic skills to the limit.

Sarah was no problem, of course. We were now unofficially engaged, having both agreed that Daddy was not quite ready for the news. Marjorie, beaming triumphantly, brought me evidence of Harcourt's private life: addresses, times of weekly visits, the odd name. Yet when I coolly peppered the target with warning shots – the heavy hint, the passing remark, the gamy wink – Harcourt responded with nothing more than polite curiosity. Someone saw me where? Maida Vale. Surprising since I've been here all week. The cold stare. Perhaps I have a double. More wine, Sarah?

But no man, as the saying goes, is an island vis-à-vis his own particular point in time. The mighty loom of history contains many threads. We're all part of the pattern, as Christy Harcourt discovered to his cost.

Let us return to Maida Vale.

It is 1972. We are in an agreeable modern maisonette. Laughter can be heard behind the closed door of the bedroom: the amused, contented tones of a gentleman at play, the trills and coos of a young – no, *two* young ladies in his company.

Fair enough, we think in our tolerant, post-permissive way. Or even: lucky dog. But wait! There's another sound. While our friends are playing pig-in-the-middle in the bedroom, we hear the click, the whirr of a camera in a small adjoining room. Bloody hell, we're among sophisticates, it seems. Tactfully, we tiptoe away into the street outside.

So what? you're saying. We've all done it or, if not, we've thought about doing it. Maybe not the snapshots but, if our friends here are into candid camera, what's it to us?

Yet this humdrum domestic scene marked the end of an epoch. It was the moment when the Gentlemen finally drew stumps and made way to the Players.

Of course, the Gentlemen had enjoyed a good innings. The Macmillans, the Douglas-Homes, the Lord Hogg of Hailshams, men who worked the budget out with matchsticks, whose idea of foreign policy was to suck up to the Americans while sneering at their lack of class, who dropped and picked up peerages when it suited. We knew they were up to all sorts of tricks, always had been. Gladstone and his tarts, Lloyd George and his secretary, Bob Boothby and Lady Dorothy. Not to mention the small regiment of officers in the pink army, the left-footers, the incidents in the urinals at Piccadilly Circus, the mud-wrestling with guardsmen in Hyde Park, the joyful thrashings of one another at the Monday Club. No matter, we thought. Everyone needs a hobby. Tough business, running the country, and who does it better than the Gentlemen, kinks and all?

All the same, we gave the Players their chance in the sixties. Wilson, Brown, Frank Cousins – names you could trust, faces that looked you straight in the eye, solid, married types without so much as a whiff of scandal about them. But they turned out to be dull, pious bastards, with a sort of self-righteous smugness about them we Britons tend to distrust.

So we tried again, this time with Players of a different persuasion. Heath, Walker, Barber – professional, hard-nosed technocrats with a proper respect for money. For a while, it seemed we were getting somewhere at last. These were no goody-goodies, they were in power to clip the wings of the nosies and noddies of Whitehall, make the world a fit place for your average wealth-creator, profit-taker, achiever.

Yet, as the seventies unfolded, there were signs of a revival among the Gentlemen. There emerged an odd, atavistic yearning among the common people for the old style of politician, chaps in plus-fours who addressed the nation as if giving instructions to the beaters on their estate. The Players faltered; not for the first time, Lord Hailsham of Hogg allowed it to be known that the idea of Prime Ministerial office was not entirely odious to him.

It was at this precise moment that a languid, junior minister playing for the Gentlemen's Second XI in the House of Lords was caught indulging in his favourite pastime.

We're back in the maisonette now. The camera was not, it appears, part of the game. It was operated by a sewer rat on boggle patrol, working for the *News of the World*. He had not been invited.

When the story broke, it was generally held that the Gentlemen had gone too far this time. To be snapped blissfully naked in the company of a professional woman might have been dismissed as no more than unfortunate. And if being entertained by a brace of business girls suggested a certain degree of over-indulgence, then after all conspicuous consumption was back in fashion. Even the fact that he was pulling on a king-sized reefer could be overlooked at a time when pot was still an acceptable tipple among the liberated classes. But to be lolling about, stoned out of your box, indulging in God-knows-what with a couple of tarts and all – here was the stinger – *in the middle of the afternoon* was, it was widely agreed, simply going too far.

This was no amusing peccadillo, a spot of playful how's-your-father after a busy day in the House; it was a full-blown, daylight group-sex drug orgy. Badly let down by their tailenders, the Gentlemen were, finally and definitively, out.

Forgive the foray into political history but just as that innocent scene – three pie-eyed lovers on a king-size bed in Maida Vale – was to alter history so it was to influence the private life of Jonathan Peter Fixx, once and for ever.

'In France, no one would have turned a hair.'

Sarah and I were down at Colevile Hall shortly after the scandal broke. It was another of Harcourt's weekend gatherings, his mini-Camelots, which were frankly becoming increasingly irksome to me. A sprinkling of the best and the brightest were there – MPs, businessmen, the odd jumped-up journalist – and the subject over dinner on the Saturday evening naturally turned to the affair. It was some wife or other who had made the perceptive remark about our French cousins' lack of public morality.

'In France,' Harcourt sat at the head of the table with a sickening man-of-the-world smile on his face, 'the scandal is when a minister *doesn't* have a mistress.'

We laughed dutifully.

'And yet I wonder,' I said, after a moment's pause. There was the mildest *frisson* of apprehension around the table, as there so often was when I was a guest at Colevile. Now what was Sarah's enigmatic and dangerous-looking boyfriend going to say? 'I just wonder whether it's as insignificant as all that.'

'We're not worried,' said a stupid, red-faced back-bench MP who liked to talk as if he were already in the Cabinet.

'You wouldn't be,' I said. 'On the face of it, the whole thing's ridiculous. Which of us, after all, has not enjoyed the occasional . . . fling?' I managed to dart a quick, conspiratorial leer at Harcourt, who flinched visibly. 'But has it blown over? My information is that there's more to come. And that it's pretty hot stuff.'

'And where exactly does this information come from?' said the MP stuffily. 'The Crown and Anchor public bar?'

'Hardly.' I glanced in the direction of a well-known journalist. 'We're off the record here, are we?'

The best and the brightest nodded vigorously as if the very question was an insult.

'There's a man called Collin,' I said. 'Was a senior snoop on the *Sunday Times* Insight team. Used to work with David Frost. These days he's – '

'Yes yes, the BBC,' said Harcourt impatiently. 'I think we all know who Brian Collin is.'

'First-class man,' said one of the senior sewer rats. 'Bags of integrity.'

I noticed that Harcourt and the MP appeared somewhat unsettled by Collin's reputation. It was a moment of enormous satisfaction to be deploying to such good effect the man who had caused me so much grief with Mila. There was a certain poetic justice to it.

'*Bags* of integrity,' I agreed. 'It appears that he's been working on this story ever since it broke. He thinks there's a lot more to come. More names, more girls, more kinks. D'you know that one of the men insists on being strung up – '

'Spare us the details, Fixx,' said Harcourt. 'There are ladies present.'

'Tip of the iceberg, he told me. Could bring down the government.'

'Bloody BBC Trots,' said one of the double-barrelled Deirdres, the wife of a banker.

'I suppose I could have a word with the DG,' said the MP unconvincingly.

'That's the problem,' I said. 'Brian seems to think the dirt he's digging is so important that, even if the BBC don't run with it, he'll go to Fleet Street. The public has a right to know, he says.'

'And why did he tell you all this?' Harcourt now had a dangerous, pinched look about him.

'We're old school chums. Went on a bit of a bender after a reunion the other night. Discretion flew out of the window in the wee small hours. We've no secrets, old Collers and I.'

There was a thoughtful silence around the table.

'Oh well, sod the media, I say,' said Harcourt finally, with a fine show of cheerfulness. 'Who's for pud?'

To give credit where it's due, Marjorie had done me proud. In her eagerness to corral me back to her bed, she had tapped sources that the average sewer rat could only dream about. A list of girls' names and addresses was not enough, I had told her. I needed evidence, details, the full poop.

It is not the object of this modest account of my life and achievements to drag the reputation of public figures through the mud. So Talbot was revealed to be a cheap crook; I note it, and pass on. Mila destroyed her career with drugs; I spare you the details. And Lord Harcourt liked to be dressed up as a baby and disciplined by a couple of highly paid business girls; I reveal it only because certain members of his family have taken to making various allegations about myself. Of course, it's a free country. They have the right to slander me, just as I have the right to make publicly available, if circumstances require, some of the really quite hilarious photographs – His Lordship snoozing thumb in mouth, swathed in king-size nappies, being awoken roughly and stripped by his nannies, quaking with excitement as he receives his punishment – that are in my possession.

As I say, Marjorie had done a good job.

He was a cool one, Harcourt, I'll give him that. Beyond being rather more distant towards his guests and almost friendly to me, he behaved normally for the rest of the weekend and it was Sunday afternoon, while we were out walking the dogs, before he finally raised the subject again.

'This Collin fellow,' he said, as we watched Sarah throw sticks for one of the labradors to retrieve. 'Any chance of my meeting him informally, d'you think?'

'Of course,' I said helpfully. 'I could arrange lunch at Bentleys next week.' We walked on. 'Except . . . ' I frowned, as if tussling with a weighty moral dilemma.

'Go on,' said Harcourt impatiently.

'I love him dearly, but Collin's a slippery sod. I can't help feeling that he might just use an approach like that against the government in some way – or even against you personally. You know how journalists are.'

'Ah.'

'And he has got an awful lot of information, apparently. Addresses in Maida Vale. Names of girls: Suzi, Paula, Linzi.' Harcourt started slightly at the names of three of his favourite girlfriends. 'And some of the details he gave me were certainly pretty fruity.'

Making sure that Sarah was some distance away, I pulled out my wallet.

'Give yourself a laugh, Christy,' I said, passing him some Polaroids. 'Look – Baby being winded.'

Harcourt gulped as, for a moment before looking away with a shudder, he examined the photograph of his wizened body, crouched like a Muslim in prayer. He was wearing a nappy.

'Baby being changed.'

There was an odd whimper from Harcourt. Although Baby's face was obscured in all the photographs, it was clear that he recognised the scene.

'And here, Christy – Baby being smacked by his nannies. Linzi and Paula. Very strict.'

Harcourt swallowed hard and passed them back to me like a child playing Pass the Parcel.

'Are there any more?' he asked weakly.

'Masses, apparently. I've not seen them myself.'

'He's got to be stopped. The – the government's work is too important to be put at risk by this sort of nonsense.'

'Oh, I agree,' I said. 'It's all so ironical. I know a few things about Collers's early days that he would give a lot to keep under wraps. Now he's the Mr Clean of the BBC. Extraordinary.'

It took Harcourt less than a second to rise to the bait.

'Maybe *you* could . . . '

'Could what, Christy?'

'Discourage him, somehow. Get the negatives from him. Put a bit of discreet pressure on the fellow.'

I shook my head firmly.

'I'd like to,' I said, 'but I've got my career, my future, to think of. I really don't want to get dragged into this. It wouldn't be fair on Sarah.'

Harcourt started.

'She hasn't seen the photographs, has she?'

'Good Lord, no. I wouldn't want to expose her to that sort of thing. Particularly when we're both going through such a difficult period.'

'Difficult? Why?'

I half-turned away from him.

'We want *very* much to get married,' I said. 'But only with your blessing – that's very important to both of us. And at the moment . . . ' I tailed off miserably.

'Maybe,' said Harcourt, in a curious, flat voice, 'I could be persuaded to change my mind.'

'You *wouldn't*. Oh, Christy, if you did, I'd be enormously grateful. I mean, I'd do anything for you.'

'Would you?'

He looked at me coldly. For a moment I felt sorry for the man, well and truly hooked as he was. Then I hauled him in without further ado.

'Just say the word.'

'Perhaps you could speak to your friend Collin,' he said. 'And get those negatives from him.'

'Well, maybe I could. If I did, would we have your blessing?'

'Of course you would have my blessing,' he said wearily.

I shook him warmly by the hand. 'Thank you, Christy. I won't disgrace the family, I promise.'

'I'm sure you won't, Fixx.'

'Christy,' I smiled. 'I'd like it very much if you called me Jonathan.'

'I'm sure you would,' he said.

'What was that?' I said more sharply.

Harcourt sighed.

'Nothing, Jonathan,' he said.

It occurred to me some time later that, amid all these complex and exciting manoeuvres, I had omitted to square things with Sarah regarding the actual date of our marriage. It was not a major problem since, in those distant days, she was quite besotted with me but, now that I had stymied Harcourt and Marjorie, it would obviously be tidier to get us hitched as soon as possible. Sadly, this ruled out the great society wedding at Gloucester Cathedral on which I had set my heart but then again we all have to make sacrifices on these occasions.

Funnily enough, my announcement that we should get married immediately was not greeted as warmly as I had anticipated. Yet no man could have done more to make it go smoothly: dinner at La Pomme d'Amour was the way I planned it, on to Annabel's, a couple of minutes of romantic gush, propose, date for her diary at the Fulham Registry Office which I had taken the trouble to book two days hence, waiter appearing bang on cue with a bottle of Moët and POP! What more was she expecting?

But no. Instead of being swept off her feet by my romantic impetuosity, Sarah was distinctly panicky. When we should have been drinking gaily to our health, she bombarded me with a series of idiot questions.

Was I sure about Daddy? What about her career (she bought and sold paintings a bit, even then)? Of course she must pursue it. Would I want children soon? In our own time, my darling. Where would we live? London or Studley Grange – the choice was up to her. Why couldn't we have more time? I had already booked our honeymoon in the Seychelles. Was I sure – sure sure sure – about all this? Yes, my sweet, I was sure – sure sure sure. Eventually, after shedding the inevitable tear or two (nerves? excitement? fear? search me), she capitulated and, in a nightclub that was now almost empty, we raised our glasses to one another.

'To Mr and Mrs Fixx,' she said.

'Née Harcourt,' I said.

The champagne was warm and flat.

I remember little about the Big Day. Sarah was given away by Lucy Geddes, a schoolfriend with auburn hair and, I noticed through a haze of emotion, very passable legs. The best man was Pringle, one of my commodity brokers who, as luck would have it, had a cancelled appointment that morning. Generally speaking, it was a low-key, almost dull occasion.

It came as no particular surprise that my own mother was unable to be present at the wedding. She was swaggering about in the Australian outback somewhere, boasting about her book, and had claimed that it was difficult to abandon her trip at two days' notice. The fact that the most important day in the life of her only son took second place to squeezing a few dollars out of a group of hairy Australian feminists tells its own story, I suppose. Catherine flew back and cried prettily during the brief ceremony, which was nice.

As it happens, I was unable to tell Marjorie to her face that, far from discouraging me from joining the Harcourt family, the filth she had dug up about Harcourt and his nappy rash had actually helped my cause. It would have been a painful scene and, in my vulnerable emotional state, I might have been tempted to say things to her I would later regret. Menopausal angst I did not need at this point in time. To tell the truth I almost forgot to leave her a letter explaining my sudden departure for the Seychelles. Having written several tender, regretful pages in my head, I clean forgot to get them down on paper.

In the end, I jotted down a crisply worded note on the back of an amusing postcard and mailed it from the airport.

14
Plus ça change

– Has she really changed that much?

– Who?

– Sarah.

– Beyond recognition. She was a sweet simple girl, full of love and wit and generosity. She listened to me, marvelled at my stories, laughed at my jokes. Before we were married, she was everything a wife should be. Her rapid deterioration was a great sorrow to me.

– Of course, she would say that then she was a fool, that she has grown up since.

– Became a total person, that's what she'd say. A total person in her own right.

– Perhaps it's true.

– Probably. Yet if she had never met me, what would have become of her? A suitable marriage to some bovine, tweed-suited wally, children, acres of rolling parkland on which to exercise the horses. Wealth, security, staff – everything she now claims to detest. It was I who helped her blossom or, as she would say, fulfil her potential.

– Put that way, she seems oddly ungrateful.

– You said it.

Diversification. That was the name of the game as my career and my personal life, in perfect step as usual, entered this particularly interesting phase. Change, variety, spread – I was everywhere in the seventies, everywhere.

In these bright days of growth and opportunity for the right-minded go-getter, it's difficult to recall the dense grey fog of defeat and depression that enveloped this sceptr'd isle at that time. The white heat of the technological revolution now barely warmed the fingers. The noisy throng of gurus who had once seemed to have the answer to everything were silent – dead, disgraced, or working on the Stock Exchange, false prophets of a false dawn. Political activism, once so chic, was as dated as the mini-skirt. Where there had been revolution, there was Jim Callaghan. Where there had been Young Meteors, there was Edward Heath. The pendulum years swung no more, the New Permissiveness having given way to the New Celibacy. The nation lay, slumped, in a torpor of post-coital *tristesse*. At some point, inflation reached 30 per cent, the lights went out and ambulancemen stayed at home, causing the death of countless thousands of pensioners, to no one's particular surprise.

The winter of discontent, they called it. More like the decade of discontent.

Under the circumstances, the duty of every share-owning patriot was plain: get the hell out of the place until things cheered up a bit. You didn't have to be Peter Jay (a big-eared bamber and probe-merchant widely rumoured at the time to be the most brilliant man in Britain) to know that, at the end of the day, the wealth of a country and its businessmen are inextricably linked and that, if the best way of protecting an entrepreneurial nest-egg was to shift it to a foreign nest pro tem, so be it.

In what we used to call 'the global village', folk like myself were after all no more than modest burghers, plying their trades as best they could. So if John Bull the grocer on the High Street was in difficulties, what could be more logical than to take our business to the other side of town – to Franz or Jacques or Sukimoto? When old Johnny was once again back on his feet, we would no doubt return to him.

The familiar, ill-informed whining from the sewer rats on City patrol that speculators were somehow 'anti-social', that they were 'bleeding the country dry', was an accusation that we in the international business community did not deign to refute; if the Little Englanders failed to understand the complexities of world markets, that was their problem.

Not that it was easy for the wealth-creator to stand aside in his sunny tax-haven as the government of our once proud land was obliged to call in the official receiver, a team of hatchet-faced noddies from something called the IMF, but then the role of the entrepreneur, what I call 'the long-term patriot', was ever thus.

Calm in a panic; decisive in a boom. That was, and is, the way of Jonathan Peter Fixx.

Over a matter of two or three years, I had divested myself of many of my domestic interests in favour of international investment. Out went Fixx Properties (UK) Ltd; in came Control Corp Inc., a South African-based concern supplying troubled Third World governments with badly needed security tools. The spirit of '68 – civil disobedience, lack of respect for authority and general bloody-minded bolshiness on the part of the civilian population – had spread like wildfire throughout the world and I'm proud to say that indirectly I helped restore the grip of many an unsteady government with my new product range. Riot-control vehicles in Singapore, shackles in Central America, new and highly effective plastic bullets in Belfast – Control Corp was indeed one of the decade's unsung triumphs of new technology and international co-operation.

Then, ever alert to the growing problem of over-population, I set up a small laboratory, called Fixx Lacombe, in Berne, backed up by a significant number of distribution centres in Zürich, Hong Kong and Lusaka, with a view to cracking the market for cheap contraceptives and food.

Within two years, we had struck gold. Our miracle pill, Menson, a contraceptive which needed to be taken only once a month, had reached world markets and, despite cavilling objections from the jealous, mean-spirited scientific establishment, was outselling all other contraceptives in the Third World.

Why not make it available in the West? asked the naysayers. And why was it taken off the market after three years?

There were, as with so many great medical breakthroughs, one or two teething problems – in particular, a rather higher incidence of leukaemia among regular Menson users than might normally have been expected. Yet, such was its popularity, that several months after some group of professional busybodying eggheads had claimed that there was a 'grossly unacceptable' mortality rate among patients, there was only the smallest dip in demand. In the market-place, where it mattered, the attractions of my pill were generally felt to outweigh its drawbacks. The consumer in his mud hut, kraal or back-street slum ignored the so-called experts and continued to buy 'Massa Miracle', as the local distributors touchingly called it.

In the end, taking the responsible line, I agreed to withdraw Menson from sale pending one or two further tests and to shelve plans to market it in the civilised world on the condition that certain lawsuits in the international courts were dropped. It was not an easy decision since Massa Miracle had certainly, one way or another, proved its worth in keeping the Third World population figures down which, I had always understood, is what contraception should be all about.

Diversification. Just as I spread my investment generously around the world, so I found that new areas of experience were opened to me by the fact of my marriage to Sarah.

I am, I confess, something of a traditionalist when it comes to married life. I have the modest, not unreasonable expectations of the average husband. Give me a clean shirt, a well-run household, a decent hot meal of an evening and, when the time's ripe, a couple of well-mannered children, and I'll have no complaints.

You'd have expected Sarah, coming as she did from one of the country's most respected families, to hold a similarly responsible view. Marriage is all about teamwork, leadership. I was to provide the thrust, the direction and the funds (now swelled, I agree, by a handsome family trust paid over to Sarah on her marriage), while she – just as important in her own little way – would provide the back-up, the support, the general context within which I could work fruitfully on behalf of us both.

Yet, within the first week of our honeymoon, I could tell that I had backed the wrong horse matrimony-wise. Something about having 'Mrs' tacked on to her name changed Sarah for ever.

Little things, first of all. Not looking up from her book when I entered the room. Allowing her attention to wander as I told her an amusing or instructional anecdote from business life. Ordering directly to the waiter at dinner rather than through me. Laughing at an alleged mispronunciation of one of the dishes on the menu (a gay, light laugh, but laughter all the same).

Then more serious problems. I am not one of those autobiographers who is only too happy to tear the sheets back from the marriage bed to reveal every wart and stretch-mark of the woman who once shared it with him. Sheet-sniffers need read no further. The after-lights-out behaviour of Sarah Fixx will remain, to use a peculiarly apt metaphor, a closed book.

Yet, since this is a true account of my life thus far, there are certain painful facts that cannot – that will not – be glossed over.

And one of them concerns our first night.

Busy as I was in the days leading up to our wedding, I had still found time for a few moments of soft-focus fantasising about that magical moment-to-be.

I saw the champagne in the silver ice bucket beside the opulent, spacious hotel double bed.

I saw the white silk sheets on the bed.

I saw me, waiting in bed, calm, in control, and yet, in spite of all my experience, just a touch nervous.

I saw her, standing in the doorway from the bathroom in the discreetly provocative nightdress I had given her, a picture of virginal loveliness.

I heard my voice, soothingly reassuring.

I heard her bashful, girlish request for the bedside light to be turned out.

And then I – sure, tender, firm, confident, solicitous, insistent – and she – soft, trembling, pliant, sighing, wondering, breathless – are soon (yet not too soon for I was never one to rush such moments) to become Us. As one. The girl-wife becomes a woman. The man-husband claims his prize.

Together at last.

The reality was not like that at all.

I waited in the large bed for what seemed an age as my new wife prepared herself in the bathroom adjoining our ruinously expensive honeymoon suite. We had dined well, with Sarah drinking more than usual, presumably to quell her first-night nerves.

'Darling.'

I looked up from the magazine I was reading. Sarah was standing in the doorway, framed by the bathroom light. Rather to my surprise, she had elected to make her entrance completely naked. She looked good – much better than I had anticipated, in fact – but there was something about the way she stood there which I found unbecoming.

'Aren't you going to put on the nightdress I bought you?' I asked tenderly.

'Oh,' Sarah seemed taken aback. 'All right.' She disappeared into the bathroom. When she re-emerged in the silk, peek-a-boo nightie, she looked perfect. It was exactly as I had imagined it.

'Come, my lovely,' I said, putting aside the magazine and stretching out a welcoming hand.

She walked slowly towards the bed and knelt beside me. I held her close.

'Wait,' she whispered in my ear. 'I have something to tell you.'

'Shoot, my darling,' I murmured, expecting in my innocence some saucy, charming, girlish confidence.

'This – ' she hung her head abjectly. 'This is not my first time, Jonathan.'

'Come again?' I could hardly believe my ears.

'I'm not a virgin.'

Wonderful, wasn't it? My girl-wife was already a woman. The prize had been taken by someone else.

Don't get me wrong. I'm no champion of virginity for its own sake – indeed, on the many occasions when it has fallen to me to relieve some quaking teenager of her maidenhood, I tend to regard the chore as something in the line of social work – a thankless, often messy, task, but there again someone has to do it.

But then, when you marry into one of the great families of England, you expect the old morality to pertain. This was not some grocer's daughter I had given myself to – it was a Harcourt and you don't expect to get Harcourts shop-soiled, for God's sake.

No wonder I responded to Sarah's halting confession with an uncharacteristic harshness.

'It was only once, Jonathan,' she whispered miserably.

'And it only takes once,' I said, now standing by the bed. 'Unless where you come from virginity is assessed on a sliding scale.'

'It was nothing – ' The tears were in evidence now. 'A cuddle after a hunt ball that turned into – '

'Nothing?' I asked, unable to keep the hurt out of my voice. 'Have I married a girl for whom the sacred gift of her own body is nothing?'

I was angry, of course I was. As she sobbed her apologies once more, I found myself throwing on my clothes. All my dreams were shattered, my sweet tender fantasies.

'I wish I hadn't told you now,' she wailed.

'I'd have found out,' I said coldly. 'Men can tell, you know.'

By now I was at the door.

'Why are you dressed, Jonathan? Where are you going?'

'I need a drink. I have to think things over,' I said. 'Don't wait up . . . darling.'

And, on that telling point, I left her blubbing in the honeymoon suite and repaired to the hotel bar.

Later, while drowning my sorrows, I fell into conversation with a rather amusing German air stewardess who, like me, found herself alone with time to kill. She was hardly my type – tall, big-boned, with too much make-up – but I was in a vulnerable state and, when she made her move, I was frankly in no mood to resist.

It was as memorable a night as a no-future, loveless one-night stand can be – that is, very memorable indeed. All the pain, the need, the disappointment within me found powerful, wordless expression as the air stewardess and I grappled back at her room, two lonely animals bringing savage comfort to one another as best they could. Maybe the German had something on her mind too because she fought and clawed at me, her harsh incomprehensible cries of encouragement rising to frequent crescendos of ear-splitting ecstasy which echoed through the warm night (I remember this detail in particular because, by an unlucky chance, her room was three doors down from the honeymoon suite and she had insisted on keeping the window open).

When our bodies had covered more or less all the options open to them, I took a brief nap, then slipped into my clothes and wandered off down the corridor to my wife.

It was just getting light. I felt mellower, more relaxed. Maybe I had been hasty. With a pleasant weariness, I glanced at the sleeping figure of Sarah. In a moment of optimism, she had taken off her nightdress.

She stirred and opened her eyes.

'Jonathan?' she said, covering herself with the sheet. 'Where – ?'

I placed a finger to her lips.

'Not another word,' I said softly. 'Let's let bygones be bygones.'

'Could we move rooms, Jonathan?'

'Why on earth should we do that?'

'We have,' my wife looked away shyly, 'noisy neighbours.'

'Not to worry,' I said. 'They're probably checking out today.'

As I stumbled into bed, I kissed her briefly on the cheek before turning over and falling into a deep, dreamless slumber.

I shall cast a veil over the ten days we spent together in the Seychelles. Suffice it to say that our journey of mutual self-discovery was rather more storm-tossed than either of us might have expected.

She discovered, for instance, that the world of business waits for no man and that it is quite possible for a series of crucial board-meetings to be addressed over the telephone by the modern go-getter, even if he is in his honeymoon bed.

I discovered that, despite her hunt-ball indiscretion, Sarah was 'all at sea' when it came to her basic marital duties ('There's a place for finishing-school politesse,' I joshed her during the course of yet another fumbling, after-you-my-dear-no-no-I-insist-after-you fiasco, 'and three a.m. in your honeymoon bed ain't it!').

She discovered that I had no objection to her taking lengthy shopping trips while I recharged my batteries with an internal concept session back at the hotel.

I discovered that Seychellois hotel maids will do virtually anything for the price of a hamburger.

It was not the most joyous and trouble-free of honeymoons but, then again, which honeymoon ever was?

In spite of my wife's shortcomings, I returned to London refreshed and ready for the fray. At last everything was going right. My business affairs were expanding into international markets. At home, I had a lovely little wife who adored me and brought amusement and comfort to those few evenings when I was not working late or entertaining. And, as a member of the revered Harcourt family, it was only a matter of time before the faintest question mark vis-à-vis my standing in society would be erased.

Having set Sarah up in an agreeable family home, I took the high road to Heathrow and busied myself with foreign projects. Control Corp had just cracked the Chilean market with a rather clever electrical contraption, the laboratory in Berne had perfected an astonishingly economical form of dried milk taken from spoilt barley husks. Deals had to be done, contracts exchanged.

I considered it prudent to spare Sarah the details of my business life, certain aspects of which, I sensed, she was not yet sophisticated enough to understand. That my brand of personal hands-on management was never a nine-to-five affair, for instance. That the average Third World wide-boy expects the odd perk to be waiting for him, smiling and available, in his hotel bedroom. That to travel abroad without a young, attractive assistant in tow is likely to give the man on the other side of the desk in Manila, Hong Kong, Karachi or wherever the impression that he is dealing with some kind of stick-in-the-mud. In short, that good business and fast company belong together.

'You look after your side of things,' I used to tell her, 'and leave the business to me. It's complicated.'

In fact, like many husbands at the time, I had become a convert to a new lifestyle system which had recently become popular on the west coast of America, that of 'Open Marriage'.

For two or three weeks following my honeymoon, I had tried in all earnestness to keep my hands to myself. I received calls at the office, of course, the usual offers – old girlfriends, adulterous colleagues, secretaries on the make – but I was not the easy touch I had been when I was single. Just this once, I'd say, but don't make a habit of it.

No one could accuse me of not working at my marriage. For weeks on end, I had tried to direct my over-active libido more or less in the direction ordained by the so-called wedding vows – to introduce into our marriage the spice and originality the experts in these matters advise, only to find that Sarah recoiled in embarrassment and confusion from my well-intentioned suggestions and requests.

In the end, I stopped trying. Some of us have a taste for the exotic, some don't. Some like oysters, others can only manage fish fingers. In the end, I sought my oysters elsewhere. It was only logical.

No wonder I embraced the philosophy of Open Marriage with such eagerness. It was a lifeline for me and I was convinced it would be for Sarah – at least when I got round to explaining it to her. She took a while to adjust to new ideas, and so I decided to take Open Marriage slowly, one step at a time.

For the moment, my side of the partnership would be open. Once that was working satisfactorily, we could very possibly discuss some sort of reciprocal arrangement.

No marriage begins and ends in the boudoir. While, thanks to my efforts to take the pressure off the wife by playing away from home as frequently as possible, Sarah and I had achieved a sort of compatibility vis-à-vis after-lights-out activity, all was not so simple in the day-to-day running of our life together.

She changed. She lost weight. She smiled less. The dimpled, old-fashioned innocence I had once found so attractive gave way to a tough, contemporary worldliness. There was something about living with a highly charged over-achiever that transformed Sarah from a gentle, well-spoken young lady into a strident, angry woman of modish egalitarian views, often and loudly expressed. Were it not for my doubtless unfashionable belief in a certain decorum when writing about one's ex-wife, I would simply dismiss her as just another mad harridan. As it is, I'll merely say that she was a considerable disappointment to me.

An example. During the odd soirée that I innocently and misguidedly arranged for influential friends and colleagues, she would startle the assembled gathering by speaking out of turn, contradicting me even. There's a certain protocol on these occasions: mine host wittily and modestly directing the conversation, the lady wife twittering about decoratively in the background. People don't expect opinions from the distaff side, particularly on matters outside its experience (business, politics, life); they're frankly embarrassed when a wife speaks out of turn. What made these sudden, surprising attacks of opinionated braininess all the more irksome was that many of the guests who moments before had been listening politely to their host actually turned away as the hostess took it upon herself to sparkle independently of him.

It wasn't on. I hadn't married to have attention at my own parties wilfully diverted away from me. I'm as broad-minded as the next person when it comes to the equality of the sexes but, for the support act on these occasions to jostle the male lead aside, frequently reducing him to the status of a spear-carrying wally in the shadows backstage while she pranced about like Glenda bloody Jackson, was going too far, you'll agree. In company, I smiled and kept my peace but when the party was over I would become a snarling tiger. Sometimes I refused to speak to her for days.

Naturally, much of this new confidence in Sarah was the result of being married to an achiever, what we in the business would call 'the knock-on effect'. Yet there was more to it than that. A hidden hand was at work, undermining me, sabotaging my plans, turning the head of my innocent little wife.

I award no prizes for identification of the owner of that ever-busy, ever-destructive hand. It was, of course, Sarah's new best friend, her mentor, none other than her famous literary mother-in-law.

Yes, Mother was at it again.

15
Call to arms

As it happened, I had little opportunity to worry about domestic distractions since my business affairs had become the subject of various impertinent investigations conducted by cohorts of professional nosy-parkers. I was surprised at the time. All right, so I had sailed close to the wind, muddied my hands, skated on thin ice – show me an achiever who hasn't – but, really, was that sufficient reason for the Inspector of Taxes, HM Customs and Excise, the City Takeover Panel, the Monopolies Commission, the Solicitor-General, the Fraud Squad, Interpol, UNESCO and the World Bank to take such an unwelcome interest in the way I earned my crust?

I sent my legal people into bat for me. They returned to the pavilion with long faces. The game was up, they said. The noddies had failed to understand the way I worked. Further explanations were needed. In the meantime, I would be well advised to take an extended break, preferably somewhere obscure, sunny and extradition-proof.

Naturally, I declined to turn tail and run. Such is not my way. I had one or two cards to play, of which my father-in-law Harcourt was only one. Fortunately for the old fraud, he soon became surplus to my requirements.

'Mr Fixx?'

The man waiting for me in my office one fine spring morning in 1976 was the type with whom, a matter of months previously, it would have been a pleasure to deal. The expensive tweeds, the tie of significant stripe, the nicotine-stained moustache of a military man well past his prime. They used to come to me in droves, these old buggers, looking for a job, hoping to sell out of some hopeless enterprise. One or two of them tried to brazen it out, briefly treating me like some damned jumped-up subaltern; others would get straight to the point. The result was always the same: the shoulders would sag, the hard Sandhurst eyes would slide away from contact, the authority would drain away from the voice. Give it ten minutes and generations of breeding would count for nothing. They were supplicants. I was in control. Normally, I would give them a stiff lecture on the facts of modern business life before showing them the door. The old school tie cuts no ice with Jonathan Peter Fixx.

'How the bloody hell did you get in here?' I asked, ignoring his outstretched hand. During my current difficulties, my secretary had strict instructions not to make appointments for me with strangers.

'Never mind that,' said my visitor. 'Give me five minutes. You won't regret it.'

Before I could reply, he had sat down in my guest chair and was looking at me in a curious, appraising manner. He was not just another loser, I could see that. There was something different about him.

'You're in the shit, old boy, aren't you?'

'What on earth makes you think that?'

He gave me a brief, unnervingly accurate account of precisely why I was in the shit.

'My information,' he concluded, 'is that there's an awful lot more to come. They're out to get you, Fixx.'

'They?' I said coldly, still infuriated that this man, who was clearly some sort of senior Whitehall snoop, had been allowed in. 'You mean "we", surely?'

'I mean "they". Although I admit we have contacts among them, a certain influence. When we say "Jump", the Inland Revenue don't ask how high.'

'Nor the World Bank, I suppose.'

'The World Bank, we find, is always open to persuasion.'

'And who exactly are you? Who's "we"?'

'That's not relevant. All you need to know is that if you wish the various Jonathan Fixx dossiers to be taken out of the in-trays of various interested bodies, and placed in "Pending", all you have to do is help us.'

'Why not the shredder? I'd prefer them there.'

'You know bureaucracies. "Pending" can be a very long time. Pending can be a euphemism for never.'

'I'm listening,' I said.

The espionage lark is not nearly as dull as you would believe from reading the pretentious yarns of the professional fantasists. It rarely involves the lugubrious, screwed-up public-school loser mooching around with his tiresome, old-fashioned hang-ups about class, country and sex. Many so-called spies are like me – open, easy-going, amusing. I keep in touch with them to this day. We have a laugh about old times. There's a lot of job satisfaction in being a spy.

When my visitor, who called himself Colonel Scott, first briefed me, I was frankly sceptical.

'We're looking for someone used to travelling around the world,' he said, 'someone at ease among foreigners, who keeps himself to himself, who's generally sound and . . . anonymous.'

I laughed good-naturedly. Anonymous? *Moi?* Either MI5's research department was every bit as unreliable as it was rumoured to be, or Scott was proving to have an over-developed sense of humour. And yet he appeared to be in deadly earnest.

'Anonymous and reliable,' he said. 'We know your history. Melton. Kray. Talbot. We know just the sort of man you are. Your country needs you.'

So, the call had come at last. Looking back, it was inevitable that Her Majesty's Government would finally see fit to employ the services of one whose career was even now blazing across the sky of British life like a small, perfectly formed meteor. Achiever. Captain of industry. Show-business luminary. And now, do-or-die soldier of fortune in the war against world communism. It was a logical progression.

'What,' I asked casually, 'would be in it – ?'

Colonel Scott ran through a very reasonable financial scheme, involving the monthly transfer of a significant number of Belgian francs into a Swiss bank account. 'Then there's the relief from your current difficulties and, if all goes well, your contribution to national security may just be recognised by Her Majesty.'

This was more like it.

'You mean,' I touched my lapel significantly. 'Ermine?'

Scott feigned surprise.

'You didn't hear it from me.'

Of course. It was only natural that HMG would, for the moment at least, be anxious to avoid blowing my cover by conferring a peerage on me too hastily. No doubt, the powers that be would 'see me right' in the fullness of time. I supposed they would use the old 'For services to exports' line, when it came to my inevitable trip to the Palace. I didn't mind. A nod's as good as a wink to the *crème de la crème*, amongst whom I was now proud to include myself.

'It all sounds rather interesting,' I said finally. 'So long as you are who you say you are.'

'Watch the post,' he said. 'By the end of the week, you will have received a sign that we have it in our power to help you. I'll meet you for lunch at the Garrick on Friday to give you a fuller briefing. In the meantime, it's essential you speak to absolutely no one about this.'

'Of course not.'

'Not even your wife.'

'You can trust me, Colonel.'

– *Talking of which, we've found a translator.*

– *Excellent. Agency job, was it?*

– *You're joking. More like a Russian-waiter job. But John says he's reliable. He'll do what he's told.*

– *He'd better.*

The gentlemen of MI5 were as good as their word. The following day, I received a letter from the Customs and Excise people explaining that they had decided to shelve proceedings against my companies indefinitely for 'administrative reasons'.

Naturally, I told Sarah nothing of my recruitment as an international spy, or of my impending knighthood. In fact, the temptation to use my new status for personal purposes proved irresistible on only one occasion that week. At a business dinner, I found myself seated beside a blonde fashion designer who clearly found me attractive. Table-talk led to small-talk which led to pillow-talk; one or two indiscretions may have been let slip in the heat of the moment back at her place in the wee small hours. I felt rather bad about it the following day but, since the blonde had clearly forgotten most of what I had said the previous night, thought no more of it, comforting myself in the knowledge that, like so much in life, security is a matter of practice.

That Friday, I told Colonel Scott that I was prepared to work for him.

'And you've spoken to absolutely no one about our conversation?' he asked, as we celebrated my recruitment over a glass of the club champagne.

'Nope,' I said briskly, judging that the minor gaffe of an unzipped moment was hardly relevant to the great task ahead of me.

Scott smiled, as if enjoying a private joke.

'I think,' he said, 'that you're going to be perfect for the job we have in mind.'

'And what is the job, Colonel?' I asked, already looking forward to my new life of adventure. 'Where do I go, what do I do?'

'You simply do what you're asked. Without question.'

'But what sort of work will I be used for?'

'Straightforward tasks to start with. Drops, swaps, that sort of thing. Then perhaps on to more complex schemes. Precisely how we use you will be kept confidential.'

'Even from me?'

'Especially from you.'

By a curious paradox, it was at the very moment when I was setting aside personal concerns to become involved, albeit in a covert capacity, in the public arena that Mother's private life took yet another dramatic turn in its downward spiral into demented self-obsession. After several years devoted to earnest, much-publicised navel contemplation, her attention began to stray inevitably, inexorably, to points south.

Tempting as it is to gloss over the various excesses of the Mary Fixx Self-Stimulation Workshop, to dismiss the entire episode in a brief, sardonic footnote, I will nonetheless summarise it here. After all, right or wrong, this loony was my mother; her story, unfortunate as it may seem to the neutral reader, is inextricably linked with my own.

'The New Woman', to quote from an article written by Mother for a feminist magazine (doubtless called *On the Rag* or some such), 'has taken responsibility for her own life. With growing confidence, she has taken the first steps along the road to true gender independence. Economically, politically, socially – in the West, at least – she has made significant progress. But the true struggle is not on the street, or at the workplace, or even in the home: it is within ourselves. To confront and overcome male dominance, the New Woman must relate to herself, to become truly self-sufficient spiritually, emotionally – and, yes, sexually. She needs, quite literally, to regain her own space, that space that has been so frequently invaded by the male. For it is here that we are short-changed most often. Shere Hite has revealed that only three in ten women achieve that basic right of all adults, the sexual climax, with their male partners. It is up to the New Woman to liberate herself from the notion that the best sex is shared. "The ability to orgasm," says Hite, "when, where and how we want, to be in charge of our own stimulation, represents owning our own bodies, being strong, free and autonomous human beings." It is to provide the pre-orgasmic woman with help and advice – above all practical advice – in this area that the Mary Fixx Self-Stimulation Workshop has been established.'

'She's gone too far this time,' I said when my wife – my wife, no less – showed me this evidence of Mother's latest enterprise. 'Even you have to agree that.'

'I don't know,' Sarah said airily. 'It seems rather a good idea.'

'After all I've done for her – supported her, found a publisher for her book, never said a word when she rabbited on about her past, shamelessly using family secrets to advance her own career. But really, when your own grey-haired mother stands up and announces that the country's womenfolk should learn to play with themselves, lines have to be drawn. There is a limit. What did you just say?'

'It's a good idea. The need's there, after all.'

'A need that's better not discussed in public. Really, would you like it if your mother showed a late-flowering interest in orgasms?'

'If my mother had known about orgasms, she might never have run off with the Spanish groom.'

'A decent mother wouldn't know what one was. Self-stimulation – it's disgusting.' I found it slightly annoying that Sarah was now reading Mother's articles with interest. 'Anyway,' I continued, 'who the hell is this pre-orgasmic woman?'

And where was she? I was tempted to add, but refrained from doing so out of deference to my wife's feelings. In my experience – past and present – the modern woman was more than capable of getting her fair share of orgasms in the average one-on-one situation; as far as the man was concerned, providing them had simply become part of the deal, like tipping a taxi-driver at the end of a journey, something you did out of politeness, duty or fear, depending on the circumstances.

'She exists,' Sarah murmured.

'Well I've had remarkably few complaints in my time.'

Something about this remark appeared to agitate my wife to a quite extraordinary degree.

'Well you're getting one now,' she said, somewhat harshly.

'You're not telling me that – '

'It's not a race, you know,' she said, putting down the magazine. 'It's not a bloody Olympic competition. There isn't a panel of judges awarding you marks at the end of your performance.'

I tried a conciliatory smile, which was ignored.

'Sometimes I feel I might as well not be there,' Sarah ranted on (I resisted the temptation to tell her that frequently she wasn't). 'It's as if I'm a sort of prop for an over-rehearsed solo act. If you must know, not once in our marriage have I – '

I allowed her to indulge in a series of personal allegations, the details of which (had they been true, which they weren't) are not relevant to this account, before attempting to put a stop to this bizarre outburst with a well-timed shaft of wit.

'It would make rather a good Olympic event, wouldn't it, darling?' I said. 'Technical merit? Artistic impression?'

'Fixx, Great Britain, 2·3, 1·9,' she said mystifyingly. 'Anyway, I might even try the workshop myself.'

'Wise up, darling,' I said with no more than a hint of roughness in my voice. 'It's just a bunch of plain, middle-aged women with nothing to do. The devil finding work for idle hands. Not,' I added waspishly, 'that there will be many idle hands around, if Mother has her way.'

Chortling softly at this witticism, I left Sarah reading her copy of *On the Rag*.

Your average man has certain expectations when he finally gets down to selecting a wife. He may be looking for no more than a clean-underwear provider, or a cook, or a shoulder to cry on. Most frequently, he's after someone to keep him straight, in order, out of trouble. Mother, mouse, regimental sergeant-major – your average man tends to find the wife he deserves.

Such was not the way of Jonathan Peter Fixx. I just wanted a *wife*, for God's sake – a basic, nice, easy-going helpmeet, a comfortable, undemanding human support system. A wife.

Heaven knows, my expectations were hardly excessive. A certain order in life, an easy routine of an evening, a how-was-your-day-darling over the gin and tonic, a measure of mindless domestic chit-chat to soothe the nerves after the cut and thrust of corporate life, a meat-and-two-veg with a bottle of plonk, a shoes off and feet up in front of an agreeable situation comedy on the television, an early night, maybe, to enjoy a leisurely constitutional around the foothills of desire, our modest bedroom needs meshing comfortably before, weary, content, we drifted off to a shared dreamland. Night, darling. Night, darling.

It was surely not too much to ask, even in a modern marriage.

Apparently it was. Sarah, I was soon to discover to my cost, wanted more. Sharing a life with an entrepreneurial high-flyer had convinced her that she too deserved treats, invitations, trips abroad. 'But what have you *done*, dear?' I would remind her gently. 'These events are for doers, achievers, not hangers-on, however amusing and decorative they may be.'

Sadly, my wife lacked the breadth of vision to see it my way. Indeed, to remind her that she too had a job, very important in its own domestic way, was to risk serious injury from one of the flying objects which had become quite a feature of life at home. I should have foreseen the trouble, of course – headed it off with flowers, flattery and baby talk – but I was really rather too busy at the time to give domestic issues too much thought. My government work simply had to come first.

The stories I could tell you about the espionage game, were it not for the Official Secrets Act – the things I did, the characters

I met! Spooks. Counterspooks. Spooks who were in it for the money, for the glory, for the sheer hell of it. Spooks caught with their trousers down. Left-footed spooks in cocktail dresses and high heels. Fake spooks who weren't really spooks but who distracted the attention of the other side's spooks from the spooks who were. Spook businessmen, spook journalists, spook members of the Royal Shakespeare Company (don't press me for details). Spookettes, easy on the eye and highly trained in seduction techniques that only spooks in cocktail dresses could resist. Spookettes who could seduce with one twitch of the finger, kill with another. Spookettes with fake nipples concealing camera, tape-recorder and first-aid kit for emergencies. Moles. Countermoles. Moletraps. Molettes who –

But no. Unfashionable as it may seem, I shall not be joining the ranks of disaffected ex-spies, prepared to put the lives of former colleagues at risk with boastful, self-serving memoirs. Betrayal has no place in the world of the man whom intelligence chiefs called 'F'.

There were scrapes, of course there were – times when, had it not been for quick-thinking and a certain raw courage, I might today be languishing, pale and unshaven, in some distant gulag rather than dictating these words in my penthouse, Katrina at my side.

On one occasion, Paterson, the junior naval attaché who acted as MI5's ringmaster in Moscow, sent me to a small country railway station in the Kiev region in order to collect some photographs which were to be part of a routine sabotage operation. Having found the film concealed in the way we used most often – rolled up inside a fake toilet roll in a gent's lavatory – I was perturbed to discover that the station was stiff with Russian soldiers.

Thinking quickly, I re-entered the lavatory where, as luck would have it, an ancient ticket-collector was washing his hands. 'Sorry about this, Ivan,' I said, strangling him with the standard-issue length of piano wire kept in the buckle of my belt. After a quick change of uniforms in one of the cubicles, I walked calmly to my train past the soldiers who, I now noticed with a certain wry amusement, were members of a local militia band!

It is, incidentally, a myth that life behind the Iron Curtain lacks excitement of the personal, sophisticated kind. Often, relaxing in a restaurant or hotel bar after a successfully accomplished mission, I would fall into conversation with a fur-clad lovely, apparently eager to further the cause of international friendship with an off-the-record chat, followed by a spot of traditional hospitality back at her place. Unlike their world-weary counterparts in the West, who are likely to react to tales of personal heroism with a shrug and a sneer, the *ninotchkas* were wide-eyed with wonder at the few carefully edited titbits I threw to them as they fell under my spell.

'У тебя есть время?' asked a tall, dark-eyed girl with whom I happened to be sharing a carriage on the train back to Moscow after my close shave in Kiev.

'Если у тебя склонность!' I quipped in reply with a frank appreciative smile.

The girl looked away. 'Очень смешно', she said softly. 'Я думаю, что следующий вопрос было бы так: "До куда ты едешь?" '

I shrugged, temporarily taken aback by the directness of the girl's approach. 'Ладно,' I said, coolly playing it her way. 'По-моему ты девушка которая была повсюду. Едешь ли далеко?'

An attractive blush had come to the girl's face. For a moment I thought she was going to throw herself across the carriage at me there and then. 'Отвяжись!' she said suddenly, her shyness and modesty forgotten in the heat of the moment. 'Отвяжись, или я возму кондуктора!'

It was going to be an interesting journey back to Moscow.

Returning one Sunday evening, tired but satisfied after a routine weekend trip to East Berlin, I was somewhat taken aback to find my wife poring over estate-agents' catalogues at my desk.

'Sorry for interrupting,' I said affectionately, 'but I was wondering if a spot of dinner was on the agenda.'

'Darling!' Sarah leapt up and embraced me rather roughly. 'How did you get on?'

'Fine, fine,' I said, extricating myself. 'What on earth are you doing?'

'Nothing much,' she lied. 'Just a little project. Something your mother suggested.'

Something my mother suggested! Suddenly the full weight of my domestic responsibilities came crashing down on my shoulders. I slumped wearily into an armchair.

'Shoot,' I said. 'Tell me the worst.'

'It won't interest you,' said Sarah, with a fine show of phoney embarrassment. 'I'm opening a gallery – for women painters. It's never been done before.'

'What fun,' I said without enthusiasm. 'And what will you be using for capital?'

'Daddy's helping me. He thinks I need a job. The outlay's quite small anyway.'

I pulled a pocket calculator from my top pocket. 'Run the figures past me then, darling.'

'Figures?'

'Budget, projected turnover, production costs, overheads, stock write-down, tax structure, profit streams – the usual things.'

Sarah laughed and kissed me annoyingly on the nose.

'Perhaps you can help me with all that.'

I sighed. I was all for Sarah finding a hobby but really this was testing my patience to the limit. No budget, Daddy's money, and some half-arsed scheme that would doubtless involve her scurrying about the garrets, studios and art colleges of the country, consorting with God-knows-what sort of riff-raff and scrounger – it was hardly a suitable occupation for the wife of a seasoned entrepreneur.

'Who's going to look after the house?' I asked reasonably. 'Homes don't run themselves, you know.'

'Perhaps we could get someone in,' she said, clearly miffed at the note of realism I had introduced into the discussion. 'Like other people do.'

'Get someone in?' I laughed. 'For the cooking, the entertaining of my guests? Get someone in?'

'Yes.' Sarah was now pouting like a little girl being denied a treat. 'Staff.'

Of course. Staff. Where she came from, staff were the answer to everything. Husband, house, children – staff were always there to look after life's boring trivia, releasing one to attend to more important things: organising jumble sales, running the local Women's Institute, dashing around in aid of a charity ball or, in Sarah's case, setting up some damnfool all-girl art gallery.

I pointed out, as calmly as I was able, that I had hardly married her to 'have someone in', that it was unacceptable for a man in my position to have a wife that worked, indeed that reliable staff were almost impossible to find these days.

Sarah had returned to the desk and was looking through her papers once more.

'I'm doing it, Jonathan,' she said grimly. 'Like it or not, I'm doing it.'

The Harcourt Gallery (naturally, Sarah dropped the Fixx name as effortlessly as she abandoned the last vestiges of loyalty to her husband) opened its doors in a back street of Islington in the summer of 1977. Resisting the temptation to embargo the entire event, which might have appeared mean-spirited, I escorted my celebrated young wife to the occasion.

I remember little of the evening that is relevant to this account. Somewhere in the general haze of jostling bedenimed bodies, Strewel Peter hairstyles, the smell of earnestly puffed Gitanes, I recall there was a sense of a new age dawning – yet another bloody new age. Because, it was true, something had changed. Something that had nothing to do with the sexual politics, environmental politics, Third World politics that preoccupied the unkempt ninnies as they gazed distractedly at the 'work' hanging on walls and littering the floor.

The men – if the luckless, emasculated, apologetic creatures shuffling about in their faded jeans could be described as such – spoke in quiet respectful voices, frequently allowing themselves to be interrupted by their womenfolk, nodding eagerly in agreement at anything, however outrageous or fatuous, they said. Those who, hardly five years ago, had stood tall, proud and hirsute in their Cuban heels, now wore flat sandals, shoulders stooped in an unconscious effort to make themselves look smaller, the occasional prematurely balding pate peeping like a pale winter moon through wispy clouds. Apart from Lord Harcourt, who paid a brief courtesy visit, fighting his way through the scruffs (with barely concealed distaste written all over his face) to congratulate his daughter before very sensibly leaving for dinner in the City, I dare say I was the only real man in the place. The rest had checked their balls in at the door.

The women, I must confess, were something of a surprise. Frankly, I had expected a rabble of big-bottomed lesbians but, apart from the few bruisers that customarily formed Mother's bodyguard, they were almost all attractive – tall, square-shouldered, confident, Amazonian.

Victory had done something for these women. There was a new

sparkle beneath their studiously unplucked eyebrows. Of course, we were among the élite – Sarah's new-found independence fell some way short of mixing with the less stylish members of the sisterhood. This was an evening for the Generalissimas – the movement's unlovely spear-carriers and envelope-lickers had been confined to barracks.

As I wandered, with an increasing sense of bemusement, around the exhibits (a Diana the Huntress constructed entirely out of tampons leaps unbidden to mind), thoughts of an undeniably revisionist nature began occurring to me with a nagging persistence – thoughts of seducing a sister, frolicking with a feminist, nuding it with a New Woman. My innocent daydreams would doubtless be categorised by guests at the Harcourt Gallery as Body Fascism, Genital Aggression or Sexual Terrorism but, dammit, even at the dawning of a new age, a man's a man for all that. And who knows? Perhaps some of these lovely, liberated creatures secretly enjoyed reactionary fantasies of submission and simple adoration of the man for whom political compatibility was insignificant beside the simple yes or no of powerful physical attraction.

Wrong again. I looked a tall, black girl in the eye. She turned away. I winked at a shock-haired redhead. She nudged a friend who stood beside her and both girls laughed openly before returning to their conversation. I gave a girl in a boilersuit an open, attractive smile and she actually mocked me, widening her eyes and allowing her jaw to drop in an unpleasant pantomime of the frustrated male boggler. I was all for feminism but, not for the first time, I found myself wondering why it had to be so confoundedly ill-mannered. These women spoke of role reversal, yet were unprepared to make the first move. For them, the pleasure of rejecting a desirable and powerful man appeared to outweigh the more conventional forms of gratification. Despite their obsession with the right to orgasm, the sisters seemed particularly unwilling to experiment with an acknowledged master in the field.

At some point during that interminable evening, it occurred to me that it was precisely because Sarah had led a pampered and privileged life that she was such an easy prey to the sisters. While many of the women in the room had, if they were to be believed, been brutalised by a legion of randy uncles, benighted parents, loutish husbands and lovers, Sarah's deprivation derived from the soft cocoon in which she had passed her childhood and adolescence. She actually longed for a taste of life's harsh realities but no one had been allowed close enough to be more than mildly beastly. That was her great tragedy.

The talk all around me of self-realisation, self-fulfilment and self-gratification provoked in me feelings of justified resentment.

'You realise this has been set up with Harcourt money,' I told an American woman who appeared to be somewhat over-impressed with Sarah's work. 'Daddy's money.'

The woman shrugged. 'A woman can't choose the prison she's born into. Sarah's was velvet-lined. So what? She escaped. That's what matters.'

This was too much, even for a man of my legendary tolerance. 'But she escaped thanks to me,' I said, rather more loudly than I had intended. '*I* introduced her to the real world. If there was a prison, *I* released her from it. As for the gallery, it took her father's money and my . . . encouragement.'

'And her balls.'

'Not everything is a result of the sexist conspiracy,' I continued, choosing to ignore this particularly stupid remark. 'Sarah might have been an unhappy, inadequate person because that was the way she was. I don't blame her for my problems, if I have them – why should she blame me? It's ridiculous. It's . . . unfair.'

The woman shrugged. 'I may cry,' she said, and walked away.

When Mother (naturally in her element here) asked me to accompany Sarah and a select band of sisters to a celebration dinner at a nearby vegetarian restaurant, I pleaded a headache. There is a limit and yet more earnest self-regarding conversation over disgusting, brown food was some way beyond it.

I needed a dose of reality. Spending the evening in close proximity with the pride of unfettered, loose-limbed modern womanhood had left me longing nostalgically for someone pink, soft and adoring, someone with whom conversation was not an assault course of politically correct attitudes. I wanted a woman, not a person; better, I wanted a girl.

I left the gallery and hurried to a nearby phone-booth. Luckily I had brought with me my trusty little black book, which contained the numbers of countless girlfriends always happy to see an old friend when he was off the leash.

There was no reply from the first number I called. Or from the second. The third was engaged. The fourth – a divorcee, normally a banker on these occasions – actually offered me a bed in the spare room. She was tired, she said.

So was I. As the woman warbled her excuses, I hung up and, pocketing my little black book, walked to the car. It had been a long, dispiriting night.

I must have suffered from some sort of blackout on my way home because, at some point in the early hours of the morning, I found myself, quite inexplicably, cruising the dark streets of Mayfair. On an impulse, I decided to park the car and take a stroll in the night air.

'Looking for business, darling?' said a voice from the shadows.

'As always,' I quipped, smiling at the young black girl with absurdly long legs who now ambled lazily towards me.

After a brief round of negotiations, I allowed her to take me to a small hotel room behind the Playboy Club.

'Any specials?' she asked, removing her shoes.

'Yes,' I said wearily. 'No talk.'

– Losing your touch, were you?

– Do me a favour.

– You must have been approaching forty by now.

– I kept myself in trim. I had filled out a bit, lost some of the swagger of youth. I still looked good although, I confess, my freelance options became somewhat restricted at this stage. More deletions in than additions to the little black book.

– And that had nothing to do with Old Father Time?

– Nothing at all. It was history. There was something about the late seventies, a sort of weird, lop-sided morality. Some of the girls got married and played the fidelity game for a couple of years. Others slowed down. Some became lesbians. There was a lot of that going on.

– How could you tell?

– Easy. Walking down a London street, say five years previously, I'd get a few appreciative glances from the ladies. Nothing gross, mind – but it was there. Suddenly, they'd march by as if I wasn't there. Not interested.

– Lesbians?

– Precisely. Then some of my regulars actually took to feeling sorry for my wife.

– And that was new?

– Of course. All of a sudden, sisterhood was everywhere, even in the bedroom. I'd tell them what went on between Sarah and myself was none of their business but, to tell the truth, they rarely bought it.

– How annoying for you.

– Not really. There's nothing more tiresome than a mistress with a conscience. It takes all the fun out of it. As soon as it gets heavy, I move on.

– So you spent more time with Sarah?

– Good Lord, no. I spent more time in Eastern Europe.

– With the girl on the train.

– And others like her. Are you sure about that Russian waiter, by the way?

– Your translator? John said he was fine.

– It's just that he translated 'I need it now, Englishman!' with the phrase 'Отвяжись!' I thought that meant something like 'Piss off!'

– You're the traveller.

– Just as long as no one's playing games.

A less determinedly self-absorbed woman than Sarah might have detected subtle changes in her husband's lifestyle and behaviour at this time – the growing interest in the politics of the Cold War, the scrambling device installed on a private line, the cool reticence, secretiveness even, of her nearest and dearest.

But the fact is that Sarah's thoughts were elsewhere. The Harcourt Gallery had been something of a success. Artists, dealers and punters engaged in the now fashionable Relevant School sought her out. She was frequently asked to appear on late-night, minority viewing, egghead television programmes. And such was the dearth of reasonably articulate, tolerably good-looking experts in the area of Relevant Art for the modern woman that my wife – my dear little wife, not so long ago the mouse of Colevile Hall – actually became something of a minor celebrity.

I am not by nature a jealous man. If I found myself regretting that I had allowed myself to get hitched to a common-or-garden, publicity-hungry bandwagon-hopper, I had the generosity and breadth of vision to keep such thoughts to myself. So this was the Age of the Woman. *Et alors?* As a lifetime admirer of the fair sex, I was not about to object. For, in a way, the Fixx marriage could be seen as a microcosm of how men and women operated at that time – Sarah, wafting around self-consciously in a cloud-cuckoo land of modish ideas and pseudo-issues, and me, quietly earning real money in the real world and contributing in a real, if discreet, way to national security.

All I asked was that she kept her infernal little business out of the family home – but even this mild request was used against me. I wasn't interested, I was told. I was patronising. I was, to use Sarah's favourite adjective, pompous.

I never stooped to deny these absurd allegations. If it was 'pompous' to insist that Sarah held her joke meetings of like-minded scruffs anywhere but at the house, then I suppose I was pompous. If refusing on principle to pass on telephone messages from fellow-Relevants betrayed a lack of interest, then I guess I wasn't really interested. And if it was patronising to chuckle good-naturedly to myself, while reading a paper, as Sarah earnestly expounded her freshly discovered world view to some new victim then, yes, maybe I was a touch patronising.

Yet, heaven knows, I tried. When she diversified and bought a second gallery – the Artisanne Gallery, she called it – I actually visited the thing the day before it opened.

'Good Lord,' I said as we entered a vast room full of scaffolding and rough, half-finished carpentry. 'They're leaving it a bit late, aren't they?'

'Who?'

'The workmen. You open tomorrow and they haven't even finished the place.'

It was the wrong thing to have said. Apparently the Artisanne Gallery was actually *meant* to look like a building-site. Its cultural significance was that not one plank or rivet in the place had been touched by a male hand. It was, I learnt from the *Guardian* later that week, 'a boldly imaginative comment on sexual stereotyping in contemporary society'.

I mean. How the hell was I to know?

After a while, I began to lose patience with Sarah and her blasted career. She was tiring herself out and, rather more importantly, she was distracting me from work of a more serious kind. It was about time, I decided, that she slowed up and returned to the important business of being a wife.

By a happy coincidence, I was closely involved in work on the Menson pill at the time. Other birth-control pills were, we knew, being restyled away from the attractively feminine nursery-pink colour motif that had once been the vogue to more contemporary, non-sexist colours – blue, yellow, green. I ordered a consumer test, for which my people in Berne were required to produce dummy packs of our rivals' products, packaged authentically but containing placebos.

With the benefit of hindsight, I can see that it was a mistake to bring my work home, particularly when that work happened to be an entirely ineffective packet of birth-control pills, identical to the type Sarah used. Mistakes can so easily happen. The wrong pills can be left by the bedside, the right ones thrown away with other samples.

There followed a month during which I cancelled all trips abroad. I courted Sarah. We had been drifting apart. We should spend more time together. We decided to take a second honeymoon in Paris. Sarah blossomed under the warmth of my attention. She relaxed. She even took to wearing make-up now and then. She wasn't such a bad old stick, I decided. And she was going to make a wonderful mother for the baby which, five weeks after our return, she announced a trifle tearfully was on its way.

Paradoxically, I was rather more excited by the news than she was.

Something changes when two discover that, within the year, they will become three. A shift of perspective. A softening of attitudes. An awareness, deep down where it matters, that you are now part of a process incomparably more important than the hustle and bustle, the hurly-burly, of everyday life. Career, money, pleasure – all those things that, only yesterday, were at the centre of your universe – are now no more than laughable distractions. You are about to bring a new being into the world – a vulnerable, feeble, pink, trusting little thing that will depend utterly upon you for years to come. Your life changes. You start talking about the nursery, buying minuscule, fluffy articles of clothing, thinking of names. You become proudly aware that you, a mere couple, are about to become society's investment in the future. Parents. Mummy and Daddy.

At any rate, so I've heard. Personally, I had work to do, and the old in-tray was gaining weight even faster than Sarah was. That month dedicated to Operation Pudding Club had played merry hell with my schedule and now I was suffering from a bad case of the black diaries. Scarcely had the Bollinger hit the bin before I was obliged to catch up with some old contacts on a lengthy trip around the Eastern bloc.

When I returned two or three months later, I was touched to find that Sarah was already showing signs of motherhood. It does something to a chap, that little swell in the wife's stomach, doesn't it? I've known normally quite sensible men spend hours gazing at it, prodding it, making damnfool goo-goo noises at it, and I'd be a liar if I didn't admit that, as Sarah waddled about the place, it did something for me too, made me a happier, more relaxed person.

Because, at last, I had found something to slow her down. Her movements became more stately every day. She hardly referred to her galleries at all now. She grumbled at the work. She delegated responsibility. She stayed home whenever possible. What an anchor that little devil turned out to be – and what an asset! Here was something for which you couldn't 'get someone in'. Not before time, Sarah was beginning to act like a proper wife, mooching around at home, leaving me to attend to the world outside.

Already I could sense that fatherhood was going to suit me.

It was while I was abroad showing my new personal assistant Trudi the ropes vis-à-vis the Bangkok market that I received a telegram from Mother telling me that Sarah had produced a baby girl. It was a bit of a blow, to tell the truth. Girls are all right when they grow up and visit you at Christmas and generally make a fuss of you, but in the mean time they're nothing but an expensive nuisance. Suppressing my disappointment, I responded with a suitably gushing cable of congratulation and confirmed that I would be home as soon as matters in Bangkok had reached a satisfactory conclusion.

Four

'Great spirits have always found violent opposition from mediocrities.'

Albert Einstein

16
Compassion fatigue

– Does the term 'cluck' mean anything to you?

– Now what?

– 'Transmitter'? 'Talking head'? 'Disc jockey'? I understood they were used in intelligence.

– Some of our operatives enjoyed speaking a sort of private gobbledegook. Personally I never had time for it. I had work to do.

– I've been reading around the subject for the deep background you requested – the touches of authenticity for the second draft.

– And?

– I came across this passage in J. M. White's History of British Intelligence Since 1945. *I thought it might interest you.*

– Shoot.

– 'The policy of "disinformation", supplying the other side with deliberately misleading information, reached its apotheosis during the early 1970s. Hitherto the service had used professional operatives, double-agents who had been "turned", for this work but it soon became clear that the KGB were able to ascertain within weeks which of their agents were providing them with bona fide information and which were not. By using agents who knew that the secrets they were supplying were phoney, British intelligence was, it seemed, playing into the hands of the Russians.

'In 1972, MI5 in consort with the CIA adopted a new approach with an operation that was codenamed "Talking Head". A number of new, inexperienced agents were recruited – businessmen, mostly, but also some journalists – and were given apparently top-secret assignments. None of the new boys was told that the "secrets" they were delivering were worthless, indeed to this day many of them believe that they were an essential part of the service. In fact, they were no more than an elaborate network of false trails and leads, a smokescreen behind which the genuine operations worked.'

–Interesting but irrelevant.

–'A key element of Operation Talking Head lay in the recruitment of the "agents". Unusually, the service was looking for characters who travelled to Eastern Europe as part of their job, who would be willing to work for the government, but above all who would be entirely unreliable. It was essential that they should be susceptible to any ploy or distraction – sex, money, blackmail – the KGB laid in their path. Thus, in their cups or in their hotel bedrooms, they would unwittingly supply the other side with disinformation. In other words, a particular type of agent was needed – weak, garrulous, open to every kind of flattery and temptation. These characters were known by MI5 as "transmitters" or "disc jockeys"; at CIA headquarters, they were nicknamed more colloquially as "clucks" – frightened chickens that ran pointlessly hither and thither making as much distracting noise as possible.

–Ah, Talking Head. Yes I knew about that, of course.

–You weren't part of it?

–I was one of those behind the smokescreen. Now leave me alone. I need to work.

–Of course.

–Anyway, would a cluck really be of interest to the service today, be as sought after as I am?

–You certainly appear to be sought after. They're still down there, you know. Waiting.

–Let me just finish.

On the occasion of my fortieth birthday, I sat in the summer house at Colevile Hall and reflected. It was a warm evening and, in the gathering gloom, bats could be seen darting in and out of the croquet hoops on the Great Lawn. The only sounds to be heard were the distant hooting of owls in the park and, from the house, the dull throb of disco music. My guests were at play in the Pleasure Lounge.

Where am I going? I asked myself in philosophic mode. Where have I been? Has it all been worth it? How can one truly estimate 'worth'? Achievement, money, peer-group popularity, Colevile, a family, the imminent prospect of my greatest romantic adventure – were they true 'worth'? Indeed, what was I 'worth' – me, personally? Pondering these and other of life's big questions, I totted up a few numbers on my pocket calculator. Yes, it appeared that I was 'worth' quite a lot.

There were items on the debit side, of course there were: casualties that littered the path behind me, a certain notoriety of reputation. It was regrettable, yet there was no point in dwelling on the disappointments of the past.

If that sounds harsh, remember that I, like many others, was suffering from what the experts call 'compassion fatigue'. Of course, I was sorry that the older generation – Mother, Harcourt, Marjorie – had paid the price for their wilful selfishness. Naturally, I felt bad that my wife, confused by the conflicting demands of domestic life and her ridiculous chain of galleries, was tottering from one tiresome emotional crisis to another. It gave me no pleasure whatsoever to note that my contemporaries from Melton Hall – stooped, ridiculous balding creatures these days – had already given up on life, hoisting the white flag at the first whiff of grapeshot. And, yes, I worried about Catherine, who spent so much time flopping about gormlessly with a bunch of part-time anarchists in a South London squat.

I felt terrible about all this, but what, at the end of the day, could I do? Get on with it, that's what. From the summer house, I glanced across the Great Lawn. Yes. Get on with it, and cultivate my garden.

By now it was quite a garden, to tell the truth.

Even before the *annus mirabilis* of 1979 when, with the long-awaited arrival of the businessmen's government, we corporate tigers could at last break cover and roam the plains at will, those of us at the sharp end of national life had formed what I called the 'New Establishment'.

The age of the wealth-creator, the good marketing man, was dawning, the country was soon to bask, as it does today, in the warmth of robust self-interest. Yet at this time, the great British public – Mr and Mrs Average Loser on the Street, that is – still clung to the absurd notion that certain standards of public life still pertained, that the concerned backbench MP, the mercilessly correct TV probe-merchant, the incorruptible silk were somehow above the quick in-out, no-questions-asked, keep-your-nose-clean financial deal, that they actually lived off their *salaries*, for heaven's sake.

Today we can smile at such quaintness but then it was important for those in the public eye to appear untainted, to be 'above suspicion'. Of course, it was too much to expect. We in the New

Establishment knew that money was interesting again, greed was back in fashion; Joe Public would doubtless wake up and join the party five or six years hence, but in the meantime there was work to do, fortunes to be made.

It soon became known among public life's coming men – and women, I was pleased to note – that a discreet financial interest in the concerns of Jonathan Peter Fixx would inevitably yield a respectable (or, if you were particularly lucky, unrespectable) return. Nothing on paper, mind – no names, no questions asked, the noddies of Company House, HM Customs and Excise and the Inland Revenue left chasing their tails. Dividends payable to my influential backers tended to arrive in the form of consultancy fees for obscure West German corporations, or one-off payments from august Scandinavian institutes researching into arcane social problems.

Not that I was some form of vulgar broker – the gambles of the average City spiv interested me not one jot – but if you had power where it mattered (in the House, the High Court, the loftier reaches of the media), Fixx was your man.

Now is not the time to bewilder the ordinary reader with the complexities of my business concerns. Arbitrage, commodity pillaging, overnight mushroom financing – I'll spare you the details. It is merely relevant to note that during my travels, on behalf of the government as well as that of Control Corp, Menson and other businesses, I had found myself becoming increasingly involved in certain markets not normally listed in the City pages of the *Financial Times*.

My work as a highly confidential public servant was also paying dividends vis-à-vis the right contacts in the right places. To be sure, the mention in despatches, the call to the Palace, had been rather slower in coming than I had anticipated but then, I reasoned to myself, peerages were no longer the meaningless baubles they had become during the sixties, when every sort of party hack, goody-two-shoes lefty and payola peer of the Talbot variety had thronged the Upper House. Today the concept of ennoblement once again meant something; peerages were there to be earned; it took time.

Not that I was content to wait my turn. A spy, at the end of the day, is more than just another civil servant, nose-picking his way through the paperwork in the sure knowledge that his mindless devotion to duty will be recognised, probably when he's too old to enjoy it. He's a playmaker, an improviser. If events are not happening quickly enough, he goes out and makes them happen. That's how it is in the world of espionage.

It had become clear that the relatively low-level work I was doing for Colonel Scott was getting me nowhere career-wise in the intelligence game. I was cool, courageous, reliable and yet, when all was said and done, I was being used as no more than a delivery boy.

So when a female friend in Berlin casually introduced me to a senior figure in the East German Foreign Ministry, I was content to play it her way. When this man, whose name I am not at liberty to divulge, invited me to deliver and collect material from some really quite well-known names in British society – vice-chancellors, newspaper editors, minor members of the Royal Family – I hesitated for not one moment. Single-agent, double-agent, Fixx was never one for doing things by halves. It was promotion, after all. Doubtless, at some later stage, when my Eastern bloc friends had shown rather more of their hand to me, I would shop the lot of them to MI5. If that failed to bring me recognition and promotion in the service, nothing would.

Thus it was that new doors were opened, invitations to the High Table at Poncyface College, University of Cantab, extended to me. 'I gather we have friends in common,' a pompous old traitor would say out of the corner of his mouth, having sidled up to me at one of the many nobby receptions I now attended as a matter of course. 'Why not come and have dinner with me at Whites next week? We ought to get to know one another.'

Life became much simpler, with both the New and the Old Establishment in my pocket. I discovered that, as if by magic, I wielded a certain influence that was of benefit to my affairs, business and personal. Tiresome legal problems involving the activities of some of my companies failed to reach the courts. The efforts of dogged smear-merchants found their way on to the editor's spike. The odd personal assistant who, through her own carelessness, found herself in difficulties (too virile for my own good, that's me) was attended by the best medical attention Harley Street could offer. Life's little irritants tend to fade away once you know the right people in the right places.

Or, at least, most of life's little irritants. While my professional affairs, thanks entirely to my own enterprise and efforts, were taking off into the stratosphere, my domestic concerns remained firmly earthbound.

I press the 'Search' button on my life as a young father, husband and provider in the hope of finding the briefest cameo of normal family happiness, but in vain. Boredom, disappointment, resentment, discord – the scenes flash painfully before my eyes. There must have been the odd moment of reconciliation, tenderness, but I'm damned if I can find it.

And yet I tried. The trinkets acquired at airports during my foreign tours, the guest appearances at the occasional neighbourhood cheese-and-wine parties for which Sarah had developed a liking, the quality time I devoted quite often during the evening to the child Jennifer (dull name, I always thought, but I had to be away for the christening and, needless to say, no one saw fit to consult me), the ruinous expense of a loft extension for the infant and its nanny – these were the contributions of a man who took seriously his onerous new responsibilities as a 'family man'.

The fact is, Sarah and I were drifting apart. It was not little Jenny's fault – in her subdued, amenable way, she was quite an acceptable child, if slightly clinging – nor, to be fair, was it entirely my wife's. Somehow, time had been unkind to us: while my horizons broadened, hers contracted. She actually seemed to enjoy the pointless dinner parties, the tennis-club gossip, the messing about in the garden of a Sunday afternoon, the swarms of cute-faced children scrounging on the doorstep for this and that every Hallowe'en and Christmas, the school runs, the mini-scandals, the chumminess, the rivalries, the chit-chat over privet hedges. For Sarah, former daughter of the manor, suburban life was a new experience; for me, it was like returning to prison.

A more imaginative person might have understood that, for an international entrepreneur and sophisticated intelligence operative, the experience of jostling with faded mediocrities and their infernal kiddies in the outer reaches of Fulham lacked a certain excitement, but sadly Sarah's ability to understand the complexity of the man of action she had married was fading as quickly as her looks. Motherhood did something for a woman, I knew that – gave her a voice, a confidence, a territory to defend – but quite why the relatively straightforward business of producing and rearing a rather ordinary child transformed the simple girl I had married into a terrifying, round-the-clock grouch was beyond my understanding.

Dinner times were the worst, as I recall.

'Evening repast not to Sir's satisfaction?' she might say as I picked at the bland, homely fare defrosted for the occasion.

Or, when I tucked into one of the more edible meals with a degree of no-nonsense enthusiasm, 'You don't have to go at it as if you haven't eaten for a week.'

'How was your day, Sarah?' she said to herself one evening, with the steely sarcasm she had taken to affecting. 'Oh, my day was just great, thank you very much. I took Jenny to the doctor – you remember we have a daughter, well she's been ill with croup – then I had to visit the gallery and do the shopping. Then I came back to slave over the meal you're pigging down this very minute. Another great day for Mrs Fixx.'

'Congratulations,' I said good-humouredly.

Now and then, if I was lucky and Sarah's hormones were not playing her up, such outbursts of domestic guerrilla activity would gradually give way to a sullen ceasefire. 'I'll be out tomorrow evening,' I remember saying on one occasion. 'So you won't have to slave then.'

'Another working dinner?' she asked in a dangerously cheerful voice. One of the most difficult aspects of Sarah's behaviour were her unpredictable mood changes – from violent anger to sniffling self-pity, from sarky woman-of-the-world to pathetic little-girl-lost. It was enviable in a way, this ability one moment to lob a glass of gin across a room with accompanying expletives, and the next, before retaliation could be meted out, to crumple pitifully to the floor in a fine display of terminal wretchedness. Only someone as cunning as my wife would have dared to try it.

'As it happens, yes,' I replied. 'I'm needed to close a deal at the Caprice.'

'Couldn't someone else close it? Just this once.'

Sensing that Sarah was moving into sodden, woe-is-me mode, I attempted to head her off.

'Wish they could,' I said tenderly. 'Deal's too big to delegate.'

'As usual.'

'It's the way I work.'

'Don't tell me. Hands-on management.'

I smiled – there were times when I thought Sarah was getting the hang of the Open Marriage game.

'Right,' I said, with an endearingly raffish wink.

Moments later, as I wearily wiped the contents of my plate from my trousers, I found myself reflecting how Sarah's attitude these days gave new resonance to the term 'no-win situation'. Exclude her from confidential plans, and I was accused of cold indifference; include her, and I ended up with dinner in my lap.

Clearly something had to give.

To tell the truth, my normal release from the grim routine of domestic life – a regular and well-organised round of infidelity – was no longer as satisfactory as it had been.

I had a nice set-up, of course – the three or four mistresses that I kept afforded me a choice mix of exotic pleasures. If I felt lost or insecure, I could visit Mary who worshipped and mothered me. For my wilder, more dangerous moments, I could submit to Juliana for whom nothing was unnatural. Then, for a spot of variety, there was always Alison and Nicola whose passion for one another, I discovered, did not exclude playtime with a third party of the opposite sex.

That arrangement would last, say, six months before I'd decide to introduce new blood into the team, letting go the girls whose tricks had become predictable or who showed signs of succumbing to a case of the emotionals, and recruiting someone new and amusing.

Yet, as widely and entertainingly accommodated as I was, something was wrong, something nagged at me even more persistently than my disgruntled wife. It was all right, this relentless thrashing about in different bedrooms, but a man of my maturity and stature needed more. I yearned for an emotional context in which to live, for someone who would put me back in touch with my deeper, nobler feelings.

Love? Possibly. Probably. Yes.

Quite why, one summer's day, I found myself on the wrong side of the river, jostled by members of London's underclass, on a train bound for Stockwell of all places remains a mystery. I had been scheduled to visit Juliana but suddenly the idea of an afternoon being knocked about by a sado-masochistic nymphomaniac, however beautiful, had seemed more like work than play. I was looking for adventure perhaps, danger, the unpredictable.

It happened that the only address in my little black book which would take me away from my normal stamping-ground was Catherine's. She had disappeared out of my life of late, even declining an invitation to the Harcourt Gallery which was the sort of social event that, under normal circumstances, she would have liked. I worried. What was she up to in that squat of hers? Who were her friends? I wanted to stay in touch.

My concern deepened when I reached the address that she had given me. It was a large Victorian house in a derelict terrace. There were graffiti on the walls and all the windows were boarded up. Deciding that to appear on the doorstep unannounced and dressed in a well-cut City suit was unwise, I crossed the road to a squalid, run-down pub where, pushing through a rabble of unemployed scroungers, I ordered a drink which I took to a grimy table on the pavement.

After a while, a rickety, hand-painted van drew up outside the house. A young black man jumped out, ran up the steps and hammered on the door. Catherine opened it and greeted him with rather more warmth than I would have wished. She called over her shoulder and three other people, a couple of rather plain girls and another man, emerged. They opened the back of the van and, with a certain amount of shouting and laughter, manhandled a large bed up the steps and into the house. Minutes later, they came out again and chatted on the doorstep. Catherine glanced over in my direction. She had seen me. She said something to her friends and walked over to where I sat, coolly smoking a cigarillo.

'What's going on?' she said, pushing her dark curls away from her face, which was still glowing from her exertions. I took a sip of my drink and smiled. In her colourless T-shirt, torn jeans and thick-soled shoes, she could have been a model for squatter chic in the *Tatler*.

'I wanted to see where you lived.'

'We have a phone.'

'I didn't want to intrude.'

'Of course not.' Catherine sat down at the table opposite me. 'Want to come in? Meet my friends?'

I glanced across the road where the group outside the house were still talking.

'I'd better get back,' I said. 'Some other time perhaps.'

'Right.' Catherine stood up.

'How about dinner on Thursday?' I said quickly. 'It's been a long time.'

She gave me an odd, quizzical smile and shrugged.

'Why the hell not?' she said.

We met and then, a few days later, we met again. I showed her around the office, chatted about business life, revealed one or two amusing tricks of the fast-money trade. Despite a convincing show of nonchalance, Catherine was intrigued by my world, I could tell. After all, here people actually did things, achieved; it was quite a novelty.

On our second date, she spoke more openly about her fellow-squatters, who were all, as I had expected, artists, students, would-be writers – time-wasters of that ilk. Her best friend, she said, was the lead singer with a group called Swinging Bollocks and the Bendover Boys. I nodded seriously. Was he, did they . . . ? Catherine smiled and shook her head. 'We're *friends*,' she said. The sense of relief which I felt quite took me by surprise.

Almost without noticing, we began to meet regularly. It was a relatively quiet time for me, with the business running itself and Sarah apparently too absorbed in domestic nonsense to need me at home. As for Catherine, she liked to joke that it was only the prospect of a square meal in a warm restaurant that kept her coming back. I knew that, for both of us, our secret family outings were special.

'This isn't getting strange, is it, Jon?' she asked me one evening over dinner. I had inadvertently let slip that Sarah believed I was meeting a visiting Wall Street broker.

'Strange? How?'

'If Sarah doesn't know, it's almost as if we're, you know, seeing each other.'

I smiled. 'Listen,' I said, quietly but firmly. 'You may not know it, but you're helping me through a very difficult period. It's what families are for.'

'And what are wives for?'

'I'll tell Sarah eventually. She has problems of her own right now.'

'I don't like it,' said Catherine.

Fortunately, at this point, the main course arrived and, by the time Catherine had worked her way through her plate (and most of mine), Sarah had been completely forgotten.

Although it would be harsh to blame her directly for the death of her father Lord Harcourt, I fear that Sarah's hands were not entirely clean.

It began with a problem of accommodation. Concerned that my wife's brain was turning to muesli, that my daughter was being raised among unacceptable role models and, more importantly, that my address at the dull end of Fulham was hardly suitable for a man who was about to become a peer of the realm, I resolved to move the entire Fixx ménage out of London.

There were predictable squawks of resistance from the distaff side (friends, school, gallery, the usual excuses), which rose to a crescendo when I suggested that the obvious family residence was now Colevile Hall.

'And what about Daddy?'

'Rattling about in that enormous house? It's time he found something more suitable for a man of his age. One of those nice farmhouses on the edge of the estate. I'm sure he'll see the logic of it.'

Sarah laughed in a rather vulgar, horsy way.

'Daddy would rather die than leave Colevile. You must know that.'

'He'd be near his beloved only child,' I said with a hint of sarcasm.

'Try it then. Ask him. I can't wait to hear what he says.'

As Sarah well knew, old Harcourt and I were not on the best of terms these days. The fact that, before she went mad and died on a hunting field in Ireland, Marjorie had blown the seamy details of Project Harcourt to him hardly helped, I suppose.

'Perhaps you could have a word with him,' I suggested.

'Perhaps,' said Sarah, 'I'll do just that.'

She let me down, of course. Within days, I had received a typed letter from Lord Harcourt. It read:

Dear Fixx,

Sarah tells me you have it in mind to move into Colevile Hall, notwithstanding the fact that I am in residence here and had until recently intended to remain so for the rest of my life.

Your characteristically crude initiative has, in fact, clarified certain matters pertaining to inheritance which had been concerning me for some time. The thought that, after my death, you will become the master of Colevile Hall is, for reasons that you above all will understand, deeply troubling to me.

It was therefore with considerable relief that I heard from Sarah that she cannot foresee any time when she will want to move from London, indeed that she would be delighted if the decision as to what to do with Colevile Hall were taken off her shoulders.

To be brief, we decided that I should indeed move from the house forthwith into one of the farms but that, rather than put it on the market, we shall donate it to a suitable cause.

Sarah tells me that the Home for Battered Wives is looking for a headquarters and this, given what she has told me of some of your recent behaviour, appears to be an apt beneficiary.

The papers will shortly be drawn up and I will amend my will accordingly. Thereafter the matter will be closed.

Yours,

Harcourt

The double-agent moves in a strange, shadowy world. One day, it's a discreet chat over port and cigars with a senior civil servant and mole, the next an urgent case conference in a Soho strip club with a semi-literate busboy and fox. Moles talked, foxes acted. Right now I needed action.

'Is Carlos there?' I asked the manager of the Xstasy Club. 'Tell him he's needed for a football match.'

I sat watching one of the girls put the club snake through its paces. It was a quiet night with only a few solitary punters dotted about the dark room.

'Problem?' A swarthy little man with a head like a billiard ball sat down at my table. I knew of Carlos only by reputation, but he was said to be effective.

'I think my cover's blown,' I said, staring at the stage, where the girl was laconically performing an unnatural act with her pet.

'Who?'

I told him.

'Just teach him a lesson, will you,' I said quietly.

'I teach only one lesson.'

I frowned. It was hardly the moment for a detailed discussion of the man's business methods.

'Go for it,' I said.

After the tragic events of that week, I realised too late that it had been a mistake to talk to Carlos. A retired terrorist who now kept his hand in by doing odd jobs for the Russian embassy was unlikely, it turned out, to understand nuance, subtlety, the sensitive approach. He had gone too far. My inexperience at the sharp end of the intelligence game let me down badly, I admit it.

I still find it faintly shocking that the murder of a senior Conservative peer, blown sky high in front of his own house, could cause so little fuss. The nation was stunned, of course it was – a car bomb at Colevile Hall, whatever next? – but, so hardened to outrage had we become, there was no particular surprise.

Within hours of Harcourt's death, no less than three separate terrorist groups, all of them Irish, had claimed credit for the attack, the great and good had put out the usual sombre, good-hearted nonsense about the evils of political violence, unnamed Intelligence sources had refused to comment on reports that Harcourt worked for them, and the wave of national paranoia had pushed the government up a couple of points in the opinion polls. The sewer rats, of course, had a field day.

Tributes poured in: from the Queen, from ministers, peers, captains of industry and, of course, from his own family. On the day of Harcourt's funeral, I delivered a few heartfelt words on the steps of his beloved Colevile Hall. I was prompted to reflect, I said, how the saddest occasions can serve to unite those previously riven with discord. Overcome by quiet, manly emotion, I was unable to continue.

Together we stood for a brief photo-call: the dignified head of the family, the weeping wife, the solemn child; behind us, the lovely old house that had meant, and would continue to mean, so much to the Harcourt family. There was hope for the future here, strength in a family dynasty that, even in these troubled times, would stare tragedy in the face and survive.

It was all very moving.

Unfortunately, before the flowers on her father's grave had withered, Sarah was back among the rubber-glove set, all semblance of loyalty to her family and its ancestral home having been abandoned.

Disappointing as her ill-tempered departure was to me personally, it was not without some advantages. The various rationalisation plans I had in mind for Colevile Hall were going to be almost impossible to put into operation while she mooched about the place, lugubriously sorting out clothes and weeping over old teddies discovered in bottom drawers. Then again, she insisted on treating the staff like old friends – never a good idea, but particularly unwise at a time of change and reform. Naturally, sensing a certain robustness in their new master, the servants turned to Sarah for their daily orders. I let it pass pro tem; their time would come.

It turned out that, somewhat carelessly, Harcourt had annulled his will the day after he had sent me his ill-advised poison-pen letter and that he had not yet met the Battered Home sisters in order to finalise the transfer of Colevile to their dubious cause. There was therefore no will. According to my lawyers, all legal precedent pointed to the house, the land and all its contents being made over jointly to Sarah and myself.

There were threats, there was hysteria, there was much hand-wringing and boo-hooing when I announced that I planned to move to Colevile Hall immediately. At one point Sarah threatened to take me to court, but the fight went out of her when a thick file of legal documents prepared by my people arrived the next morning. She insisted that, if I lived at Colevile, it would be without her and Jenny; I agreed that, at least while I set the place in order, we would spend less time together.

'And you'll look after the staff?' she said in a quiet, defeated tone.

'Of course.'

'This is it, you know.'

'We'll see. You're upset now. We'll look at the situation in a couple of months.'

Streamlining an establishment which is only a couple of wings short of being a stately home, a house that has been allowed to tick over in more or less the same way for generations, is a delicate operation, requiring patience, tact and diplomacy. Unfortunately, there was no time for any of that and I was obliged to dive straight in with my radical rationalisation plan.

On the afternoon of Sarah's departure, I assembled the staff of Colevile Hall and told them they were all dismissed. I could tell from their bewildered expressions that this spot of belt-tightening – the place was overmanned, mostly with wizened retainers whose gloomy, shuffling demeanour I found depressing – took them aback but I chose not to give my reasons to a group of throwbacks, who could hardly be expected to understand modern business methods.

The head butler, a watery-eyed old fool called Johnson who had been with Harcourt for a good half century, stepped forward.

'I was given to understand by Miss Sarah – '

'*Miss* Sarah, Johnson?'

The fact that the head butler was unable to grasp the change in my wife's status since her father's death was somehow indicative of the sloppiness of the place.

The old man tried again. ' – by *Lady* Sarah, that the staff would remain unchanged.'

'Really?' I said coolly. 'She had no right to tell you that, Johnson, particularly since she has refused to live here. As you know, His Lordship's death hit her very hard. No, Johnson, I'm in charge now and, death duties being what they are, I have to make certain economies.' One of the parlour-maids was sniffing into her handkerchief. 'Believe me,' I concluded, 'this hurts me more than it's going to hurt you.'

Over the following days, Johnson, showing surprising spirit, mounted something of a rearguard action, ringing Sarah, even involving the local press, so that I was finally obliged to abandon the civilised, low-key approach I normally favour.

'Drop this nonsense once and for all,' I told him one evening, having summoned him to my study, 'or I'll be forced to reveal that you systematically cheated my father-in-law for over fifty years.'

'Cheated?'

'I happen to know that you helped yourself, on a weekly basis, to three pints of beer, a bag of coal from the cellar, and that every Christmas you enjoyed a bottle of his best brandy.'

'At His Lordship's insistence, I did, yes.'

'An agreement, was it? In writing? Part of your contract of employment? Perhaps you could let me see it.'

'We have no contract. Colevile is not like that. Or at least it wasn't.'

'I make that over sixty thousand pints of best bitter, eighteen tons of coal, and a good fifty bottles of brandy you owe me.'

Johnson sagged visibly.

'There's not going to be much left of that month's salary I promised you, is there?' I chuckled winningly. 'Don't take on the big boys, Johnson. It's not worth it.'

In the end, I agreed to let the entire staff go with six weeks' pay, an official waiver covering the various items stolen from their employer over the years and an adequate reference for each of them. As an afterthought, I kept on the gamekeeper since I didn't have to see him every day and I was rather looking forward to inviting my friends down to shoot some birds.

As a final lesson in life to the rebellious old butler, I bounced Johnson's cheque and wrote out a new one only after his stumblingly ill-written begging letters began to irritate me. I doubt if he has tried to out-box an employer again.

Now that I was a member of the landed gentry, I might have been expected to embrace a more dignified, middle-aged way of life, ease off, slow down, take stock. Yet I was damned if I could stop myself cranking up the merry-go-round of sybaritic pleasure once more. I was rich, successful, attractive; I had my own stately pile in which to play and, as long as my wife continued to sulk in suburbia, I was free.

Fun was back in fashion for the first time since the late sixties; indeed, this was much better. Then it was on the street, democratic, shared, a political act, play-power. Now it was just play, and only those in the new élite could join in. Other people – I thought of my visits to Stockwell – were having rather a bad time of it. The world outside was more squalid and run down than ever, which in some indefinable way made this, the feverish round-the-clock fooling around with forbidden substances and/or each other, even better.

We had worked for it, hadn't we? We had earned it, paid our dues. Now it was our turn.

In fact, had Sarah not vowed so solemnly never to set foot in Colevile Hall again, she might have been quite startled to see the old place now. It was unrecognisable.

The Great Hall had become the Dance Room, complete with tables, banquettes, flashing lights and outsize video screen. The library had lost most of its books, the general feeling among my pals being that ancient leatherbound tomes of high learning were somewhat out of place in what we now called the Pleasure Lounge. The dining-room had a snooker-table, the sitting-room was a television lounge, complete with an extensive collection of exotic videos. A well-disguised double-mirror had been fitted in the guest bedroom, affording those in a small adjoining room – me, a couple of totties, maybe a guest celebrity – an intimate and often hilarious glimpse of unwitting new guests at play.

Colevile, in short, had been modernised.

My only disappointment was that, throughout this exciting and fulfilling period of my life, Catherine had declined my repeated invitations to visit the new family home. 'Will Sarah be there?' she would ask. Of course not. 'Maybe some other time then.' Didn't she trust me? An odd look. 'What do *you* think, bruv?'

I understood. It was not me that she didn't trust, it was herself. And maybe she was right – the weaker sex were never more so than when I was on song.

In the end, I outflanked her with an invitation she was unable to refuse: a weekend at Colevile with Mother and a few close friends to celebrate my fortieth birthday.

'Welcome to Jonathan's mid-life crisis,' was Mother's characteristically sour verdict, as one of the attractive young parlour-maids I now employed showed her into the Dance Room.

Behind her, Catherine gave a low whistle of surprise.

'Approve?' I smiled.

'It's different,' she said. 'I'll give you that.'

It turned out to be an amusing, but largely uneventful weekend. Mother took every opportunity to nag at me about Sarah and the child. When was I going home? Was it not time I faced up to my responsibilities? Surely I owed it to 'little Jenny' to be at least a part-time father. Resisting the temptation to riposte that a grandmother known in certain circles as 'Madam Diddle', whose main claim to fame was as an expert on self-abuse, was hardly in a position to pronounce on family responsibility, I coolly deflected the conversation away from domestic matters. This was hardly the moment. I had guests to entertain.

The small group I had invited for my birthday was an agreeable mix of friends, celebrities and ex-lovers. There was an advertising millionaire and his teenage research assistant, a former actress who did louche, interesting things in the publicity line, a marquis with a small drug habit, a fun-loving chat-show host, a couple of versatile models and – an afterthought, this – my friend Nicola, whose affair with Alison was going through a rocky patch and who was, as she put it, 'anxious to meet new people'.

If that social mix failed to divert Mother's prurient attention away from Catherine and me, nothing would.

My little step-sister, I concluded that weekend, was improving with age. Now twenty-seven, her attempts to play down her wanton, natural beauty with a no-nonsense, one-of-the-lads style had never appeared more futile. Even the studiously sexless clothes that she wore, by making not the slightest concession to the astonishing figure they contained, merely served to accentuate it.

She didn't fool me. I sensed that, from behind the veneer of modish, seen-it-all indifference, a warm, vibrant, sensual woman would one day emerge. It was only a matter of time.

Yet she had no boyfriends. It was strange. I began to worry. Was it possible that those formative years spent surrounded by Mother's dubious camp followers had diverted her from the straight and narrow? I knew how to find out and, having had a word with Nicola (who required little encouragement), I set up a controlled experiment. It was risky but, as head of the family, I needed to know where I stood.

Sitting in the summer house, alone and deep in thought, I stubbed out my cigar. Catherine would be in bed by now. As luck would have it, I had put her in the main guest room – the Mirror Room, as those in the know had come to call it – and I would be able to check out the action at first hand . . .

By the time I had positioned myself in the small room next door, Catherine was lying in her dressing-gown, reading a book on the bed. For some minutes, I watched her through the double-mirror as, absorbed in her book, she relaxed, toying with her hair, scratching her leg, stretching.

After about half an hour, there was a knock at the door. The hidden microphone in the room picked up Catherine's surprised 'Come in'.

It was Nicola, of course.

'Hi,' she said softly, almost as if she were expected. 'D'you have a moment?'

'Sure.' Catherine smiled and put down her book.

Nicola walked in and sat on the end of the bed. She was wearing dark red lipstick – an odd choice of make-up, I thought, for someone who claimed to be preparing for bed. It made her look older than she was, predatory, decadent.

'I couldn't sleep,' she said with deceptively innocent girlishness. 'I felt like a chat.'

'It must be the excitement,' said Catherine, sitting up on the bed.

Nicola laughed. 'What a bunch, eh?' she said.

They talked for a while and joked about some of the guests. To my annoyance, I discovered that both of them were finding the weekend's entertainment less than enthralling.

After a few minutes, Catherine grew restless.

'Well,' she said, with a fake yawn. 'Time to turn in.'

Nicola didn't move from the bed.

'I was rather hoping to stay here,' she said in a quiet, insistent voice.

Catherine looked only slightly surprised.

'Ah,' she said.

For a moment, there was silence in the guest bedroom. Next door, I was caught up in a turmoil of conflicting emotions. Of course I was interested to see what would happen next – show me a man who wouldn't be – and yet I knew that my natural curiosity would quickly be stifled by the sense of pain and betrayal if Catherine succumbed.

'Nicky,' she said, looking down. 'I'm not – '

Without a word, Nicola made her move. Leaning across the bed, she interrupted with a soft but determined kiss. Apparently too astonished or too terrified to react, Catherine sat bolt upright. It was only when Nicola stealthily introduced a hand into her dressing-gown that she broke free.

'What I was going to say,' she said, standing up, 'is I'm not . . . like that.'

'None of us are until we try.'

Catherine walked to the door and opened it. 'I think I'll take that on trust,' she said, less flustered now. 'I enjoyed our little chat.'

'It's nice, you know.'

'Goodnight.'

Nicola shrugged and walked slowly to where Catherine stood.

'Pity,' she said. 'Some other time perhaps.'

Pecking my little step-sister on the lips, she left the room.

It was a relief, as you can imagine. For a moment, sitting there alone, I had found the prospect of yet more deviance in the family (was I to be the only Fixx with normal, straightforward appetites?) oddly unsettling. Catherine locked the door and, deep in thought, wandered towards the mirror. She stood there, not two feet away from me, and stared into my face. Then, with a soft 'phew' of relief, she let the dressing-gown slip from her shoulders to the floor.

Have you ever used a double-mirror? It's unnerving, I can tell you. You want to reach out and touch the other person, make contact; it's natural – or at least it would be under other circumstances. I felt uneasy, yet unable to leave.

Suddenly, to my horror, Catherine put her face close to the mirror as if she had seen something moving behind it. As coolly as possible, I turned away and pretended to tie my shoe-lace, expecting at any moment an angry knock on the glass. After what seemed an age, I had the courage to glance back into the room. Catherine, as naked and unconcerned as before, was taking a closer look at her face. There was the slightest shadow of lipstick around her mouth, where Nicola had kissed her. She licked her lips and wiped them roughly with the back of her hand, as if she had tasted something unpleasant.

Breathing more easily now, I felt a sharp pang of affection deep down where it mattered. Whatever it took, I would save this girl from her unsavoury, low-life friends. I would bring her back to the world of civilised values.

Catherine turned out the light.

'Goodnight, little sister,' I said softly. 'Sweet dreams.'

– Perhaps, at this point, I should make my excuses and leave.

– I need you. Soon we'll be away from all this.

– How?

– I'll think of something.

17

Change and decay

For some time now, I had been ignoring Colonel Scott's increasingly tetchy requests for a meeting, or 'global de-brief', as he put it.

His impatience was, I admit, understandable. Offered attractive, high-level work by the other side, I had been letting slide my various chores on behalf of British Intelligence. When I saw fit to present my secret dossier to Scott (or, more probably, his superior), the balance of power in the espionage game would shift westwards, perhaps for ever. Promotion would be assured. Or I might even retire, a legend in Intelligence circles. I could hardly wait to see the Colonel's face when he realised with what devastating effect I had cut through his precious bureaucratic system. Doubtless he'd be fired.

Then one morning, quite out of the blue, a letter from a Mr Brown of Customs and Excise arrived at Colevile. I was to make myself available for a meeting the following week. It was regarding certain tax irregularities. At the request of the Director of Public Prosecutions, my file had been reopened.

No more than mildly perturbed by this turn of events (we were in the entrepreneurial eighties, after all – my over-enthusiasm in the fiscal department was nothing compared to what the new generation of achievers were up to), I dutifully appeared in Brown's office at more or less the appointed hour.

'We have evidence to suggest a significant degree of fraud, tax evasion and irregularities in share dealings within your companies over a period of some ten years,' Brown, a snaggled-toothed idiot with an annoying voice, announced self-importantly.

I replied with detailed references to some of my entirely legitimate shell companies and use of tax shelters.

Brown cut me short. 'Save it for the court,' he said nastily. 'We have the evidence and we're going to use it.'

'Oh, all right,' I shrugged, opening my briefcase and producing a cheque book. 'What's the damage?'

Brown glanced at his watch. 'Several millions, I believe,' he said. 'The cheque book won't be necessary, Mr Fixx. The DPP wants to see you in the dock.'

'Couldn't we square it now?' I said, trying another tack. 'Just you and me.'

'Sorry,' said Brown, making a note on the pad in front of him. 'And we need your passport, by the way. Just until the case comes up.'

I objected, of course. This went way beyond a joke. I had foreign commitments. I was an international businessman. 'Certain people in government will be none too pleased with you if I'm grounded,' I added with a certain quiet menace.

'I'll take that risk,' Brown smiled unattractively. 'If your passport has not been delivered to this office by close of business today, a warrant will be issued for your arrest.'

'Let me see your superior.'

Brown stood up. 'I am my superior,' he said, taking a buff envelope from a drawer inside his desk. 'A colleague asked me to give you this.' I recognised Colonel Scott's writing.

'Couldn't he use the post?' I asked acidly.

'You know Whitehall,' said Brown, holding open the door. 'The cuts.'

Out on the street, I opened the envelope. In it was a typed note. It read, 'STP PLYNG SLLY BGGRS. MT 1500 HRS TMRRW. RY42.'

It was time to play my trump card.

I was preoccupied when I met Catherine that night, I'll admit it. There had been moments over the past few weeks when I had been tempted to tell her about my secret career – the tensions, the complexities, the excitements of life as a senior double-agent – but until now I had resisted them, merely revealing past adventures in the fast lane.

'Jesus, Jon,' she'd say as, chin on hand, dark eyes alight with youthful scepticism, she listened to some exotic tale. 'You're such a liar. Then what happened?'

But no. It would be wrong to involve her. In the world of spying, knowledge is dangerous. I was on my own.

It was possible, too, that she might misunderstand certain aspects of my government work. Close as we were in many ways, we still held different attitudes. I, despite my temporary difficulties, was an optimist; she, like so many of her generation, was a full-time doom-merchant. I pointed to the thriving stock-market our wealth-creating government had encouraged, the lads scarcely out of their teens making six-figure salaries in futures and commodities; she pointed to the inner-city slums, the unemployment figures, the bolshy pinched faces of underpaid nurses and teachers. I expounded upon my philosophy of robust self-help and enterprise, enthused about the joys of good business, overnight money, healthy bottom lines; she saw money as a prison, ambition a treadmill. She'd never work in an office, she said – reading one good book was worth a hundred good deals. I spoke of the pleasure of love (we knew each other well, remember), she dismissed it light-heartedly as no more than another appetite, generally overrated and somewhat old-fashioned.

'One day you'll change your mind about that at least,' I said confidently.

'Somehow I doubt it.'

Funnily enough, I had found myself spending more and more time in the strange London underworld where Catherine felt most at home. It was interesting for me, and not quite as depressing as I had imagined.

'Like it?' she shouted in my ear as, one night in the back room of a Stoke Newington pub, we bounced up and down to the discordant sounds of her friend Swinging Bollocks with his Bendover Boys.

'Very good,' I lied gamely. 'Very . . . swinging.'

– What were you really thinking?

– It's true, I was interested. They wanted nothing to do with the world of jobs and getting on in the world, these people, and yet they seemed happy. No jobs, no prospects, no future. They didn't give a damn. It was odd.

– Yes, but what were you thinking?

– I'll tell you. What a waste. All this youth, this undirected energy, spent so pointlessly.

– And you wanted to reclaim them. Bring them back into the real world.

– Not them. Only her.

– And she thought she was reclaiming you.
– It's possible.

'Problems?'

On the eve of my meeting with Colonel Scott, Catherine and I were sitting in my car outside the squat. Ever sensitive to my moods, she had noticed that I was not my normal outgoing self.

'Nothing I can't handle,' I said, touched by her concern.

'All right, bruv,' she said. 'How about coming in to meet the folks?'

'Not tonight,' I smiled.

I liked this new reluctance to say goodnight. Something had changed between us. Even her brisk, pursed-lip farewell of old (that swift, this-far-and-no-further peck was closer to a head-butt than a kiss) had given way to a softer, more affectionate embrace.

She leant across now and kissed me.

'Another night then,' she said. 'Take care.'

I watched her as she ran up the steps to the house. She didn't look round.

Given its history of scandals, you would think that the last place British Intelligence would meet its top operatives would be in a brothel. Yet that – a back room in a Chelsea knocking-shop – was 'RY42', Colonel Scott's chosen rendezvous.

'Nice spot, Colonel,' I said cheerfully as a dumpy middle-aged woman who called herself 'the manageress' showed me into the room.

Scott, who was sitting uneasily on the end of the double bed which occupied most of the floor space, looked at me with as much dignity as the circumstances permitted.

'Take a pew, Fixx,' he said automatically.

'Where?' I glanced about me. 'On the bidet?'

He gestured impatiently to a stool in front of a small dressing-table with a cracked mirror.

'Let's get on with it,' he said gruffly.

'Handy too.' I was determined to pace the interview at my speed.

'What?' The pin-striped pillock on the bed looked confused.

'Ever avail yourself of the facilities, Colonel?' I chuckled appreciatively. 'RY42, eh? You scallywag.'

'Sit down, Fixx,' the Colonel snapped. 'Shut up and listen.'

'Yessir.' I sat to attention on the stool.

'I'll be brief. You'll recall the conditions under which you were employed. We helped you, you helped us. Drops, swaps? And no questions asked, least of all by you.'

'I remember it well. So perhaps you'd be good enough to explain why you've put Chief-Inspector Brown of the VAT on my case.'

'We did not, if memory serves, mention anything about living out adolescent James Bond fantasies, or blabbing desperate, boastful nonsense about your work in a pathetic attempt to get into the knickers of any passably attractive strangers – '

'Not that pathetic, as it happens.'

' – all of whom worked for the other side, of course.'

'My methods were unconventional, I admit,' I said, preparing to put the Colonel out of his misery. I reached into an inside pocket for the lengthy list of British establishment spies that I had drawn up. I handed it to him with a cold smile. 'Perhaps,' I said, 'you'd care to peruse the evidence of my penetration of – '

'No I would not!' Scott's bellow of anger must have startled those at play in the next bedroom. 'I know precisely who you've penetrated, when and how often.' With a look of intense distaste, he took some Polaroids out of an envelope he had been holding and threw them on the bed. I glanced at them long enough to tell that they were pornographic, with me in a starring role.

'You're a bloody fool, Fixx,' the Colonel continued more quietly. 'You've been turned more often than a pig on a stick.'

'Look at the list, Colonel,' I said grimly.

'Did you really think that we're not aware of who's working for us and who's working for them?'

'Really,' I said, beginning to lose my sense of humour. 'So you'll doubtless know that a member of the Royal Family is involved in top-level espionage, will you?'

'We know everything. They know everything. It's all under control – so long as we don't make the mistake of employing bungling amateurs. And even they don't last long.'

Concluding that it was not the moment to point out that the agreeable game Scott and his friends were apparently playing with the Russians might account for our decline in the league of spying nations, I casually asked him when I would be getting my passport back.

'You won't,' he said briskly. 'There's no call for a passport where you're going.'

'You don't mean – '

'No, not prison. It would be fearfully expensive to bring your absurdly clumsy frauds to court. You're going back home.'

'To Colevile?'

'To your employers. To Russia. Or to East Germany, if you prefer.'

I laughed uneasily at what I assumed was another of the Colonel's unpleasant jokes.

'I spoke to them yesterday,' he continued. 'We've got a naval attaché in Moscow who's gone mad and has been arrested for exposing himself in Red Square. We'd prefer to get him back quietly without an unpleasant trial. Petty Officer Flasher goes one way, you go the other. Back to your Uncle Ivan.'

'You agreed all this? You talk to the KGB? You swap people around as if they were bits of diplomatic baggage?'

'We keep the wheels turning. Help one another clear up our little messes.'

'How could you do it? I can see why they would like a major-league entrepreneur, a senior spy, batting for them but how could you agree to it?'

The Colonel looked at his watch and stood up.

'As it happened, it wasn't easy,' he said, smoothing out the bed. 'They tried to persuade us to keep you – they wanted you even less than we did. Tough Cheddar, we said – you used him, he's yours, take him. They'll be in touch within the month to tell you which windswept beach in South Cornwall they'll pick you up from. The little lifeboat, flashing signals, then on to a Russian trawler, it's all quite straightforward.'

He held out his hand and, still dazed, I shook. 'Good luck, Fixx,' he said. 'Shame it didn't work out.'

'Where can I reach you?' I said, determined not to be shaken by this news. 'I have another plan.'

'Don't try anything clever, old boy. Otherwise it could be – ' the Colonel made a brisk upward stabbing motion ' – poison-umbrella time.'

It was a shock, I'll admit, to be betrayed so casually by my own side, particularly after the highly dangerous confidential work I had done for them. Clearly I was going to need all my legendary calmness in a crisis to avoid the grim scenario that the Colonel and his Russian friends had planned for me. Jonathan Peter Fixx, exile, yesterday man, whiling away his days in a grey Moscow apartment, pining for Walls pork sausages, paying vast black-market prices for back issues of *Punch*. Even with countless *ninotchkas* at my beck and call (and would they still find me as attractive as they once had, now that I was no longer at the sharp end of the spying game?), even with caviare and vodka and the Grand Order of Lenin on the mantelpiece, it wouldn't be the same. I had to move, and move fast.

Had the Colonel been telling the truth when he had said Ivan would be coming to get me? Frankly I doubted it. The man was clearly rattled by the inroads that I had made, independently and without assistance, into East European Intelligence. All the same, I took the precaution of avoiding lonely, darkened streets and left answering machines on my various telephones. Needless to say, there was not the slightest sign of interest from the KGB.

Mother, on the other hand, called every day. Dismissing this unusual behaviour (she was normally too involved with her diddling enterprises to take an interest in her son) as some sort of hangover from her exciting weekend at Colevile, I ignored her increasingly hysterical requests for me to call her. Did I need a lecture on sexual morality, family responsibility, the dangers of mixing with drug-crazed members of the aristocracy and raunchy Page 3 girls at this point in time? I did not.

In the end I received a letter from her, and quite a surprise it turned out to be.

Dear Jonathan,

Where on earth are you? I've been needing to speak to you urgently for the past fortnight but you seem to be avoiding me. I would have thought that, by the age of forty-three, you would have learnt at least some manners but it appears not.

I was hoping to discuss this matter face to face – in fact, I had always hoped it would not be necessary to discuss it at all but recent developments have forced me to grasp the nettle, painful as it is likely to be for me and possibly for you.

We've not been terribly close over the past few years, have we, me with my writing and activism, you with your several mysterious careers? There have been times when I've wanted to talk to you, to penetrate that cold private world in which you live and find out what you're really up to, and whether I can help. Because you may have achieved this and that but it doesn't take much to see you're as restless and dissatisfied as ever. (*Restless is right, Mother – cut the patronising guff and get on with it, will you?*) All the same, I hope you'll now set the past aside, and consider what I have to tell you very carefully. This is important, Jonathan.

It's about Catherine. (*Aha.*) I've watched you two together at Colevile – your little chats, your private jokes, your walks together in the garden. At first, I thought, that's nice, brother and sister getting on so well after all these years. Perhaps they're both growing up at last. Then I thought again. Catherine is quite an innocent in her way – under that tough exterior she's easily led, I believe. And you – well, you're Jonathan, aren't you? You've always been a dreamer (to put it politely) but sometimes you're just mad enough to try to turn your off-centre fantasies into reality. Frankly, the idea of you dating your step-sister would concern me, even without the secret I am about to tell you now. I hope, once you have read this, you will behave with a sense of responsibility and tact that have hitherto not been evident in your behaviour.

When your father and I adopted Catherine, we told you that it was because we were lonely. You were at Melton, I was unable to have another child, we wanted company. That was only partly true. The child, in fact, belonged to the housekeeper Miss Whiting. She was pregnant when she left us – indeed that was why we had to let her go. Now, during that ghastly evening when she was finally dismissed, she made various allegations which may or may not be of relevance to the situation today. Jonathan, this, I hope in my heart of hearts, will be a shock to you: Miss Whiting claimed that you had 'pestered her', as she put it, that you had – despite your extreme youth – finally seduced her. The child she was bearing was, she said, yours.

Naturally your father and I dismissed all this as the ravings of a discontented domestic. But after Catherine was born, Miss Whiting paid us a visit. The child, she said, was going to be adopted. She wanted us to have her. Well, we felt sorry for the woman, guilty even, and, after all, it was a bit quiet around the house and the baby, of course, was adorable. Then we had perhaps both been thinking some more about you. Such a strange little boy, you were, so isolated, so determined, so emotionally underdeveloped in some ways, yet so mature in others.

And that's what happened. We banished all thoughts of the paternity of the child from our minds, cleared it with the adoption agency and (with a certain amount of relief, I must confess) bid a final farewell to the dreaded Aunty Bar-Bar.

You'll probably find all this ridiculous (*I do, Mother, I do*), in which case please ignore and destroy this letter. If, on the other hand, there was something – *anything* – in what the housekeeper said, that there's the slightest possibility that Catherine is in fact your daughter, I hope you will know how to behave towards her from now on. Either way, say *nothing* to her – it can only confuse and upset her to discover all this.

So there we are, Jonathan. Only you and Catherine's mother know the truth. I hope sincerely that this letter is as bewildering (or even amusing) for you to read as it has been difficult for me to write.

As you know, I'm leaving on a European publicity tour with members of the Workshop next week. When I return, I shall *not* expect this sensitive subject to be a matter for discussion between us.

Your loving
Mother

In an odd way, my mother's ham-fisted attempt to soil the unsullied relationship between Catherine and myself strengthened the affection I felt towards my girlfriend, step-sister, daughter or what you will. If, as now seemed quite possible, she was a close blood relation (and, let's face it, that would explain her exceptional combination of poise and beauty), need it necessarily mean an end to the happy times we spent together? Briefly, I was tempted to share the contents of Mother's letter with her but, on reflection, I resisted the impulse. Somehow if the acute, well-timed advice I gave her on how to deal with life's problems were tainted by the paternal tone, it would lose much of its value.

Frankly, I was much more concerned about Mother. For a woman with only limited natural gifts, she had enjoyed a fair stint as a public personality and now, I feared, the strain was getting to her. She was a Williams, after all, and a female Williams; it was inevitable that what I privately called the Williams Loony Factor – an unfortunate curdling of the genes which sent the women of the family clean round the twist when they reached a certain age – should assert itself. It might well be that Mother had toppled off her trolley long ago, when she set out to betray the family name by writing *The Second Front*. In normal times such eccentricity would have been tolerated or even ignored but times then were anything but normal; briefly, the Williams Loony Factor had seemed to afflict the whole of womankind, allowing Mother, its personification, to become an absurd, unlikely mini-celebrity.

I worried, of course I did. But she was having fun; and doubtless the liberation binge indulged by the sisters would eventually peter out and normal services would be resumed. Naively, I had underestimated Mother's lust for glory; dotty she may have been, but the flair for self-promotion remained. Going digital: that was a popular hobby as yet unexplored in the magazines and on the chat-shows. As a topic, it had it all – it could be universally enjoyed, it aroused prurient interest and now, thanks to Mother, it was a political statement. Enter Madam Diddle, the tireless hand of liberation, a myth for her time.

Good God, it was obvious, had been for years. The woman had flipped; she was barmy, certifiable. And now she had taken to writing bizarre letters to her only son, in which her diseased imaginings were revealed to have taken another, unpredictable and potentially embarrassing turn.

No. She had to be stopped. Even if her allegation regarding Aunty Bar-Bar and myself contained a grain of truth, Mother had pushed me too far this time. Ten years ago, I might have taken it, but not now. I had grown up.

– She was trying to help you.

– Never. She was cranking herself up for another literary exposé at my expense. I could tell the signs.

– She was worried. Any mother would be.

– Look at the facts. Here was a woman who had built her career on the back of her late husband's insanity and her only son's troubled upbringing. She had even used her own solitary vices as 'material'. D'you really think she'd hesitate to use a story which had everything – child abuse, incest, top-level cover-ups. It couldn't fail.

– Maybe. One of the papers said that Sarah was going to write a book.

– Surprise, surprise.

– 'FIXX EX-WIFE TO TELL ALL'. I kept the cutting.

– Ex-wife! I swear that's the most beautiful phrase in the English language.

Regarding Mother. The Russians had by now made their move (hardly cloak-and-dagger, as it happens: a note, 'Mullion Cove, 0200 on 21/7, be there or else', left in my cubby-hole at the Garrick), and I needed to resolve tiresome family matters as quickly as possible.

I rang Mother to arrange a meeting. At first reluctant, she finally agreed and we had tea at her London flat, the day before she left. It's all lies, I told her. The housekeeper must have been spiteful, deluded or both. Mother switched on her loving-parent manner and we parted amicably, after I had given her a farewell present of an expensive pigskin suitcase for her next round of travels.

'Jonathan, you really shouldn't,' Mother gushed. 'It looks so expensive.'

'It was,' I confessed. 'But worth every penny. From a grateful son.'

'You mean we're friends at last?'

I smiled warmly. It was good to make up family quarrels, I decided. After all, who knew when I would see my mother again?

'Yes. Friends,' I said, embracing her. 'At last.'

What would you have done in my position? The KGB steaming towards the English Channel to snatch you from your native shores, your controller at MI5 traitorously abandoning you to your fate, various high-flying tax noddies rifling gleefully through your somewhat irregular business accounts, your mother swanning off on yet another self-publicity tour, oblivious to the fact that she may never see her son again, the one and only love of your life alleged at precisely the wrong moment to be your own daughter? You'd have cracked, I bet, gone mad, found a lonely park bench and burst into tears, caved in.

Personally, I liked the challenge. Never more effective than when the odds are stacked against me, I remained calm – icily, dangerously cool. I withdrew to Colevile, where Catherine would often visit me, and waited for my moment, for the grand plan to unfold.

More specifically, I was waiting for news from Africa. It was like this:

Fixx Lacombe, my highly sophisticated drugs company based in Switzerland had, following the unwelcome interest of UNESCO in Menson and the low-protein milk substitute, addressed the less controversial area of chemical weaponry. It was a shrewd business move: the demand for various silent, invisible, non-explosive anti-personnel products was increasing, in spite of the inevitable opposition from various whinging willies at the United Nations.

Almost by accident (how often major scientific breakthroughs happen this way), one of our top boffins had fluked upon a man-made virus that was selective in what he jovially described as its 'target audience'. The professor, a fish-eyed geriatric called Getzler whose chequered career had over the past forty years taken him from his native Germany to Peru, Costa Rica, Chile and now back to Switzerland, outlined in unpleasant detail how his pet virus was transmitted. It was, unfortunately, he concluded with undisguised disappointment, 'only interesting to men of homosexualist persuasion'.

Thinking no more of it at the time, I allowed Getzler to take a team of researchers to a jungle in the Central African Republic where certain of our confidential field experiments were often conducted. A year or so back, he had flown to London with the news that those natives who had been injected – the poor saps having been told they were being given vitamin jabs – had achieved what he called 'a highly acceptable mortality rate'.

The practical significance of this pure research only became clear when Colonel Scott started cutting up rough. Where was MI5's most urgent problem? Apart from certain weak links in the management chain (viz. the Colonel himself), British Intelligence was clearly infiltrated at the highest level. And what did the traitors have in common? Obvious: an affection for a certain left-footing lifestyle, pink wallpaper, opera, Campari soda with a spot of rough trade in a leather lounge off the Earls Court Road; above all, a deep and tremulous affection for one another. Clearly the controlled deployment of Getzler's evil virus would go through the service like a dose of salts. Result: an infiltration-free MI5 comes up brand new and smelling of roses.

'Get Ivan off my case,' I'd say to the Colonel, 'and your worries are history.'

All I needed now was the word from Getzler that an effective antidote (lacking any sense of social responsibility, the professor had resisted this idea to the last) was available. As soon as certain routine tests had been completed in darkest Africa, I would receive a call from Getzler's headquarters in Bangui that would solve all my problems at a stroke.

Never trust a so-called expert. That's my advice. He's never quite as bright as he thinks.

'Experiment completed,' the professor reported at last in a late-night call on a crackling line.

'Congratulations, Prof,' I said warmly. 'Courier the full results to me tomorrow. I need them urgently.'

‘ – but not successfully, Mr Fixx.’

‘How do you mean?’

‘The antidote is not entirely effective. In fact, not effective at all.’

I thought quickly. Maybe the Colonel would accept use of the virus without a controlling factor pro tem. The problem was urgent, after all. Perhaps the antidote could follow along later.

‘Send me the details anyway,’ I said crisply.

‘There is another problem, Mr Fixx. It appears that our little baby can walk more quickly than I anticipated. Run, even . . . ’

I listened aghast as Getzler’s distant voice explained that his experiment was no longer quite as controlled as he had planned. The virus had spread from the jungle to the capital of Bangui. It was proving to be highly contagious and it had recently been reported that the regulars at a bar where itinerant foreigners – high-living American airline stewards and the like – hung out had been falling like flies.

‘You mean that your virus could, even now, be winging its way to America?’

‘I fear that may be the case.’

‘Then, what?’

‘That all depends on how your average air steward behaves when he gets back to his Greenwich Village.’

‘My God.’

I could hardly believe what I was hearing. A perfectly respectable experiment, aimed at strengthening our defences against the communist menace, had gone horribly wrong. Worse than that, Fate had cruelly snatched from my hand the last trump card that I had to play. I sighed wearily.

‘Getzler, you’re fired,’ I said.

No, of course I don’t feel good about it. To be responsible, albeit at second-hand, for the greatest medical catastrophe to have faced mankind for five centuries is a terrible burden which quite often keeps me awake at night. The fact that the madman who developed the virus shortly afterwards scurried back to South America (renewed interest in his distant past by a group of Israeli investigators having appeared to alarm him unduly) merely added to my sense of impotence. If only I could do something to help in some way. Unfortunately it’s too late, I can’t and that’s all there is to it.

Worse was to come. Four days later, as the staff at Colevile prepared the house for one final party before I left on an extended holiday, there was shattering news concerning Mother.

It appeared that, acting on some sort of tip-off, police at Stockholm airport had, with remarkable courage given the size and average weight of the Self-Stimulation Workshop entourage, searched the group's luggage. In addition to one or two undeclared items (diamond-studded Japanese love-balls? I found myself wondering idly; high-tech quartz vibrators?), the Swedes had been astonished to discover a quantity of pure cocaine with a street value of half a million pounds in the lining of one of Mother's suitcases.

There were headlines, there was hysteria. Madam Diddle was all over the front pages. On several occasions, Mother's solicitor telephoned me from Stockholm but, as I explained to him, the burden of her defence – that the suitcase had actually been planted on her by her only son – merely confirmed my growing concern that she had lost her already feeble grip on reality.

To make things worse, it appeared that the Swedes had recently announced a crackdown on this sort of thing and that several other unresolved drug-smuggling charges were quite likely to be laid at Mother's door. After all, she frequently travelled around Europe, she had the perfect alibi and, who knows, perhaps her much-vaunted liberal approach to sex extended also to drugs.

Catherine was naturally devastated by the revelation that Mother was no more than a common criminal. She begged me to help.

'It's up to you, Jonathan,' she said at one of the miserable dinners we had together during this depressing period. 'You always claim to be an achiever. You get things done. Now get Mother out of this.'

'Darling,' I said, adopting the daffy, bewildered expression that the occasion demanded. 'There's something you should know.' Quietly, emotionally, I told Catherine of my business problems and of the threat hanging over me. 'So you see – ' my voice may have cracked slightly at this stage ' – my hands are tied. I don't even have a passport, for heaven's sake.'

'Do something, Jonathan. Please. She's your mother. She's innocent – you know she is.'

I sighed. 'I don't know what I know any more. The world's gone mad.'

There was a certain amount of blubbing. Eventually, more for a quiet life than anything, I agreed to write to the Swedish authorities pleading my mother's innocence (or, as I finally put it, genetic insanity).

It was the least – and paradoxically, the most – that I could do under the circumstances.

Frankly, the idea of Mother languishing in a foreign jail put something of a crimp on my eventful last party at Colevile.

It was not, by the way, the unbridled debauch later described in lip-smacking detail by certain unscrupulous sewer rats. There was music, yes, there was food and drink. Other stimulants may even have been consumed in dark corners – the good host never imposes house-rules. But the story that a coachload of cocktail waitresses had been booked for the occasion was an absurd fabrication. Nor was there a queue for the Pleasure Lounge, at least not that I saw. And the suggestion that the theme for the night was Madam Diddle Goes Down, that guests arrived provocatively dressed as jailbirds, that whips, handcuffs and French Tickler headgear were distributed by miniskirted WPCs at the door is the grossest of libels – not least upon the many glittering celebrities who amused themselves thoroughly but innocently that night.

Personally, I was not at my best. I circulated, I smiled, I acknowledged the affectionate greetings of friends, I participated in the odd silly game, but inside I was a cauldron.

Was this it then, the end of an era? And at the very moment when my life looked like achieving the sort of stability I had always yearned for? So it seemed. After all, on that very night, a Russian trawler would be waiting for me off the south coast of England. Tomorrow I would be a wanted man. And even if Uncle Ivan eventually lost interest, there were others who were turning against me.

Colonel Scott, naturally, was at the head of the queue. Old duffer he may have been, but there was something implacable about him which I found unnerving. It would offend his sense of order, the idea of an ace Intelligence maverick on the loose. Then there was his sheepdog, Brown of the VAT, corralling me towards the Old Bailey with his scrupulously documented allegations against my companies.

At least, Mother was not around to stir the pot. Yet even that sad business had added to my worries. Within days of her arrest, I had received several unpleasant messages from a gruff-voiced virago claiming to represent a group known as 'the Snatch Squad'. 'We are the cutting edge of the women's movement,' she said, leaving little doubt as to what would be cut if I failed to square things vis-à-vis Mother's drug-smuggling rap.

My wife, it goes without saying, was also in the pack, baying for blood. She (or rather a little man she had got in) had taken to harassing me for money, quoting some piffling court order for maintenance. My explanation – that every penny of my earnings, and indeed of my wife's family trust, had been spent on the upkeep of Colevile, the family home – had fallen on deaf ears.

There were even rumours that my old friend Collin was at work on a muck-raking biography of me, having persuaded some dimwitted publisher – Marc Shelley, perhaps – to finance his vengeful little enterprise. But he was just another with a vested interest in my failure. I dismissed him, too, with a weary wave of the hand.

I wandered among the revellers in search of Catherine. Some of the fight had gone out of me, I'll admit it. More worrying than the growing army of losers and malcontents who were ranging themselves against me was a sense of inner futility that was entirely new. Had it all been worth it – the pain, the effort, the tears, the deals, the seductions promising so much and delivering so little, the shattered lives, the ever-increasing bodycount on the bloody battlefield of my career? Call it mid-life crisis, the coming of wisdom, executive burnout – the fact is that, for the first time in my life, I was becoming prey to doubts.

'Let me take you away from all this,' I said to Catherine when I found her, quiet and unnoticed, on the outer fringes of a group of television personalities. She stood up and took my arm as we wandered out of the house into the garden.

'I'm really not into parties,' she said.

'Nor me.'

We sat on a bench in the rose garden. Nearby, on the Great Lawn, some of my guests were playing a drunken game of croquet in the half-light.

'Anyway,' I said. 'It's all going to change soon.'

She looked at me curiously.

'Are you up to something, bruv?'

Briefly, I considered telling her of the dramatic and radical solution

I had hit upon to solve all our problems at a stroke. No. She would find out soon enough.

'I'm always up to something,' I smiled. 'You know that.'

Catherine sighed. 'If only Mother were here,' she said.

'We'll get her out soon. As long as we're together.'

She moved away slightly, murmuring, 'When you say together – '

'I mean together.' One of the girls on the lawn screamed and giggled as she was chased by her boyfriend.

'Let's get away from these people,' I said. 'I want to show you something.'

– You're going to write about the summer house?

– It's important.

– Careful.

– Trust me.

Have I mentioned that the summer house had been modernised too? It was quite comfortable now, with its little fireplace, its curtains, its bed in the corner – a modest, homely retreat amidst the grandeur of Colevile.

'Well, well,' said Catherine, as I led her by the hand into the little room. A fire had been lit, and there was a bottle of champagne in an ice bucket by the bed. She ran a hand down the neck of the bottle. 'Expecting visitors?'

'Only one.' I locked the door.

'Jonathan,' she said. 'This is wrong.'

Of course it was wrong. We kissed, leaning softly against one another in front of the fire. By normal standards, it was all wrong, what we were doing now. She knew it was wrong and so (to a rather greater extent, I admit) did I.

'Catherine,' I said, searching for the right words. 'This means more to me than – '

She broke away from me and, kicking off her shoes as she went, walked towards the bed.

'Just don't say anything,' she said, unzipping the back of her dress. 'Don't say a word.'

I felt faint and closed my eyes briefly. There was the click of a light-switch and the rustle of clothing. When I opened my eyes, she was standing there, her body lit only by the flames from the fire.

'Coming?' she said softly.

Does guilt make it better? Was it all the pain and problems of the world outside that made that night so strangely different from anything I had experienced before (or have since). And yet nothing that happened between us was unusual. We made the time-honoured moves in more or less the traditional manner. Why was it that suddenly all those lovers, all those bedrooms, all those conquests – the pushing and pulling, the gasps and groans, the pitiful attempts to kick-start the libido with ever more exotic variations on the same old theme – never seemed more futile than they did that night in the summer house as I lay with Catherine in my arms? Or maybe I'm romanticising and we were simply good together, like some people are. Search me – that night, I was a lost soul. A fallen soul. Nothing else mattered.

'What time is it?' I asked, some time in the early hours, as our bodies took a brief respite from one another.

Catherine groped on the floor beside the bed for her watch. 'Five to three,' she said.

I went to the window and drew back the curtain to look at the house which had meant so much to me. The noise was dying now, the lights were going out. I would miss it.

It was three-fifteen when two cars drew up and parked halfway up the drive to the left of the summer house. Eight figures emerged from the cars and ran towards the house.

'We have visitors,' I said calmly. 'Get your clothes on quickly.'

Catherine sat up in bed.

'Who is it?' she whispered.

'I don't know.'

The intruders had stopped at the front door. One of them appeared to be bolting it in some way while the others ran around to the back. From the lights of the Pleasure Lounge, I could see that they were each carrying something.

'Where's your car?' I asked urgently.

At this point Catherine's eyes widened in alarm. 'It's by the stables but . . . shouldn't we do something?'

I looked back at the house. It was now clear what the men were up to. At a signal, one of them lit a torch, which flared in the night. Within seconds, flames were licking around the base of the door.

Soon the great, timber-framed hall was ringed by a circle of fire. The figures ran back to their cars and drove off at speed, this time with their lights on.

'Jesus,' Catherine muttered as we ran across the Great Lawn. We tried the front door but it appeared to be locked, and the heat from the blaze was already unbearable. All the same, it took some persuasion and a small amount of force to get Catherine into her car and away from Colevile.

– You could have called the fire brigade – the police.

– Stop at the next call-box. Then keep going to London. I'll explain later.

– They'll find you.

– Not a chance. So what do I call him?

– Who?

– Swinging? Mr Bollocks?

– I'm frightened, Jonathan.

– Morning, Mr Bollocks. Bendover Boys up yet?

– His name's John.

18
Catherine

He did a runner in the end, of course. Or rather not the end. He was never one for seeing things through. Get involved, screw up, move on. That was his style.

The waiting had got to him, he said. He yearned for action, to be in the front line. Stroll on, I thought to myself. You won't get nearer the front line than this.

Anyway, thank God he's gone. I was getting more than a little pissed off hanging around in the cold and dark as he droned on into a tape-machine. That's no life for a girl. There's a limit to family loyalty.

So, after Colevile, we spent the longest six months of my life at the squat. I didn't have the heart to kick him out, what with his face all over the papers and being wanted by the police. He used to have these nightmares. He was being deported to Russia. Contract killers were waiting around every corner. The VAT man was going to bankrupt him. He'd be dragged through the courts, humiliated, dumped on by his wife. (Poor old Sarah, the last time we spoke, her only request was never to have to talk to him again.)

It could have been quite a heavy number, in fact. The word in the press was that it was he who torched Colevile for the insurance. His financial affairs were apparently in a real mess. John said he should come clean and say it was the KGB or whatever. After all, not even he would want ten people to die (most of the guests escaped through the windows but apparently some were too wasted to make it) just for a bit of cash. For a while, there was talk of an accident – some tosspot freebasing in the library, blowback, bang, curtains go up – but when they found traces of kerosene, it was all over.

He wasn't exactly a natural-born squatter, that one. After a week or so hiding out in his room, he started hanging around the kitchen, the sitting-room, talking about this and that, a bit of boasting here, a lot of whining there. I used to tell him to fuck off and then escape to my room from which he was now banned. Then he started on John. He really got up John's nose.

Which isn't easy, to be fair. Give John a Vonnegut, a bottle of whisky, and a Little Richard tape blasting through his headphones and he's a pussy-cat. You have to be tolerant in a squat, but John takes the biscuit. Psychos, junkies, banged-up teenies, failed anarchists, mothers with weird, fucked-up kids, dogs that crap in the kitchen – provided they leave John alone they can stay as long as they like.

It started with really stupid jokes about the name of John's group. All right, it's a silly name, but he didn't have to go on and on about it. How did they get the name? He couldn't wait to see how they'd be announced on Top of the Pops. *Hilarious, particularly since the group had just broken up.*

Then he talked. Jesus, he never stopped. Not just the usual stuff but stories that made him out to be the biggest fascist bastard that ever drew breath. John would sigh, close his eyes and turn his tape up louder. He's a saint, that man. He only reacted once, as I remember. He said at the end of a particularly absurd story, so you're personally responsible for the AIDS *epidemic, are you? Yes, goes Dickhead, it's a heavy burden. John laughed at that, but it was a weary, deeply pissed-off sort of laugh. It must be, he said.*

The final straw was when he began sticking his nose into the way we run the house. All right, so John's not an 'achiever' but there's one thing he's really good at, and that's squatting. He can sus out the best places, get the electricity on, square it with the local pigs, negotiate with the council, the lot. Give John a week and he can turn a hovel into a home. He's been doing it for years.

And of course he has his own ideas as to how the place should be run. No power trips, just a basic understanding between us all that we do it his way. For instance, he likes it to look like a squat – not squalid, but definitely not too tidy – if it's that neat, you might as well live in a sodding flat and have done is his view. So when the Master of Colevile Hall announced he wanted to paint the door of his room, John sat up and took notice. You what, he says. I just don't like graffiti on my door. Graffiti? says John. Yes – TAKE YOUR FUCKING BOOTS OFF – *I don't know who put it there but I don't like it. That's not graffiti, says John, it's a community message. Well it's not very nice. John puts his headphones back on and closes his eyes. Leave it, he said. And our friend – being, in fact, a bit of a wimpo when it comes to an up-front confrontation – leaves it.*

So John decided to eject him (it was his suggestion that what the squat needed was some kind of management structure that finally did it), but he did agree to get him in somewhere else, which was nice of him under the circumstances. There was a tower block by the Thames down Wapping way which was about to be demolished to make private flats for City bastards. John got us in, set us up and left us to it.

You'll be wanting to know about the sex. There's not much to tell, thank God.

The day after we moved into the squat he spent hours staring out of the window at the strip of urban wasteland which was our back yard. Eventually I asked him what the matter was. We need to talk, he said. Sure, I said. Are we alone in the house? We were. So then it all spilt out – the intimate confessions of Jonathan Peter Fixx, family man, step-brother, seducer of his first-born.

I was shocked. Well, you would be, wouldn't you? It was dodgy enough living with the idea that I had made it with the man I regarded as a brother without being told that he was my long-lost dad. Incest I could do without. But then, after I had kicked a few walls and shed a few tears, I found myself thinking, what the hell? It was only once and there had been no danger of getting pregnant (you want to know his first words, afterwards in the summer house on that romantic, star-spangled night? 'Are you safe?' Of course I bloody was).

Funnily enough, I had been thinking that something odd was going on. He had hardly touched me since that night – I didn't mind, but it seemed out of character. So, having let off a bit of steam, I took pity on the poor bastard, slumped there staring into space. I went over to him, kissed him lightly on the head and said, 'Hi, Dad.' And, d'you know what? He burst into tears, the silly sod.

Anyway, it wasn't all his fault. I may have had the idea that sleeping with Jonathan would persuade him to get Mother out of jail (I knew he could help more than he was doing), but I went into that summer house with my eyes open. I'm a grown-up. I make my own decisions.

Because, to be honest, he had a peculiar kind of pull when he was really motoring and in control – a dangerous, fascist brand of charm that was quite seductive in its way. Not that the act itself was entirely memorable. Arms, elbows, legs – he made you feel more like the victim of a smash-and-grab raid than a lover.

It must have been a power thing, his charisma, because no one could have been less attractive than Fixx the squatter. Out of his context, dependent on others, he was merely pitiful, just another mid-life crisis haunted by passing time and lost opportunity.

Of course, he was still hung up on sex. Once he had settled into the squat, we used to go for little trips around London (these were the early days before the place was staked out by the heavy mob). I swear that man was in a fever of anticipation the moment we stepped out on to the street. At first I thought it was fear the way his eyes darted about the place, then I sussed that he was actually looking for prey. I mean, talk about pathetic. He couldn't step on to a train in the underground without falling in love with some bemused woman sitting across the way. By now, he saw me as some sort of weird accomplice. Here's one, he'd say as if we were two lads out on the pull, shall I say something to her? I'd pretend I wasn't with him, and he'd sit there, leering until she or we got off. Shit, he'd say, I should have said something. She was expecting it. I think she liked me. And this woman had never given the berk a second look. I mean, is that sad or what?

Why not treat it like a nice part-time hobby, I used to say to him, a way of passing the time, an occasional diversion, nothing heavy? He couldn't see it at all. For instance, he got well leery when I spent the night with John after he'd agreed to set us up in another squat. It was a sort of thank you. How could you? he squealed. With Bollocks? It's no big deal, I said, we didn't have anything better to do. (In fact, John sussed that I wasn't into it and I sussed what he'd sussed, so we had a smoke and went to sleep – but that was none of anyone's business.) Anyway, hence the bragging, the name-dropping, the stories – they were a sort of highly undignified mating dance. That's what I think anyway.

As for why I stayed with him, kept him company, shopped for him, helped with his book, allowing him to present me as some sort of blonde tart – Katrina, Sabrina or whatever – well, I'm his daughter, aren't I? He was frightened, he was alone in this miserable room (his penthouse!), he was family. And it was interesting to see what happened, to hear his version of events. In fact, now that he's gone, I'm hanging on to the manuscript – just in case.

To be fair, his final departure wasn't a total runner. For weeks, this big, clean black car had been parked in front of the flats, day and night. There were two goons in dark suits sitting in the front, just waiting. Sometimes they'd get out of the car and lean against it, smoking a cigarette and looking up at our window. At about seven every night, an identical car with two more heavies would roll up for the night shift. It was a bit unnerving at first but, once we knew they'd leave me alone when I went out to do the shopping, we got used to them.

Funnily enough, he didn't act that scared. Let me just finish this, he'd say, I'll think of something. Then one afternoon he put on his one clean shirt, his City suit, his Old Meltonian tie, checked some papers in his briefcase. I'd better be off then, he said. I'll be in touch. What about the book? I asked. Stay here for a week. I'll get word to you. He made a brave but totally unconvincing stab at an emotional farewell before, squaring his shoulders like an old ham actor about to take the stage, he left the squat.

I watched him emerge from the front door. The men in black behaved as if they'd been expecting him. One of them opened the back door for him, like a chauffeur, and, the two goons in the front seat and Jonathan Peter Fixx in the back, they drove off. And that was that.

19
The next horizon

Well, I've made it. Perhaps not quite by the straight and narrow (never the most interesting of routes) but, beyond the slightest shadow of doubt, I have made it.

Yet, even as I bring this modest account of my career thus far to a satisfactory climax, I find myself scanning the horizon in search of new challenges. And, believe me, from where I stand – in the heart of government – there's no shortage of peaks to climb.

Not that you'll be reading my name in the newspapers. Frankly, I've outgrown all that. In my line, cheap publicity – face recognised on the street, name bruited about in saloon bars across the country – is the very last thing I need.

Let me be circumspect. As you may know, the call has come from the highest level for public-spirited entrepreneurs to come to the aid of the government as it streamlines this great country of ours for the next century. Our task? To strip away the layers of bureaucratic blubber, to weed out the naysayers, the moaning, spineless enemies of progress and wealth-creation, to transform Great Britain, until recently a dinosaur among modern countries, into Great Britain Ltd – the sharpest, most aggressive outfit Europe has ever seen. It's a dream, I know, but we feel it's achievable.

Good marketing men. That's what they wanted. Men who know that to get there you need to cut corners. Men not afraid to nuke an egg factory to make an omelette. Men for whom blood on the carpet is no more than part of the furniture of everyday life. Men in tune with the exciting times in which we live.

It's my strength, I suppose. I fit in. Born to a different age, I might have been a general, an intellectual, even some sort of hairy guru leading my disciples to the path of true enlightenment. As it is, I promote, self-market, help my country by helping myself.

I happen to be working behind the scenes at the moment. What with Colevile, the Russians, Mother and the rest, the powers that be were of the opinion that a change of identity was advisable. My various international enterprises were quietly wound up, with a remarkably fair financial settlement for my good self, MI5 was given a sharp rap across the knuckles for its failure to deploy me as a man of my calibre deserved, and now I'm starting a new life with a new name.

You won't have heard of our department. Indeed, there's not an actual department as such. Working with Whitehall, we've discovered, is like driving a car with the handbrake on. Yet if the entire civil service were to work together (*quelle blague!*), its influence on the national life would be less significant than ours. We're a sort of unconventional, free-ranging task-force, I suppose. This strike, says Downing Street, sort it out, will you? Encourage the moderates, organise the opposition within the workforce, arrange a few stunts to convince the world the strikers are vicious commie hooligans, killers even. Or, education. We want to shake it up. De-stabilise it, will you? Because in order for people to accept much-needed reform, which might be a touch painful for them as individuals, they need to be shown the thing doesn't work. It might be some clapped-out nationalised industry, or the Intelligence Services, or the National Health. It's all the same to us: get involved, screw up, move on. We've done our job, the bulldozers are on the horizon. I see our little band of low-profile public servant entrepreneurs as vigilantes, stalking the land under cover of night, working boldly on behalf of the greatest cause known to man, that of freedom and enterprise.

As for my private life, that too is thriving. It turns out that the gossip-column set are not top of the pile, after all. There's a whole social world – powerbrokers, magnates, members of the serious aristocracy – that you never hear about. We have fun, get relaxed, fool about, of course we do. But we're discreet. Next month I fly to Texas for a three-week stay at some millionaire's ranch with a well-known and highly desirable member of the Royal Family. Hubby stays at home visiting hospitals, yours truly accompanies the lady wife abroad and helps her recharge the old batteries. A walker, she calls me. We'll see about that.

I'm proud to say that my position at the top of the dungheap has produced several benefits for friend and family. I had a word with the Swedish authorities about Mother, for instance; they, very decently, agreed to release her on a suspended sentence, providing we impounded her passport and required her to report to Biggleswade police station once a week. Funnily enough, her lawyer objected to our only other condition – that one word, spoken or written, about her case would see his client back behind bars – but, after a few months of pointless negotiation, he relented and Mother, silent at last, made her way home. I rarely hear from her these days which, after all my efforts on her behalf, saddens but does not surprise me. Gratitude was never her strong suit.

Naturally enough, my ex-wife has not seen fit to congratulate me on my change of fortune. Indeed, in the media clique which she now inhabits, there were rumours that she was to give her ego yet another outing, this time in the form of an autobiography. Not any more. I work with national security. We have a way with whistle-blowers. A word in the ear of Mr Publisher and the project's in turnaround before you can say 'brown trousers'. One of my people rang Sarah to inform her that, from the security point of view, we had never met. 'Suits me,' she said, tremendously witty to the last. Of course, I worry about the child growing up in an atmosphere rank with spite and greed but, since I'm denied access, there's precious little I can do beyond sending over the odd improving volume at Christmas and birthdays. I hope for her sake that she takes after her father, but frankly I'm not optimistic.

Such is my contentment with the new life I lead that it was my original intention to consign this account of my old self to the bottom drawer. The past, as Kipling had it, is another country: the allegations once made against my good name are no longer relevant; who knows, certain readers might even, in a spirit of perversity, envy or simple stupidity, misinterpret some of the actions of my youth. Yet in the end, I have decided that I owe it to my family to allow publication to proceed.

Some will doubtless carp at the inclusion in the text of occasional, admittedly irritating and irrelevant interruptions to the main narrative by the woman to whom I had mistakenly entrusted the task of typing out the manuscript. I make no apologies. These distractions, tiresome as they may be, are in a very real sense the last will and testament of my late daughter Catherine and I felt it only right to leave them in their eccentric entirety.

Poor Catherine. After my recruitment into government, she clung to the manuscript almost as if it belonged to her. What was happening in that confused brain of hers? I wondered. Did she think she could make money out of my work? Was she trying to protect me? Did she misguidedly believe that, while she had possession of what she may have regarded as evidence against her own father, she was somehow safe from the attention of the authorities? If so, how tragically mistaken she was.

I asked her, through my people, to return my property. She refused. We insisted. She took to moving from squat to squat with her unwholesome friend John. I really did need my manuscript. Finally, they were cornered in a derelict house in Paddington, the police raided the place, John was found to be in possession of a quite astonishing amount of neat heroin and, as Catherine (possibly in a drug-crazed state) resisted arrest, the gun of some idiot noddy was fired, killing her instantly.

It was a terrible shock, of course it was. I loved her, after all. Questions were asked. How could three busloads of police be required for such a straightforward operation? Why exactly were they armed? Was the fatality caused by a genuine accident? There were the predictable demands for an enquiry but, since no enquiry in the world could bring back my darling Catherine, I merely requested that the trigger-happy police constable be drummed out of the force and left it at that.

Not that Catherine died entirely in vain. To ensure that her name lives on, I have recently established, with quite a lot of my own money, the Catherine Fixx Drug Rehabilitation Centre, which is situated in Stockwell. Some of the royalties from this book will be donated to that excellent charity.

But enough of the past. There is work to do on behalf of the government, of the nation, of you, the common reader.

Not that I expect thanks, or even recognition – the satisfaction of a job well done is quite enough for me.

A NOTE ON THE AUTHOR

Terence Blacker was born in 1948 and educated at Wellington and Trinity College, Cambridge. He worked for several years in publishing before becoming a full-time writer in 1983. Since then, he has been widely published as a journalist, children's book writer and contributor to pseudonymous comedy books, as well as scripting and presenting the BBC Radio Four series, *The Seven Deadly Virtues*.

Fixx is his first novel.